ONE AGAINST MANY

Reata simply said: "You tell me where to look, and I'll start for Quinn."

"They're somewhere around Horn Spoon. That's where they want me to send the money, anyway," said Pop Dickerman. "The idea is that Quinn is my last good man. You know where Horn Spoon is?"

"I know where it is," said Reata. "The railroad goes through there."

"They sent word to me that they've got a man of mine, and if the ten thousand ain't in their hands inside of ten days, they'll slit his gullet for him. That's the news that I get from a dark-skinned hound that shows up down here one evening a week ago. There's a band of 'em, I guess."

"It'll take me two days to ride across to Horn Spoon," said Reata. "That'll leave one day for the spotting of Quinn and the saving of him. It's a short pinch."

"Sure it is," said Dickerman. "It's a short pinch. Here, Reata. You step over here and pick out the guns and the knives that you want."

Reata went to the heap of guns and looked them over with a shake of his head. "I won't have one of those," he answered, but, going to the cutlery, he picked out an ordinary horn-handled hunting knife. "This'll do," he said, glancing down the blade.

"You don't never travel with no guns?" asked the old man.

"Never."

THE FUGITIVE'S MISSION

MAX BRAND

LEISURE BOOKS NEW YORK CITY

A LEISURE BOOK®

March 2002

Published by special arrangement with Golden West Literary
Agency.

Dorchester Publishing Co., Inc.
276 Fifth Avenue
New York, NY 10001

ISBN 0-8439-4980-5

The name "Leisure Books" and the stylized "L" with design are
trademarks of Dorchester Publishing Co., Inc.

Printed in the United States of America.

Visit us on the web at www.dorchesterpub.com.

Table of Contents

THE FUGITIVE'S MISSION

Frederick Faust's original title for this short novel was "The Trail to Jerney." It was changed to "The Fugitive's Mission" for publication in the January 14, 1922 issue of Street & Smith's *Western Story Magazine* by Frank E. Blackwell, the magazine's editor. Editors have long been changing the titles of authors' stories prior to publication, with or without an author's blessing. For its first appearance in book form, the title under which it was first published has been retained, although the author's full text has been restored. It is perhaps for the reader best to judge which title is most fitting for a story that deals so much with an interplay between illusion and reality, between the past and the present.

I

"WITHOUT BANNERS"

The morning unfolded like a great song to Bill Rafferty. Every new prospect, as the trail twisted through the mountains, was a new burst of music, and the rhythm of the resounding hoofs of his horse beat out the time. On his pale hands and still paler face the warmth of the sun was good. His very skin drank up the light. He would be sadly burned before that day's ride had ended, but better the red of sunburn than the prison pallor. It was astonishingly easy to put the past eight years behind him. One breath of the dust from the mountain road, keen with the scent of the sage, was sufficient to reduce those eight years of torment to a dream. He was free. And how glorious was freedom!

For one thing the price of those eight years of pain now awaited him, *fifty thousand dollars lying snug and safe yonder in.* . . . He dared not finish even his thought. One could not tell. He had learned in prison that the walls have ears, eternally patient, listening. Because of the secrets they had extracted, it seemed that he had to serve the full eight years. Now he knew better. No matter how deeply immersed he might be in reflection, his ears were keen and his eyes were restless. There was not a motion of a wind-blown shrub on the dusty, yellow-green hillside that he did not study. There was not a trailing cloud that crossed his path without making him look keenly up into the intolerable white-hot center of the sky.

The beauty of the whole situation lay chiefly in the fact that the crime, which had been committed by two, produced fruits that only one would enjoy. Eight years ago he and Charles

Clune had deftly opened Larry Day's safe with the help of a soap mold and some soup. They had cached the loot and fled — Rafferty into the arms of the law by some cursed fate and Charlie Clune to wander in safety for three years but never able to beat back to the place where the money was deposited. Eventually Charlie was captured. He was tried on the same charge — much the same circumstantial evidence was adduced against him — and he was given a sentence of five years in the penitentiary. Charlie came to join him in confinement, just as Charlie had been persuaded to join him in the commission of the crime. When they met inside the prison walls, they swore a pact: neither was to divulge the whereabouts of the loot, no matter how Larry Day attempted to bribe them, and neither was to touch the treasure until the other was free.

Bill Rafferty chuckled when he remembered that agreement. Seven days after his own liberation — which had been only six days ago — Charlie the carefree, Charlie the reckless, Charlie the fool, would be likewise free. But he, Bill Rafferty, would have the coin. It was fitting and proper that it should be so. Fools should be made to pay for their folly, and Charlie Clune was in sad need of a lesson. Rafferty was driving as straight as the flight of a bird cross-country toward the treasure. Afterward, if Charlie wished to call him to an accounting, that call would have to be made with a gun, and, courageous as Charlie was, he had never even distantly approached the skill of Bill with weapons.

What wonder, then, that the throat and the heart of the thief opened, as he rode through the keen sunshine, and his song floated in ringing notes over the hills? He checked his singing in the middle of a strong burst. It was foolish to make noise — always foolish. After all, there was that idiot who had played the violin until late into the previous night in the hotel at Jasperville. It had put Rafferty's teeth on edge with irritation

9

to remember it. Now he drew rein, just before the trail twisted around the mountainside in an elbow turn, to survey the landscape and make sure that no one had heard him. He even turned in the saddle to look behind him, and the well-trained cow pony turned with him. That act of looking behind him saved Bill Rafferty's hide. For a sudden noise of hoofbeats roared around the elbow turn, and five mounted men dashed at him. They had been lying in wait, no doubt, but this pause of his had made them think that he was about to turn back.

For a moment fear paralyzed his nerves, his muscles, and his brain. He could neither stir nor think. In another moment he had recovered. He jerked the reins, swayed his body, and sent the cow pony scooting down the back trail, flinging himself far forward to break the wind of the running. He looked past his shoulder, and the riders were spurring and whipping, but not a gun was drawn. They wanted him alive. And no wonder. Dead, he was simply so much useless flesh, but alive and in their hands there were ways of compelling the most recalcitrant to tell all that they knew. Besides, in his past Larry Day had become intimately familiar with Indians and their ways, and Larry Day's men, no doubt, were in pursuit.

As he thought of this, the throat of the fugitive became dry. Suddenly he blessed the roan he bestrode, and the thanksgiving came from the bottom of a full heart. He was holding the pursuers even. His own weight was one huge advantage. For he had withered away on the prison fare and in the prison shadows. Compared to the bulk of the wide-shouldered, sun-nurtured riders behind, the roan was carrying only a feather-weight. It helped in the first three furlongs of sprinting. It became a decisive factor thereafter. The shouts of the men behind told of their despair. Then guns began to bark, and bullets sang out above him. Bill Rafferty hugged the neck of his horse close, and his thin face wrinkled into a grin of satisfaction. They would not risk shooting to kill, and they were idiots, in the event they did not, to think that they could frighten him. Frighten him. Frighten Bill Rafferty. As well try to scare that old murderous lion of the mountains, Hank Jerney.

Then another turn of the trail shut out the noise of the pursuit, and it seemed as if every horse and man had cut over the edge and into the ravine. Bill Rafferty knew better. They had simply shot a bolt in vain, these hirelings of Larry Day, and now they would trail him from a distance and simply make sure that he went back to Jasperville.

Back to Jasperville. Sweat poured out upon Bill Rafferty's pale forehead at the thought. It would be another priceless day lost. Tomorrow Charlie Clune would be out of prison, and, though he was a long journey away, there was no time to spare. Besides, if a report reached him that Rafferty was trying to double-cross him, might he not make a dicker with Larry Day?

Wretched, indeed, was Rafferty's mood as the roan, drawn back to a dog-trot, wound down through the hills until Jasperville was in sight. But there was no help for it. How could he have dreamed that Day's men would have spied on him so closely? No doubt there were men in Day's pay in the town, men who had been dogging his footsteps. Still others lurked in the mountains, ready to seize him. By the merest luck he had avoided capture in this first instance, but now his eyes were opened to the danger. Hereafter, if they caught him, they would catch a weasel with their naked hands.

In Jasperville he would have the formidable protection of Sheriff Sam Matthews. Not that he dreamed of complaining to the sheriff about this affair on the road. Sam Matthews dealt with crimes committed, not with those that might happen. Besides, Matthews knew Rafferty's past record, just as a horseman knows his horse. The great point was that the sheriff would extend the cloak of his formidable name and surround

Bill with it. Not even ex-criminals could be hounded during the regime and in the district of Sheriff Matthews.

Half consoled and half despairing, Bill Rafferty jogged into Jasperville, threw a salute to the surprised blacksmith, who exclaimed at his return a curse by way of response, and went straight to the hotel. He heard the violin still wailing from an upper room, as he put up the roan in the shed behind the main building, and Bill interrupted his melancholy reflections long enough to grit his teeth and shake his fist at the player. Last night he had listened, perforce, for three hours, and there had not been a single melody, a single tune. It was all just a jumble of runs, trills, showers of notes without meaning, and the whine of the instrument had nearly maddened poor Bill.

"Must be this classical music they talk about," a more patient sufferer on the front verandah had suggested.

"Classical nothing!" Bill had exclaimed on that occasion, and he pronounced the same words as he went slowly back to the main building. How could one think against such a background? Rafferty was in an excessively touchy state of mind and nerves. As he rounded the corner of the building, the wail of the violin was perceptibly diminished, and he took up his position in a chair that he tilted back against the wall, hanging his heels on the lowest rung. Presently a little blond man with pathetic, misty-blue eyes jogged up to the hitching rack on a down-headed horse. The interest of Rafferty instantly soared. His conscious brain shut out the strains of the fiddle. For he became aware of the fact that this same blond fellow had been at the hotel the evening before. Why was he returning, and from the same direction in which Bill had started? Might he not be one of Larry Day's spies? Thereafter, Rafferty became as alert as a coiled snake, though he smiled vacantly into the heat haze that rose in waves from the roofs of the houses across the street. He heard the dim-eyed man telling one of the

12

loungers that the Custer Bridge was down, and he had to come back and hit for Jericho. It was too late to start today.

That was a logical explanation. Certainly this mild-mannered oldster was not the type of gunfighter that Larry Day was apt to gather around him. Just then, as the blue-eyed man climbed to the verandah and turned away, someone blundered suddenly out of the door. The little man whirled like a flash, smoothly in spite of his speed. And he glanced not at the clumsy fellow who had stumbled into him but straight at Bill Rafferty. It was a little thing, but Bill was perfectly convinced that his first suspicion was right. This was one of Day's spies. Now every step that Rafferty took in the town or out of it would be marked and followed. And all the time fifty thousand dollars lay up yonder near the Tucker River, fifty thousand that was his for the taking, if only he could get at it before Clune arrived to claim half. Tomorrow Clune would be speeding toward him.

A black mist whirled before Rafferty's eyes, and he began to tremble like a terrier that looks on at a hopeful fight. How bound he was with invisible chains at the very moment of success. Let it be remembered that he had already waited and endured for eight years, and it will be seen why Bill Rafferty was ready for murder.

He went to the door of the hotel and opened it. Down the stairs from the upper story wavered a plaintive, whirling measure from a minuet, but there was no music in it to the hounded ear of the thief.

"Who is making that ruction with the fiddle?" he asked the proprietor.

"That's young Loftus," said the other from behind his desk, "old Harrison Loftus's boy."

II

"FATHER AND SON"

It was such a facer for Bill that he forgot his trouble for a moment, forgot even to pursue his inquiries, as he registered for a room for that night. There are certain names in the mountain desert that take on a peculiar connotation, much like the names of noble families in Europe or first families in the South. They are names that have been ennobled through two or three generations by manly men. Every county has its group of them in a small way, and every state has a larger group, with here and there a man whose name has a much wider, almost a national reputation.

The name of Loftus was in the latter category. Gilbert Loftus started the family tradition when he crossed the plains, making history with his rifle and chipping a brief record of his exploits into the butt of his gun. John Loftus, his son, was not less war-like, and he combined with his talent for gun play and his love of the impact of fists a canny business sense, building up a fine property in cattle. The son of John, Harrison Loftus, represented the business instinct a good deal more than the combative, but still he had been a fighting man in his younger days and like his father and grandfather before him a man of untainted, undoubted integrity and rugged manhood.

No wonder, then, that Bill Rafferty gasped when he learned that the incessant player of the strange airs was a scion of this line. Vaguely he heard the clerk say: "There's the old man now."

The old man, when Bill Rafferty turned, was found to be a huge, gaunt-framed stalwart of sixty. But age, which had

14

whitened his hair and lined his face, merely allowed the stern, rigid line of the jawbone to stand out more prominently, and the eyes gleamed with unabated light. His compressed lips were ever stirring a trifle, as if he were gritting his teeth in thought and resolution. He was one of those men who seem forever on the verge of making a momentous decision. He fixed Bill Rafferty with a glance that went through the thief like the pin of a scientific inquirer through an insect. Bill shrugged his shoulders and climbed the stairs. He had not intended to go up to the vicinity of that infernal violin, but the stairs offered the first ready avenue of escape from the deep-plunging eyes of Harrison Loftus, and Bill took that exit.

He was still quivering uneasily when he reached his room, very much as if he had just passed under the attention of an officer of the law after committing a crime. Such was his perturbation, in fact, that he hardly noted the thrilling whistle of the violin in the next room as it reached the last phrase of the minuet. Rather his ears heard the heavy, trudging step of a man climbing the stairs, and he knew, as well as if he saw the big, laboring body, that it was Harrison Loftus, going to his room. A moment later the door of the adjoining room was flung open and then slammed with violence.

The violin, nevertheless, continued unperturbed to draw out the final thin-spun note. The thief listened breathlessly, not so much to the fiddle as for the outburst of the father, for he was tolerably sure that Harrison Loftus was no greater lover of classical music than was Bill Rafferty. The last note diminished to a whisper, became a part of silence itself, and then ended. The meager partition allowed the passage of every sound. Bill could even hear the rattle of the bow as it was laid on the table by the player. Then his ear welcomed the deep voice of Harrison Loftus.

"How long you been doing this?"

15

"Hello, Father," responded a musical, rather high-pitched baritone. "I don't know. My watch stopped."

A chair creaked in loud complaint. Harrison Loftus was sitting down. "Your watch stopped, eh? Your brain'll stop, too, youngster, unless you wind it up a key or two. Mark, did I ever tell you why I brought you out here to Jasperville?"

"You haven't, sir," replied young Mark, with such gentle respect that the lip of Bill Rafferty writhed in derision. He could read the flabby character of the young idiot, he thought, in the very intonation of that voice.

"Have you been able to guess?" asked the father.

"I haven't tried to," said Mark Loftus. "Matter of fact, sir, you're so much too deep for me that long ago I gave up trying to fathom your reasons for things."

"Gave me up as a waste of time, eh?"

"Far from that. But you'll have to admit that it would take a pretty high order of intelligence to find out a reason for coming to a place like Jasperville."

"Don't you like it, Mark?"

The voice was gentle. A blast of sand-laden wind rattled against the side of the hotel and shook the window sashes crazily. It seemed to the thief that the wind was a truer interpreter of the emotions of Harrison Loftus than his own words.

"Don't I like it?" echoed Mark Loftus. "Well, sir, I suppose that's meant for a joke."

"A joke?" The father paused before he went on. "Mark, I'll tell you why I've brought you and left you here for three days. I wanted to give you a chance to have the country sink in, and I wanted the people to sink in. How many people have you spoke to?"

"Three."

"Who?"

"The proprietor."

16

"That fat fool isn't a man. Who else?"

"One of the cowpunchers asked me for a match. I told him I didn't need one."

There was a faint, stifled groan from Harrison Loftus. "Who was the third man?"

"Another one of the loafers who hang around on the verandah asked me what kind of preparation I used to keep my complexion in shape."

"And what did you tell him?"

"The truth . . . that a touch of cold cream was excellent for keeping off chapped hands and lips."

"Chapped hands and . . . great guns!"

"What's the matter?"

"D'you realize, Mark, that the hound was insulting you when he asked you about the cream?"

"Insulting me? Not at all. He was perfectly grave and sober about it."

There was another groan from the father. Bill Rafferty hugged himself mightily and rocked back and forth in a silent ecstasy of enjoyment.

"The skunk!" exclaimed the father. "And you let him get away with it? Well, well, what would you have done, Mark, if you'd known that he was insulting you? What would you have done, eh?"

There were unmistakable symptoms of a yawn in Mark's voice as he answered. "Insulted me? Absurd, sir. There was no insult."

"But, I say," replied Harrison Loftus, "what would you have done?"

"Why, nothing, I suppose. I understand these fellows fight with guns. I know nothing about guns."

"You'd have done nothing?"

"What can a man do against a gun with his bare fists?"

17

"Walk up to it, sir," declared the father. "Walk up to it, if that is necessary, for the honor of your name and fame and knock the insulting scoundrel down."

"Would you really do that?"

"Would I? I tell you, I have."

"Well, well," murmured the son in a sort of undisturbed, conversational wonder, "you are a hardy sort, sir."

Again Bill Rafferty rocked himself back and forth in an ecstasy.

"When you were back East at school all these years," asked the father, "what did you do when someone insulted you?"

"Turned on my heel and left him."

There was a gasp from Harrison Loftus. "What?"

"Why, of course. When one meets such a mucker, there is nothing to do but leave the room. One mustn't be rowing, you know."

"Cattle and canaries!" exclaimed the father.

He seemed unable to speak for a moment. Bill Rafferty, sneaking to the wall with his cat-like, noiseless steps, heard the heavy breathing of the older man.

"But I thought," said Harrison Loftus at length, "that you were very much interested in boxing?"

"Yes. I put in a session at that every day. With thick gloves, you know, so that a fellow won't be all scarred up. But bare fists are quite another matter. Why, sir, do you know that one may be marked for life in a low brawl?"

"I, sir," retorted the father, "am marked for life, and do you know that I'm proud of it?"

"Really?" asked Mark in his college drawl. "Of course, I don't intend to cast any imputations on you, sir, but I think it must have been unnecessary."

There was no answer. The chair creaked as Harrison Loftus rose, and then the floor creaked again as his heavy steps passed up and down the room. What agony of doubt was going on in the mind of the big man, Bill Rafferty could only dimly guess. But what he guessed pleased him. His eight years in prison had made him a specialist in pain, and he enjoyed seeing another suffer. Rafferty felt the world and society owed him many such sights to make up for what he had been through.

"Mark," said the older man at length, "what is your main ambition in life?"

"To play the violin," said the other without hesitation.

"And do you know what my ambition for you is?"

"Don't think you've ever told me."

"I'll tell you now in a word. My ambition is for you to be a man with a capital M."

"That sounds rather epigrammatic . . . in the Kipling vein," remarked the son. "Just what do you mean?"

"There's only one way for you to find out what I mean, and that's for you to go out and wander around in this country, my country, a man's country, Mark. Find out what the country is. Find out what the men in it are. Then try to be like them. Good bye for a while."

"Going so soon? Why?"

"I need air," said Harrison Loftus, and the door slammed heavily behind him.

"My word," muttered the son, "this is rare."

But presently the thief heard a lighter step begin to pace the neighboring room slowly, as a man paces when he is deep in thought.

19

III

"BAITING THE TRAP"

In the meantime his own agile mind raced as Rafferty withdrew with his dexterous, cat-footed step to the center of his compartment. He had a corner room, and he could look through the windows on two sides — upon the village of Jasperville on the one hand, or upon the raw-sided mountains on the other. Looking upon those two scenes it was strange, indeed, to think that a man bearing the name of Loftus could not refer to this as *his* country. Loftus. That name had been drilled into the ears of his infancy, had loomed great in his boyhood, and he had retained its formidable sound when he reached the age of maturity and was accustomed to use his craft to make fools of other men. From the first they had stood for law and order, these Loftus men. From the first they had been in the front rank in combating the problems of Western life.

No bad man was so dangerously wicked that a Loftus could not be found to hunt him down and crush the viper. No good man was ever in a strait so desperate that a Loftus would not go to his aid. Indeed, there was a ring of manliness to the very sound of the name, or so it seemed to Bill Rafferty. Loftus. Then, glancing over his shoulder, he cringed a little and smiled a crooked, savage smile in mockery of his own weakness of soul. In his own time of need what would he not have given for such an ally as one of these Loftus men?

A form drifted slowly past his window. It was the son, Mark, strolling on the upper level of the verandah that was a double-decker. The bowed head attracted him, for sorrow is mysteriously akin to crime. The thief stepped out onto the verandah.

They could not be seen from the street. They were alone, these two, between the roofs and the mountains. Their solitude placed them at once in confidential relationship with one another.

Bill Rafferty did not venture a straight glance at the other. As a matter of fact, Bill did not see so much in anything when he stared at it. He had learned, out of necessity, to grasp all details in a flash. One glimpse of the exposed mechanism of a lock was to the trained brain of Bill as good as a week of study. One flicker of the eyes of a man had taught him what he wanted to know about the insides of that man. And the first side-glance at Mark Loftus taught him what he wished to be taught.

Mark, except that he was larger, was in appearance exactly the innocuous sort of fellow that Rafferty, with the thin partition between them, had guessed him to be. Yes, he was very large for a middle-size man. His shoulders and chest were what Bill had heard his father often refer to as the "Loftus type." That is to say, the whole powerful Loftus family, generation after generation, was equipped with the same shoulders, not overwide, but very thick, and an arched chest, very deep also. Below the waist Mark Loftus tapered away to a slenderness that is so often seen in athletic men. Above the waist he swelled to formidable proportions, culminating in a big, heavy neck and a big, blocky, handsome head. All of these characteristics were common to the Loftus men. Bill Rafferty had often studied their pictures. Most crooks in the West had studied them in the same fashion from time to time. For bad men, of one sort or another, had an almost monotonous habit of running into a Loftus and their own finish, sooner or later. No wonder, then, that Bill Rafferty in a single glance could tell in what Mark agreed with the type and in what he differed from it. The differences, in fact, were as pronounced as the agreements. Stern resolve had not gathered the brows into wrinkles between

21

the eyes, neither had it caused his jaw to jut out a little as did Harrison Loftus's jaw. The light of his eyes was not gathered into a small, penetrating spark but was mildly diffused. The mouth was formed with feminine tenderness compared with the rigid line of Harrison Loftus's lips. And, all in all, one missed in the son the labor-hardened, danger-tried peculiarities of the father. Harrison Loftus had the head of a lion, but the head of Mark Loftus was not even the head of a lion cub.

Bill Rafferty swallowed with relief. It would be possible to talk to this youth without feeling that his own soul was being dragged out from behind folded doors, dragged out and exposed to a biting light of understanding. Those mild blue, almost misty, eyes of Mark — a child could have deceived him. As he leaned on the rail of the verandah, the plot rose and unfolded in Rafferty's mind. In a single moment it passed from a seed to a swiftly aspiring shoot, and then opened a luxurious flower at the head of the stalk. *Suppose he were actually to use a Loftus man in his own interests? Not to let Mark in on the secret, but to use the boy blindly? Suppose he made Mark the connecting link? Far off in the mountains were Hank Jerney and his band, outlawed but honest. Hank would do much for a third of fifty thousand dollars. Hank would stick by it. No doubt of that. Suppose, then, that he used young Loftus to reach the outlaw?*

This process of thought was cut short. Mark Loftus had halted and was clearing his throat, as if about to speak. Rafferty cast a glance over the heat-dimmed mountains. Yonder rode Larry Day and his men, watching for him. But would they ever dream of suspecting a Loftus? And, if they did, would they dare to lay hands on him? The thought struck like a full chime of bells in Rafferty.

"I beg your pardon," a voice was murmuring in embarrassment.

Rafferty turned, genially grinning upon Mark Loftus.

"Hello," said Bill. "Speak to me?"

"I did. I. . . ." He paused, mentally fumbling, his eyes downcast. "Do you happen to know a man named Lawrence Day?"

In spite of himself Rafferty was shocked into an oath of surprise. The question was entirely too apropos. "I do," he answered. "Why?"

"My name is Loftus," Mark hastened to explain in his gentle, soothing voice. "My father has come on here to meet Mister Day."

A bright light broke across the brain of Rafferty. He might have guessed it before. In his desperate determination to recover his lost money Larry Day had called on all his friends, and Harrison Loftus was among them. That accounted for the keen look which the man had turned on him when they passed each other downstairs. Loftus himself was one of the enemy. The blood of Rafferty turned cold.

"I know Larry Day," admitted Bill thickly.

"Ah," murmured the other, seemingly much pleased. "The reason I ask is that my father admires Mister Day a great deal. In fact, he has often told me that he wished I would use Mister Day as a model, but he has never been able to explain to me just what sort of a fellow this Day is. I wonder if you can?"

"What's he told you about Day?"

"My father is a trifle cryptic. He simply says that Mister Day is a man." He smiled faintly, as he imitated the booming voice of Harrison Loftus.

"And you allow you'd like to do what your father wants? You'd like to be like Larry Day?"

"I suppose so," said Mark Loftus. "I don't agree with all the *pater*'s ideals, but I ought to conform for the sake of maintaining peace in the family, you know."

Bill Rafferty grunted and, for the sake of gaining time, drew

23

out papers and tobacco and started to roll a cigarette. He offered the makings to the boy when he was through, and he watched Mark laboriously construct a smoke. He worked as one new to the art, but the imitation was fairly good. The result was proof that young Loftus had some aptitude.

"I'll tell you about Day," said Bill at length. "He's a fighter."

"I gathered that," replied Mark Loftus.

"Made his rep young," went on Bill. "Back in the days of the Alison-Tucker feud Larry was with the Alisons when they were penned up in the mountains by the Tuckers. Larry slipped out one night, rode right through the Tuckers, went fifty miles, raised a party, and led 'em back. He got the Alisons loose. So if you want to be like Day, son, you'd have to start out with something like that."

He glanced carelessly at Mark. The latter had turned his quiet, gentle eyes toward the mountains and was nodding to the intense surprise of Bill.

"If there were only riding to do, I can ride well enough. They do some riding in the East, you know. But they don't have feuds about here in these days."

Suddenly Rafferty became extremely frank. "My room is next to yours. I heard your dad roaring at you a few minutes ago." Mark flushed and stiffened. "And the short of it," went on Bill in the most friendly manner, "is that you have your dander up. You want to prove to your old man that you got the stuff in you."

"If it can be done without brutal brawling, yes," admitted Mark.

Bill feigned dark, deep thoughtfulness, at length peering earnestly at his companion. "The word of a Loftus means a good deal," he said at last. "Suppose you give me your word that what I tell you stays dark?"

"And by that you mean?"

24

"That you don't repeat."

"Certainly," replied Mark.

"You'll shake on it?"

"By all means." He suited the action to the word, while Bill Rafferty sighed with pleasure.

"Well," continued Bill, "I'll tell you straight. Your father and Larry Day and a bunch of other gents are around Jasperville to keep me here in a trap . . . me, Bill Rafferty. Ever hear your dad mention me?"

"Never."

Again Bill sighed with relief.

"You mean to say," went on Mark Loftus, "that my father . . . ?"

"Just what I say. And now suppose, me being trapped like this, that you was to take a letter for me and ride into the hills and give it to a gent for me? Suppose I was to stay right here and slip you out of the trap instead?"

Mark Loftus frowned. "To destroy one of my father's plans? That would surely be a singular business for me."

"And ain't it a kind of singular business for him to keep you here, without ever telling you what he's in Jasperville for? Is that fatherly, I ask you? No, it ain't. And suppose you up and bust through the lines instead of me doing it. Won't that teach him that you got to be reckoned with for a man after this?"

The son shook his head. "It's entirely wild, Mister Rafferty. That letter . . . why, I haven't the slightest idea what it contains."

"That's the whole point," said the thief eagerly. "You don't know what's in that letter, and so, if they's anything wrong, it don't fall on your head. I don't mind telling you," he added in a burst of greater confidence, "that the message won't be just what everybody would call legal news. But what you're

25

out for is to get your father's respect. Well, sir, if you carry this letter through, you'll have it. You can lay to that. You'll be doing a thing that's a dead ringer for the thing that brought old Larry Day his rep when he was young."

Still Mark Loftus shook his head.

"Come into my room," said Rafferty suddenly. "I'll give you reasons. You want a lark. I'll show you one. You want something to do. I'll give you something. Here are your father and Larry Day, both busting themselves to keep something from happening. And you step out and measure up to 'em both. It might make your father cuss a little, but what d'you care about that? It ain't going to make or break Harrison Loftus, anything that I can do. That's sure easy to see. You come in here."

Mark, still shaking his head but with a brightening eye, obeyed.

IV

"MARK SHOWS HIS METTLE"

It was fully an hour later when young Mark Loftus, his eye gleaming and his step light, came out of the room of the thief, entered his own, and hastily donned the whole outfit of silly togs — as he called the Western riding clothes that his father had presented to him on his arrival. Had he paused for a single moment, even over a worn boot heel, he would have had time enough for reflection that would have made him throw up the entire business. But he had no time for reflection, and his mind was simply filled with the prospect of a great lark.

A half hour of sober reflection would have convinced him that there were profound reasons that leagued his father and Larry Day against this stranger. Without that reflection he could only hark back to the saddened voice in which Rafferty had merely hinted at huge injustices done him in the past, injustices that he was now trying to rectify in an extra-legal, rather than in an illegal, manner. But the main point was simply that his father, in the interview earlier in the day, had goaded him to the point of rebellion, and Rafferty had caught him while he was still hot and ready for the mold.

In ten minutes he was rattling his spurs on the way downstairs. In ten minutes more he was out at the shed, throwing the saddle on the back of his horse. He would have preferred an English saddle, but this heavy contraption would have to do. As for the horse — well, that was a different matter. He had chosen the horse himself, and, though his father had shrugged his shoulders with a grunt, Mark was satisfied with the long legs and the clean-cut lines of his mount. Five minutes later he swung onto the back of the rangy bay and swept into the main street of the town at a swinging gallop. He was acutely conscious of curious eyes on either side of him, curious smiles, and, above all, conscious of the letter that rattled crisply and faintly in the breast pocket of his shirt.

But no eyes followed him with so much interest as the eyes of Bill Rafferty, sitting hunched at his window, hugging himself with his long, lean arms and rocking a little from side to side in happiness. They would never guess. How could they ever guess? There was only one danger — that Mark would open the letter. And that was not a danger, after all. The Loftus word of honor was better than a signed and witnessed contract. Mark would go straight on to his goal. The rider disappeared out of sight over the first hill beyond the village, as the door of his room opened softly, without a knock. Bill Rafferty turned abruptly to see the little fellow with the faded eyes, leaning against the jamb.

"Well, Bill," said the stranger, "the whole jig's up, I guess."

"Eh?" gasped Rafferty.

"You sure played a fool part," said the other calmly. "Don't you suppose we was watching? When you grabbed that young fool, Loftus, don't you suppose you was seen? Oh, it's easy to figure out how you got to him. He's going to make himself over into a regular man-eater, so's his daddy will pat him on the back, eh? Well, Bill, he'll deliver that letter he's carrying a sight sooner than you expect. Look up the hill, there, beyond the town. His own dad is there waiting for him. Here's my field glasses, Bill. Just train this here on the road."

Without a word, his hand frozen with fear, Bill Rafferty accepted the glasses and focused them on the road, upon the figure of the horseman who was now climbing the farther hillside. True enough, it happened exactly as the stranger had prophesied. They had laid their little ambush barely outside of the village, so that they might not be seen from Jasperville itself. Now, out of the cross trail and from behind a huge pile of red-sided rocks, rode no less a person than Harrison Loftus himself, and beside him rode two others. Before the raised hand of his father the boy drew rein abruptly, and before that raised hand the thief's heart shrank and well nigh stopped. He could see Mark Loftus, talking with expostulating gesture, but then Harrison Loftus reached out and drew away a shining bit of white. The vision of the thief was blurred. It was his precious letter with the envelope scrawled over with directions for reaching Hank Jerney. It was his letter, begging Jerney for help and offering to split with him — one part out of three — the treasure whose location he had named. Thus appealed to, there was no doubt that Jerney would have accepted the proffer. Now, falling into the hands of the enemy, Larry Day would be led straight to his lost money. And he, Bill Rafferty, would be again rounded up by officers of the law for conspiracy.

He could see Harrison Loftus hand the letter to one of his companions for safekeeping. He could see him talk with a threateningly raised hand to his son, and he could see the boy shrink under the words. What a fool, what a triple fool he had been to trust anything to that soft-headed idiot.

"It's over, eh?" asked the stranger behind him.

"It's over," repeated Bill Rafferty in a husky voice. "I suppose . . . ," but here he cried out in astonishment. There had been a sudden commotion in the group. Mark Loftus had spurred his horse ahead, and his arm lashed out. The letter was snatched from the hand of the grinning cowpuncher who held it. And, while he was brushed aside by the unexpected rush of Mark's horse, the second of Harrison Loftus's men thrust his mount across the trail. Again the arm of Mark darted out. The horseman, who was attempting to bar the way, reeled in his saddle and pitched into the dust of the road, and Mark was away through the gap, leaning far forward over the neck of his mount and spurring for dear life. With a yell of triumph Bill Rafferty leaped to his feet. "Good boy!" he shouted. "I knew the Loftus strain would tell!"

The glasses were snatched from his hand by the misty-eyed stranger who, in turn, leveled it up the road. "The fool kid has busted loose!" he exclaimed. "And his dad's pulled a gun on him . . . he's shooting."

"What?" Rafferty demanded.

"It's true. He's down. No, his horse only stumbled. Now he's around the corner of the hill. There goes Harrison and Pete after him. Joe is just getting up from the ground."

"Shooting at his own kid?"

"He'd shoot at the devil, if the devil tried to double-cross him."

It was, indeed, true. The unexpected break of Mark had caught all three of his captors unaware. He was many a precious yard away before his father recovered his wits sufficiently to yell a command after him and start in pursuit. But the long legs of the runner Mark was mounted on still put stride after stride between him and the two pursuers. Then it was that, in rage and shame, Harrison Loftus whipped out his revolver and fired twice in the air to warn his son back, and, when the boy did not draw rein, the hardy old rancher shot point-blank, not at the rider, to be sure, but at the horse he bestrode. Twice he fired, and twice his anger and the jolting motion of his horse sent his bullet wide, and then Mark whipped out of sight around the corner of the hill. When Harrison Loftus himself rounded the turn, his son was too far off for effective gun work, and the two pursuers settled down to the chase.

"Steady, Pete," he called to the man who rode beside him. "We'll get that fool kid yet. That horse of his ain't built for mountain work."

This, however, was by no means the opinion of Mark Loftus. He had found himself driven swiftly into a safe lead by the speed of his half-bred mare, and to her, he firmly believed, he owed his life. The meaning of those two shots fired into the air had not reached him. He simply knew that he was under fire, and he was convinced that his father, losing all sense of relationship, all sense of fair play, was firing at his own son, and firing to kill. Hot indignation held the brain of Mark. The brutality of it maddened him, and, for a moment if he had been armed, he would have swung around in the saddle and answered bullet with bullet.

After that he sobered a little. No, he could not send a bullet at the broad breast of his father, but he would fight him in every way that lay at his command. Bill Rafferty had been right in that exciting talk in the latter's room at the hotel. His father not only despised him but had no affection for him. He was worse than a black sheep. He was a blot on the escutcheon. In a wave of grief and shame and rage Mark vowed that he would thwart them all and carry his message to its destination. The stinging words of his father had whipped him to the outbreak to regain the letter and bolt for freedom; the hum of the bullets near him had roused a fierce and steady determination within him. No doubt he had been a fool to undertake this questionable commission on behalf of Bill Rafferty, but the point was that he had undertaken it, and he would give his life now to carry it through.

He looked back. His father and Pete were falling farther and farther behind. At every step the bay gained. But he must not exhaust her on a grade as severe as this. The pursuers were rocking along at a steady canter that, he had heard, a Western pony can keep up all day. Well, he would match it with a steady trot. At that pace, then, he wound up the steep trail, only breaking into a gallop when they reached a comparatively level stretch. An hour passed, and, looking behind him, he could see no trace of the pursuers, though the windings of the trail allowed him to look only a short distance to the rear. But, judging from the sound of the mare's breathing and the down-headed way in which she went about her work, she was nearly exhausted, and a pace that had exhausted her must have completely outdistanced his father and Pete on their cow ponies.

Accordingly, Mark drew out the envelope and examined the directions again. They were comprehensive and clear. On the one side was a little, rudely drawn sketch with names of towns and trails and distances estimated. On the other side directions were written out closely. A child could have understood them. He was still studying the writing when an echo of hoofbeats, thrown out from a cliff behind him, made him turn in the saddle. Not two hundred yards behind came his father, Pete, and Joe. How could they have kept so close?

He turned, his head spinning in amazement, and gave the bay the spurs. She responded gallantly with a reaching gallop over a level stretch, but, when she struck another hill beyond, she staggered and nearly fell. Mark, in dismay, turned in the saddle to look again. Still the cow ponies came steadily on at their rocking canter, and, when they struck the slope again, they fell into a tireless dog-trot, gaining incessantly. Where in their meager bodies, their wasted quarters, and their scrawny shoulders did they find the strength? And every one of them was carrying greater weight than the bay. He listened painfully to the gasping breath of his mount. She would be ruined by another three miles of this pace in such a country. Was she not a third of the horse he had deemed her? No, her lines were true, and he had given her a stiff trial before buying. It was simply that the dogged little cow ponies behind him had the greater reserves of strength.

It was very mysterious, and so were the men of this country

mysterious, and cruelly mysterious his own father had proven himself to be on this day. An emotion of anger and sorrow swept over Mark Loftus as he remembered. The last word, he felt, had been spoken between him and Harrison Loftus. From this point their trails through life branched out. He could never again accept support from such a man. He could never again sit with him in amity in the same room.

With a grim determination, as he reached the top of the grade, Mark turned in the saddle, looked back, measured the distance of the trio and then measured the downward slope of the trail. Here, at least, the long legs of the bay would tell in his favor. Here he would give his father reason to change his mind about the importance of breeding in a saddle horse. He let the bay go, holding onto her head just strongly enough to steady her in her stride, without decreasing the velocity of her gallop. She struck out with vim, the ground running swiftly back beneath her. Yet it was killing work on her. The rack of the downhill strain was beginning to tell on her. She was still showing signs of exhaustion.

He looked back savagely toward the pursuers. Behold, they were rocking down the slope on a loose rein, as comfortably as they had run uphill. Mark understood with a sudden burst of dismay that his father had been right. Such a horse as this mare was not meant for the mountains. In another mile she would be spent, and the little insignificant ponies behind him would still have a day's running inside their cinches.

V

"LOFTUS AGAINST LOFTUS"

It was a grim moment for Mark Loftus as he thought of facing his father in surrender. Until he confronted the immediate danger of that surrender, Mark did not realize truly how wide was the gap that had spread between him and Harrison Loftus in the past few moments. But now he knew that he had almost sooner die than give up.

He looked about him. To the left the mountainside rose sheer. A goat could not have secured a sufficient foothold in that direction. He looked to the right. The slope fell away even more sheer than it rose on the other side. It dropped to a narrow strip of farm land below, and then the steep wall of the valley shot up again and terminated in peaks that chopped high up into the skyline. Mark swung his horse so close to the edge of the cliff that she shuddered and cut down her gallop to a staggering canter. Truly she was far gone.

The yell of triumph from Pete and Joe rang in Mark's ears as he at last stopped the mare altogether and faced toward the trio. As he saw his father in that moment, he would remember him to the end of his days, sitting erect, square of shoulders, grimly placid of face, with the wide sombrero brim lifting in the wind of his gallop. He was like a rock, and, Mark shrewdly guessed, there would be as much sympathetic understanding in him as in a rock. Whatever tenderness he had received so far had been because of his facial resemblance to his dead mother, and because he had never yet crossed his father definitely. Now the gauge of battle was flung down, and he knew that Harrison Loftus would not be the first to give way. He would play the new game to the end, no matter how bitter that end might be. He would jail his own son with as little compunction as another man might show toward a hardened criminal.

These reflections passed through Mark's brain during the space of time that it took him to fling the reins away and throw himself out of the saddle. The moment his heels struck the ground, he realized what was before him. He was alone, empty-handed, surrounded by enemies, and in a country to which his only guide was the rudely scratched map and directions of Bill Rafferty. Yet his determination was taken, and a thrill of wild joy ran through him as he realized that in the great emergency he was not afraid. How many men go through life never really knowing whether they are made of the stuff of heroes or cowards?

He shook his fist in the direction of the onrushing horsemen and then sprang from the edge of the trail to the face of a boulder, some six feet to the right and an equal distance below him. There was a new tune to the shout that went up from the pursuers, a note of astonishment that did Mark Loftus's heart infinite good. He waited to hear no more but gave himself whole-heartedly to the work that lay before him. It was work to have tasked the abilities of a mountain sheep, those inimitable climbers. Only headlong anger could have driven Mark to it, familiar though he was with mountain-climbing excursions. To the cattlemen above, used to travel only on horseback, the descent seemed both insane and impossible.

Down that mountainside a litter of boulders had been poured by some huge landslide. They made a slippery, uncertain stairway down which Mark plunged. Very soon the descent was out of his own power to control. His impetus swept him along, and, his heart choking his throat, he found himself literally flying over an abyss, striking half futilely with his feet at a rock here, a crevice there, to arrest the velocity of that continuous fall. It seemed as if his body were converted to lead, and his muscles suddenly shriveled to nothing, as the power of gravity swept him down and down.

A bush projected from a meager hold on the face of a rock. He caught at it with both arms, but, though it checked his fall, it came loose bodily, and a shower of gravel and dirt descended after him. Yet that check enabled him to regain the mastery of his descent. He bounded from rock to rock. After the terrible, involuntary risks of the first part of that downward climb, things that would have turned an ordinary mountaineer pale were now nothing. Presently his heels dug deep into soft dirt and gravel. He sank back against the slope, his legs numb to the hips, his feet bruised and sore. And then, high, high above him, he heard voices shrill and small with distance. He looked up. So precipitous was that descent the cliff seemed to lean out above him, and on the trail above, as if leaning out from a parapet, were his father and the two cowpunchers. Mark Loftus dropped his head, for his brain was spinning. Only by a miracle had he gained the level going, it seemed.

When he stood up and glanced toward the trail again, his father and the other two had disappeared. Perhaps they had started back toward Jasperville to spread the alarm. Perhaps they were seeking some less neck-breaking mode of entrance to the valley. He had no time to pause and wonder. In his pocket was a well-filled wallet. In the pocket of his shirt was the map of the country. He must press ahead, as fast and as far as he could. He struck straight across the valley.

In the meantime, as Harrison Loftus and his men cantered back toward Jasperville, they rode in a dead silence. Joe, from time to time, lifted his hand and gingerly touched a sore and swollen place on his jaw where the fist of Mark had connected and tumbled him from his horse. Pete observed this maneuver with something akin to a smile that he dared not show. Neither did either of them dare to make a comment on the fugitive. He was the son of Harrison Loftus, and one did not complain to a lion about the actions of its cub. They fell back a little, letting the gray-haired rancher ride on by himself.

"What burns me," said Joe, "is that the good-for-nothing hound won't have nothing done to him for this. No, sir, he'll get off scot-free."

"Most like," replied Pete. "The sheriff sure won't bust himself to catch Harry Loftus's boy."

"If anybody else had done it," declared Joe, "they'd have the whole county out, hunting for him."

"No, they wouldn't," insisted Pete. "They can't call in the law yet. This is just a private brawl between Bill Rafferty and Larry Day, with Loftus taking the part of Day. The whole idea is that Rafferty and Clune have been punished for a theft. Now they can't be touched till they lay their hands on the loot, and Larry Day is taking the law in his own hands. He's got to before they can get the coin. He'll burn the information he wants out of 'em. Nope, they can't use the law, and they couldn't set it loose on the tail of young Loftus."

"He'll come to no good," said Joe heavily. "Remember how he was sitting there, sort of dull-eyed, until his dad cussed him out for being a fool and a coward?"

"Then I heard the kid's teeth click. He was sure peeved."

"I heard his fist click on my jaw," answered Joe, "and I'll get back at the hound one day."

"Not if you have to foller him on foot," suggested Pete.

"Nope. He's sure a wild man when it comes to climbing. Man, my stomach plumb collapsed and turned into a chunk of ice when I seen the chances that fool was taking."

"And that, after his father called him a coward," said Pete, chuckling. "A Loftus is a Loftus. I sure didn't think that the fiddler had this much gumption in him. But you can't never tell. Here's Larry Day."

The latter — a broad, chunky man with a smile that involved half of his face in wrinkles — cantered out onto the trail, as they jogged into sight of Jasperville, and swung in beside Loftus. Then, without gesture and without raising his voice, the two trailing cowpunchers observed the father tell the story about his son. In the end they saw Larry Day strike his flat hand against his thigh and break into laughter. In response Harrison Loftus reached out his hand and balled it into a fist.

"I can't help laughing," Larry Day said. "The idea of that old Loftus strain breaking out in the kid like that. Why, I thought you told me he was a softy, Harrison?"

It was in answer to this remark that Loftus made the gesture of gripping and crushing something in the thin air. "He's soft enough for me to break him," he said through savagely set teeth. "He called me a liar to my face."

Larry Day grew suddenly sober. "What had you called him first?"

"A fool," admitted the father slowly, "and a coward."

"Eh? That's going it pretty strong, even if he is your own boy, Loftus."

"There's never been a Loftus that dared talk back to his father," said the other, "and it's not going to begin now. My dad would have skinned me alive if I so much as whispered something he didn't want to hear. I'll do the same by Mark. By heaven, I will."

"Steady," cautioned his friend. "Steady, partner. Now, look a-here, Harrison. Your dad was a hardy sort, and you ain't all velvet yourself, eh? Still you're a long shot from being as leathery as your dad was, and your kid is bound to be less leathery still. You can't treat him as rough as you were treated and. . . ."

"I've made his way too smooth already," replied Loftus. "I've kept him away from me. I've kept him in the East. I've let him do what he wanted to do. That was for the sake of his mother. Now he comes out here with the air of a duke and the skin of a two-year-old. More'n that, Larry, he don't like the country and the people in it."

"How've you tried to make him like the country and the people?"

"I put him here among 'em. Isn't that the best way?"

"Not to my way of thinking. Loftus, I warn you, give that youngster rope, or he'll hang himself. Don't try to hold him too short."

"He'll learn my ways," insisted the father, setting his jaw grimly, "and he'll live my way, or I'll know the reason why. He's called me a liar. He's knocked down one of my men in front of my face. He's treated me like a stranger. Well, I'm going to treat him like a stranger. I'll bring him to time."

Larry Day shook his head.

"Day, look here," said Loftus, "don't you realize that the youngster has been sent out by Rafferty?"

"I suppose he has."

"And, if he gets to the end of his trail, d'you realize that he'll probably get that money for Rafferty and turn it over to him eventually?"

Day frowned.

"Now, Larry, how would you like that?"

"I guess I wouldn't like it, but I wouldn't see you and Mark set ag'in' one another for the sake of me and any fifty thousand dollars. No, not for a million, either."

In reply Loftus dropped his gloved hand on the arm of his old friend. "The money's only one part of it, and the smallest part, Larry. I'm going to see that you get it, every cent of it. But more important still, I'm going to teach Mark that I'm a bigger and stronger man than he is in this country. I'm going to teach him that I've only got to lift my hand, and he'll be surrounded with enemies all through the mountains. Understand?"

"Halfway," said Larry Day, still frowning and shaking his head. "But go ahead. What do you mean to do?"

"It's easy to see. Larry, all though these parts I have friends, friends that I've made, and friends that my father made, you understand that?"

"Why, Harrison, there isn't a decent man in the cattle country that wouldn't walk ten miles and swim a river for the sake of a Loftus."

"I think we're trusted," said the other with a touch of emotion. "We've always stood for what's square and right, I think, and we've fought and bled and suffered in order to build up a name for honesty. Well, Larry, d'you think I'm going to see a boy of mine throw away all that two generations of his family have labored for? Larry, I'd rather see him dead!" There was a ring of decision in his voice.

"And?" queried Day anxiously.

"I'm going back to Jasperville," said the rancher, "to get at the telegraph there, and with the telegraph I'm going to wire to every town inside of a hundred miles. I'll give them detailed descriptions of Mark and tell them that he's wanted by Harrison Loftus. I think that'll get them out hunting."

"You'll tell them," asked Day, gray with anxiety, "that you want your son?"

"I'll leave that out."

"Say, partner, d'you realize that they may go out, all set to get him dead or alive, that they may go out with guns?"

Harrison Loftus was as pale as his companion, but he answered sternly: "He's brought this on his own head. I've told you, Larry, that I'd break him to my will or smash him

40

. . . and smash him I will, if I have to."

"Loftus," declared Larry Day, "I know you, and that's why I know that it ain't any good to try to persuade you, but the day may come when you'll curse yourself for what you're planning to do, and you'll curse me for being the cause of it."

VI

"SMOKE"

It was sunset time when Mark Loftus climbed wearily to the crest of the farther wall of the valley. In half an hour more he reached, on a hillside meadow, a field of shocked hay. It was too inviting to be passed. He spread out a shock, dove into it headfirst, and stretched his aching muscles. Then he slept.

When he wakened, the ground was black with night, and the sky was brilliant with such stars as shine on the mountains only. Indeed, it seemed to Mark that he had never beheld the stars before. He had only noted dim and faint imitations of them in the cities. Someone has said — or should have said — that the stars are dear to hunted men. They were dear to Mark Loftus as he stood up and, stretching himself gingerly, rejoiced to find that sleep had restored the flexibility of his muscles. How long he had slept he could not guess, but he knew that he was sufficiently refreshed to begin a new day.

He knew also before he took the first stride forward that he was equipped with a raging appetite. He tightened his belt to the last hole and then growled his opinion of writers who recommended this as a means of staving off the pangs of hunger. Presently he swung over the crest of the hill and came in sudden sight of a village in the hollow beyond. It was a startling thing to see. He had fallen asleep, convinced that he was in the midst of an uninhabited wilderness. Now he felt a ghostly certainty that the houses must have stolen up on him while he dreamed. But, after all, he should have guessed, by the field of shocked hay, that men were near.

There was no light shining in the village, a sure sign that

it was very late. Nevertheless, every roof represented to Mark a kitchen, and every thought of a kitchen was a stabbing pain in his vitals. He stepped down the hillside, as he had never stepped before. In the main street of the village a dog came out and barked at his heels, but Mark felt no malice. A strange joyousness was spreading through him. There was no reason for it that he could trace, but he could not help feeling that he was in some way freed for the first time in his life from a bondage. It may have been only the result of the keen mountain air, the hope of a square meal, the realization that he was his own master, but at any rate the glorious sense of freedom was with him, and he felt like lifting his head and breaking into song.

He chose the neatest house that he came to, a house retired a little from the street, with some attempt at a garden in the front yard. His knock on the front door raised an echo that traveled with ghostly solemnity through the interior, but he heard no other answer. It must be very late, indeed. He knocked again, this time more heavily, and presently a window squeaked as it was raised above him.

"Who's down yonder?" asked a girl's voice.

"Me," answered Mark foolishly.

He was so surprised by the gentle sound of that voice that he blinked as he spoke. Having consigned himself to a wild adventure, it seemed to Mark that the whole range of the mountains could be filled with nothing but unshaven men.

"Who's me?" demanded the cross voice above him. "And what d'you want?"

"Food," said Mark heartily. "And lots of it, *pronto*."

He used the word as one born to familiarity with Western slang.

There was a chilly instant of silence. Then: "D'you know what time it is?"

"I've lost my watch," answered Mark.

"It's two o'clock," said the voice of the girl.

There was a dull roar from the interior of the house. "Stop that yapping, Mary. If the gent wants food, feed him. But lemme get my sleep out, will you?"

This cut short the dialogue. The window was banged down. Another interval of silence followed, then light footfalls tapped down the stairs, and a lamp gleamed in the cracks around the door. It was opened a gingerly inch, and Mark felt, rather than saw, an eye peering forth at him. He took off his hat.

"I intend to pay for it, you know," he said reassuringly. It seemed that the mention of money might reëstablish his respectability.

"Hush," protested the girl. "If you wake up Uncle Dan again, you'll never get so much as a bite of bread, I warn you that. Lemme see. Nope, I've never laid eyes on you before. Where d'you belong?"

"Yonder," said Mark carelessly, and he waved his hand.

"Oh," said Mary. "Well, I've got my orders. Come on in."

She opened the door, letting a flood of lamplight fall on his face and on her own. They both hung there a moment, staring. He saw rather frightened, wide eyes and brown hair, waving low across the forehead. He saw, moreover, slender fingers, spread about the body of the lamp, and a round, small wrist, not quite lost in the shadows.

After that instant she turned her back on him and led the way into the interior of the house. He had a glimpse of a room on his right, a room on his left. He could distinguish nothing. A sense of snug comfort stole out on him. After that, he centered his attention on the girl with the lamp. She had seemed hardly more than a child when she stood in the doorway with the shadows swarming about her, but now that her back was turned, something in the round, firm mold of her neck,

44

something in the shaping of her shoulders, something in her walk told him that she had entered young womanhood.

She brought him straight into the kitchen. Smells of food assailed his sensitive nostrils. The oilcloth on the table, where she placed the lamp, was new and caught up bright reflections. The boards underfoot were unpainted and rough from wear of shoes and wear of scrubbing. Indeed, they were scrubbed white. The ceiling slanted sharply down above the stove. *The kitchen must be a built-on shed. Probably it was terribly hot in summer. Did she have to cook here? Had those small hands done the scrubbing of the floor? Had they polished the cooking utensils that were ranged above the stove?* A myriad of slightly connected observations and reflections swarmed through his brain, and then his thoughts centered again around the girl.

With her arms hanging rather helplessly by her sides she stood, looking first at him, then at a lofty, capacious cupboard. It was as if the problem of feeding him were a baffling thing. Then she looked straight at him, smiling a little. It was a wonderfully becoming smile.

"What do you like?"

"I like everything," answered Mark Loftus. "Plain bread will do fine for me. If there's any milk, it will be better than nectar. Cold ham would be a meal for the gods, according to the way I feel just now, and boiled eggs are something to dream about."

"They are in most places around these parts," said the girl, "but we keep hens." She opened the cupboard and produced a blue bowl in which the eggs gleamed like crystal. "You make the fire, while I get things together."

He crushed a newspaper together, stuffed it with a litter of kindling into the stove, lighted it, and put the lids back in place. At once a dense white smoke began to filter up in circles from around every lid on top of the big range.

"Open the draft, quick!" said Mary, coughing.

"Which?" asked Mark completely at sea.

"Silly!" exclaimed the girl and, darting past him, leaned into the rising fog of pungent smoke and turned something on the side of the chimney.

Presently, as they stepped back, coughing in unison and rubbing their eyes, the smoke ceased rising. Mark heard a roaring of fire as the draft pulled up the chimney.

"I'm sorry," he apologized.

She merely shrugged her shoulders in a workmanlike manner that shamed him strangely. Then she removed the lids again and dropped in the cord wood. It began to make a great crackling almost at once, and a faint warmth stole through the room.

Mark stood alone, praying for something to do that would redeem him for his clumsiness in her eyes. The smoke was settling to the side of the room, twisting in ghostly little shapes about the lamp, drawing in about Mary as she walked. She continued in a most business-like way to bring out a ham and slice it, showing such strength in the little brown wrists that he wondered. Then she slipped a skillet onto the stove and dropped the rich slices into it. The ham began to sizzle softly, and an aroma more delicious than anything he had ever smelled greeted Mark Loftus. The sap in the wood sang shrill little cricket songs in the stove. The pitchy places crackled with cheery energy. Fragrance of resin joined the fragrance of frying ham. Still, she was at work, bringing out a thick loaf and dividing it into big white slices. Beside the bread she placed a slab of golden butter. Mark extended his long arms.

"By Jove," he murmured, "this is good . . . this is good. This . . . this warms the heart of a man."

Her glance flickered over him rather critically, he thought. It wavered for a second on his hands, then came to rest on his face. That was her only answer. She turned toward the cupboard again and brought out a glass of jam. He could see the seeds of the berries in it, and it had a dull-red luster. *Why did not painters paint food like this?* He glanced back at Mary. *Why did not other women dress like this, simply and beautifully?* As a matter of fact, it was a blue bathrobe of cotton cloth, faded by age and many washings, but holding a grace of line in its ample folds.

"You lost your way, I guess?" She asked the question with her back turned.

"Yep. Queer country, this, you know. All ups and downs and not much of the level. Besides, all cañons look alike to me."

"I suppose they do . . . to you," replied the girl.

He wondered if there were a touch of irony hidden here. But her voice was so gentle that he dismissed the suspicion. He went on talking. Naturally she would want to know.

"I was hunting . . . up north, yonder. Got lost from my party."

"Oh, that was bad luck."

"Wasn't it?" He leaned a little toward her, welcoming this small display of emotion. "Wandered about all afternoon . . . got into a gully . . . tired myself out climbing up to the level again . . . found a hay field . . . went to sleep in a shock, just over the hill. It's great, sleeping in hay, isn't it?"

She said thoughtfully: "That must have been Mister Cornish's hay field. No. I don't like to sleep in hay. The burrs and stickers and things tickle such a lot."

"I'm thick-skinned, I guess," said Mark contentedly.

He had never before talked so inanely, and he had never enjoyed so much before hearing himself and another talk. The smoke, the increasing heat of the stove, the smell of the cooking food, the gleam of the lamp drew him closer to the girl. Mark was drifting off into a sad-sweet dream, for he was a good

47

deal of a child in many ways.

"Are you too tired to eat?" asked a crisp, matter-of-fact voice.

He looked up with a start, hurt by this dryness of tone, and he was doubly astonished to find that she was smiling down on him almost tenderly. The plate beside him was smoking with ham and fried eggs, and he turned toward it at once to cover his confusion.

"Don't you want to wash?" asked the girl in the same chilly, drab tone.

He started up. It was like receiving correction from a tutor in the days of his childhood. He flushed redder than ever as he obeyed her gesture toward the sink. After washing his hands and face, he dried them on a rough roller towel nearby. The touch of the towel warned him that he had been well sunburned during the day. He turned back and eyed her guiltily, awaiting permission to sit down. Again, to his surprise, she was smiling, but there was something thoughtful behind her eyes that troubled him.

"What were you hunting?" she asked.

His mind cast about through vacancy. For a moment he could think of nothing but the enchanting flavor of the ham. *What in the world did they hunt in these mountains?*

"Bears," he said, "and deer."

There was a moment of pause. She pushed the bread closer to him, and he obediently took a slice. How small and how tapering were the fingers that rested on the edge of the table.

"Any luck?" she asked.

"Sort of," said Mark. "I got half a dozen bears and a dozen or so deer."

"Oh," said the girl, "I call that excellent luck."

He glanced sharply up at her, but she seemed to be dreaming.

"You lost your gun, as well as your way, I see," she said at length.

"Oh," exclaimed Mark, "I must have forgot it in that hay field. Queer that I'd do that."

"Yes, it's queer. Sleepy, I suppose?"

"Yes, sleepy."

He looked up again, and his glance met hers, only to have her eyes flicker away toward that former dreaminess. *Why was she so strangely thoughtful?*

"Not even a revolver?" she asked.

"No, I haven't one."

She walked slowly out of the room, and he had finished the meal when she returned. She was carrying a big brown cartridge belt, from which a pistol was suspended in a holster on one side.

"This was my father's gun," she said. "No one uses it since he died. You might take it."

"Your father's gun." Mark was astonished and touched. *Did this explain her thoughtfulness?* "You want me to take it?"

"You . . . you might meet a bear . . . or something, you know. Hadn't you better take it?"

"Why, I couldn't hit the side of a hill with it."

"Couldn't you? Really? Poor fellow."

"Is it as bad as all that?" he asked, attempting to laugh, but there was a sad seriousness about her eyes.

"How much for the fine dinner?" asked Mark at length, feeling a certain uneasiness rise in him.

"How much? Do you think Uncle Dan would take money from a hungry man?"

He picked up his hat. He twisted it around and stared down at it. For some reason this declaration had entirely changed their relations.

"I'm very sorry that I bothered you."

"I only hope that this will give you the strength to finish your trip." She added slowly, looking him straight in the eyes for the first time: "Your trip back to the hunting party."

What she said filtered slowly, slowly into Mark Loftus's mind. He was too busy probing those wide and steady eyes to understand the words entirely.

"I'll show you the way out," she was saying.

"Where?" asked Mark blankly.

"To the stable. I guess you'll need a horse?"

VII

"MARK AND MARY"

There was nothing explanatory of her speech in her back that she turned abruptly on him while she was taking the lantern off the peg and lighting it. Then she led the way outdoors. He found himself oddly glad to have the broad arch of the stars above him. Breathing space was what he needed, infinite room. In the cramped confines of the kitchen he had begun to feel that the girl had cornered him and read his mind too thoroughly. That accounted for the mixture of contempt and pity with which she had last spoken.

In the meantime she was walking lightly on ahead of him, the lantern swinging beside her and casting, in the opposite direction, an enormous and vague shadow that wavered to and fro through nothingness. She came to the stable and led the way down the stalls. In every one was a sleeping figure. She stopped before a gray.

"Up, Sally," said the girl softly. "Get up."

The mare started to her feet, snorting, and then turned a pair of bright eyes toward them.

"This is my horse," said Mary. "I think she'll carry your weight. She's solidly built, and she's a lamb. A snaffle is all you'll need on her." She turned. "There's the saddle . . . on that peg."

"Wait," muttered Mark Loftus. "Why are you doing all this?"

"I'm trying to postpone what's sure to come," said the girl sadly. "Oh, don't you see that I know who you are? Don't you see that I know you're Bill Rafferty's man?"

It dazed the fugitive to hear her. How could the news have shot across the country in this astonishing fashion? Did the very birds carry the tidings?

She explained in answer to his gaping stare: "The telegraph has spread the news everywhere. We had the word in town, here, before sunset. Half the men are out hunting now."

Mark was stunned. His glance wandered.

"The telegram said that you're a tenderfoot. Don't you really know how to use a gun at all?"

"Shotgun is all I've ever used," he confessed. "I don't know anything about a revolver."

"If you can use a shotgun, I have one you can take."

"Take a shotgun? You mean to fight my way out if I'm cornered?" He shook his head.

"Why not?" she asked, frowning. "Don't you know what it means if they corner you?"

"Why, they'll hold me up, I suppose. But I'll keep riding till they do corner me."

"Hold you up," she echoed with a mixture of scorn and horror. "No, no, they'll shoot you down. They'll ask no questions. All they need to know is that Harrison Loftus wants you stopped. That's enough. Harrison Loftus doesn't need to give explanations. He's a known man."

"Harrison Loftus sent the wires, eh?" asked Mark huskily.

"Yes."

"Did . . . did he send my name?"

"No. Just a description. But he described every detail, and he offered a reward."

"I might have expected it," said Mark fiercely. "But I haven't really known him till this moment. Now, if he wants to fight it out on these lines, I'll fight his own way."

"I knew you'd come to your senses. You'll take the shotgun?"

"To use on other men? No, I couldn't do that."

She grew almost hysterical. "It's suicide," she said. "How are you going to fight back?"

"I'll use my hands."

He stretched out his arms, long, muscular arms, that systematic athletics had strengthened. The girl looked at him out of frightened eyes, as if he had suddenly grown taller.

"Oh," she said at last, "why, why did you do it? You aren't that kind of man. I know you aren't. Bill Rafferty pulled the wool over your eyes."

"Perhaps he did," said Mark, "but it's my own fault. He has my word that I'll do my best, and I'll do it."

"The pity of it," said the girl, half sobbing. "Oh, the pity of it."

The contemptuous, pitying superiority had vanished from her. She was entirely simple in her grief, and it touched Mark to the heart.

"You'll let me pay for the horse and the saddle?"

"No, no, I can't take your money . . . I don't want your money."

He stared stupidly at her, seeing other things about her and behind her — dreams out of his past, in part. He saw huge, softly lighted rooms and fashionably dressed people in them — young men, young women. He heard laughter and music out of the other years and the other life. He heard brainless jests and watched foolish games. Was it the same Mark Loftus who stood here in the light of a lantern in a stable, talking to a girl in a faded bathrobe about a matter of life and death, accepting charity out of her hands? All his old ideas and all his old ideals were knocked to pieces and fell about his feet.

"God bless you," said Mark suddenly. "You are beautiful and wonderful and braver and truer than any woman in the world."

She put up her hand to wave away such an extravagant burst of compliment, but he caught the hand and stepped closer to her.

"Look at me!" commanded Mark. "Now tell me what you saw that gave you any faith in me. I came sneaking into your house, a hounded man. What made you dream that there might be anything in me worth saving?"

All at once she cocked her head a little to one side. She was trembling, and her voice was shaking a little, but she said: "Because of that silly sunburn, I guess. I don't know why, but your poor red nose made me think you couldn't be all bad."

Then, strangely enough, he was able to laugh with her. Their amusement ended with both of them grave, and he watched in wonder the changing expressions in her eyes.

"I'll come back some day," he told her, "and pay for what I've taken, if I can. Only there is one thing that I hope I can't pay for . . . your good wishes. Do I take them with me?"

"My good wishes. Yes, yes!" Her voice broke. "I must go back. Put out the lantern when you finish saddling. My uncle might miss me . . . and . . . good bye." She slipped the ring of the lantern over a peg.

Mark blocked her way to the door. "You won't forget me?" he asked, as if there were listening spies nearby.

"Never!"

"And you know that I'll come back, some day?"

She put her hands across her eyes to shut out the sight of him. "Perhaps," she said.

"Not my ghost," insisted Mark Loftus. "I know what the dangers are, and I know that there is only one chance in ten ahead of me. But wish me luck, and I'll come back."

"Let me pass," she stammered, and, slipping by him, she fairly ran for the house.

He saw her swing the kitchen door open. The lamplight

within outlined her brilliantly for a moment, and then solid blackness shut behind her.

Yet Mark, as he turned to the work of saddling, was humming softly. What made up the body of his content he could not dream, but contented he was, and more than contented.

He led the gray mare out into the dark and swung into the saddle when Sally was finally equipped. By her first elastic steps he knew that she was even better than the praises of her mistress. She broke into a swinging canter, twisting onto the main street of the little village and sweeping him up over the farther hill. There he checked her for a moment, and she obeyed the first touch of the reins so readily that he could have told at once the hand of a woman had trained the horse. Mark turned in the saddle and looked back. The village was a dark huddle in the depression among the hills. The houses seemed already reduced to little cabins, but one of them was large enough to shelter Mary.

He remembered with a start that he had not learned her last name, but only that her father was dead and that she lived with her uncle. For that matter she might even be married. A thrill of terror ran through him. He was about to swing Sally around and send her back toward the house, but he checked the foolish impulse. It would be better to keep the happy illusion until he came back. Sally took the slope, and she sailed down it like a bird.

VIII

"WHEN THE DOOR OPENED"

"When you hit the Chandler Mountains," Bill Rafferty had said, "anybody can tell you how to get to Hank Jerney . . . that is, anybody outside of the towns. He's got a pile of friends among the miners and the ranchers and the sheepherders. Hank plays in with 'em all pretty thick. They can direct you. Thing to do is just to get to the Chandler Mountains, and the small trails will bring you there."

There was sound sense in this, no doubt, and particularly since his description had been scattered abroad by his father. *By his father.* On that point his mind refused to act. His brain became involved in a great red swirl. He must keep off main trails, but in the meantime it was pitch dark, and he dreaded the thought of leaving this easy road for the sake of blind paths of whose direction he could not be sure. Once he stopped and consulted the map that Rafferty had sketched. According to that he was aiming straight at the Chandlers. Then he galloped on again, blessing the easy, tireless gait of Sally. It was amazing beyond words that the girl could give up to him this horse which probably meant more to her than any other one thing in the world.

If there were an explanation, it was one that he would straightway wring from her when he came back — if he ever did. In the meantime his father had been partially right, at least. This country — "my country, a man's country" — was worth knowing, and so were the people in it, if Mary were a sample of them.

The east began at length to turn gray. The mountains lifted

rapidly forth in great black outlines. Dipping into a hollow, where the shade of night was still thick, Mark learned the danger of clinging to main-traveled roads. He ran squarely into a trap. The danger burst on him in a single instant. The soft dust had muffled the sound of the approaching horses, and a turn in the road blotted them from view until, around an elbow turn, he ran squarely into the midst of a clump of ten or a dozen riders. He could not count them in the dim light, but they meant as much as an army to him.

He thought for an instant of putting spurs to his horse and striving to break through. It was already too late to turn in the opposite direction and double back. There was no chance for him to push through his first idea. In a single rush the strangers were about him, had mastered his reins, and jammed the hard muzzle of two revolvers into his sides.

"I think we got him!" exclaimed several men in unison. "Who are you?"

Mark blinked as the shaft of light from an electric torch snapped full into his face. He was about to throw up his hands and confess himself beaten. The crisp rustling of the letter in the beast pocket of his shirt was enough, it seemed, to betray him. Then he determined to fight it through if he could. He dipped as deeply as he dared into the vernacular.

"How come?" he asked, and he summoned a scowl. "What do you mean by jumping me like this?"

"It's him," said a man in the background. "Tenderfoot written all over him. No gun, either."

"Tenderfoot, eh?" exclaimed Mark. "Lemme at you for five minutes alone, son, and I'll show you how tender I am."

The remark brought a sudden laugh. It helped clear the atmosphere tremendously.

"Where you from?" asked he of the shrill voice, pressing hostilely closer.

Mark's mind darted back to the rudely drawn map. "I'm from Quigley," he answered steadily enough.

"You are, eh?" asked the little man. "Well, I'm from Quigley myself. I never seen you there."

Mark turned cold. There was one bluff left to him, and he used it desperately. "You from Quigley? They don't have men as small as you out Quigley way. We kick your kind out and get in real men."

It brought a terrific burst of cursing from the smaller man, but the others laughed.

"Leave go of your gun, Dick," someone said to Mark's chief persecutor. "He ain't packing a gat. Can't you see that? And I guess you don't want to talk to him none without guns."

"He sure got you, Dick. You never seen Quigley. Anybody here that has?"

There was no answer, and Mark's heart thumped less rapidly.

"What you doing clear over this way?" asked one.

"And by what right," asked Mark, "d'you gents hold up law-abiding folk on the road and shove guns under their noses? I got a mind to tear into a couple of you. What am I doing here? That's my business. If you want to know, go back and ask old man Cornwall why he sent me. If he'll tell you, go ahead and find out, but you won't learn anything from me. Now, get out of my way."

He had gone a little too far. There was a growl in response, but a gray-headed man now pressed in and quelled the hostile murmur.

"He's got a right to be peeved," said the oldest of the party. "It ain't any joke to be stuck up on the road like this. Besides, it ain't the gent we want. I mind that he looks something like the description that we got, same build, same complexion. But he's riding a hoss, and that ain't in the telegram that we got.

All in all, if we'd rounded him up yonder in the hills on a side trail, I'd be for bringing him in and letting him be examined. But even a tenderfoot has got more sense than to keep to main-traveled roads like this. He'd hit for the tall timber quick, and he'd stay there. He wouldn't have the face to come down and ride right through towns, this way."

This speech was decisive. There was still a growl here and there, but they seemed to be satisfied and even muttered indistinct apologies, as they drew their horses back. Mark favored them in return with a sound berating, and then he sent Sally on at a steady dog-trot, though his heart yearned toward a free gallop that would put many a mile between him and these hunters.

They did not change their minds and follow him. They left him in peace and with something better than peace, a great idea. The thing that had turned them in his favor was the fact that he was actually traveling on this main road between the mountain towns. What he had dreaded as a chief danger had turned out to be his salvation. And might it not prove to be so throughout? Wandering through the mountains, from one obscure and dangerous trail to another, he would probably lose his way, and, at the best, he could not help but draw suspicious attention from anyone who chanced to see him. The country must be alive with men hunting for him at the bidding of Harrison Loftus. If the cruelty of his father shocked him, the power of his father astonished him no less. The whole mountain rose at his bidding. This single unit of a dozen men, riding all night in pursuit of him, was only a sample of what must be going on in other places. The principle of hiding most securely might be that of making himself the most easily seen. He determined, though with a beating heart, to follow what seemed the most dangerous road. He would ride this same thoroughfare clear through to the Chandler Mountains, if it led him so far, and let chance bring what chance might.

It was morning when he reached the next village, and he put his plan to a test. Over the hill he jogged and into the main street, blessing the sunburn that kept his pallor from showing. People turned to look at him, but these Westerners turned to look at any stranger. He went straight to the hotel, put up his horse, and entered the dining room for breakfast. Not a word was said. He himself brought up the subject to the lady of the house, as she served him bacon and griddle cakes.

"What's all this I hear about the man that broke loose from Jasperville?"

"I dunno," she answered. "All the boys are out hunting. Got the telegram yesterday. Harrison Loftus wants him. That's all I know."

"Well," said Mark, eyeing her shrewdly, "I understand he isn't carrying a gun, either."

But she shook her head wisely. "Never can tell about these city crooks. That's what I told my Jerry and our boys when I asked 'em to stay home. But they would be out. Well, he'll be brought in pretty soon, I guess. They ain't a single path over the hills that ain't being watched for him, they say."

"What sort of a looking fellow is he?" asked Mark with interest, as he stirred his coffee.

"Oh, about your build, I guess," she answered, remembering the details, "and about your complexion. Don't you go wandering through the hills, or they'll be picking you up." And she laughed at the thought, as she went back toward the kitchen.

It was only a sample of what lay before him during the next two days as he rode steadily toward the Chandler Mountains. When the curious asked him questions, he put them briefly aside. He was from Quigley, and old man Cornwall had sent him up that way, and old man Cornwall didn't like to have his business talked about. For the rest, news came in that two men had been captured, each of whom answered somewhat distantly to the description of the messenger of Rafferty.

These tidings Mark received with profound inward content. It began to come to him that this feat of riding through the long range of mountains in a hostile country was one that could hardly be duplicated easily. Certainly, if he achieved the end of his quest, it would be a convincing proof in the eyes of his father that he knew the country and knew the people in it.

So he came to the last stage of his journey. It was the ending of the third day since he left Jasperville on the wide ride. Beyond rose the steep slopes of the Chandler Mountains. Before noon of the next day he ought to be in the heart of the highlands and have tidings of Hank Jerney. As usual, he went directly to the hotel in the little town. The stables were already crowded, so he quartered Sally in a corral and gave her a plentiful feed. He had grown almost as fond of her as he was of her owner. All through the arduous ride she had remained as placid of temper, as true to her work, as a Thoroughbred, and she had learned on the very first day to come to the hand and the whistle of Mark when he dismounted to let her labor under her own weight as they worked up unusually steep grades. He lingered now, patting her, while she began greedily on her hay, as all good horses do. He cast a glance up the difficult slopes that would test her strength the next morning, and then he went into the hotel.

There was a bed for him, even if there were not stable room for his horse. He found a place at the long table, now crammed from end to end, because the whole McKringle outfit was stopping overnight on their way north, a rough-looking, heavily tanned set of men, who ate without manners, talked without moderation, and made the room ring and reëcho with their laughter.

To Mark Loftus, the sound and the sight of them were pleasant. He would have shrunk from them in horror a few days before, but the labor of the trail had hardened him. They were no more rugged than the rocky mountains in which they lived. They reminded him of the bald summits over which he had been riding, during the past twelve hours. And he was happy to squeeze in between two of them and elbow his way to a plate, eating contentedly, drinking with gusto coffee as strong as lye, and now and again running his eyes up and down the long rows of unshaven faces. These were wild men, indeed. *A bitter day if such fellows like these,* thought Mark, *should take to his trail.*

That thought had hardly passed through his head when a sound of voices reached him with the opening of the door. Looking across the room toward the entrance, he found himself staring squarely into the faces of Larry Day and his own father.

IX

"THE BATTLE"

This was the penalty, then, for having lingered so long on the road. He heard a murmur of excitement pass up and down the table: "It's old man Loftus! It's Harrison Loftus himself!"

With one accord that wild and stern McKringle outfit laid down their forks and knives and looked with sparkling eyes toward the broad-shouldered man who stood in the doorway. In their own way they were giving him a reception of which a king might have been proud. But he made no answer, not even to the hearty voice of the proprietor, who now came hurrying toward him. He raised his hand, and, as the arm rose, Mark Loftus felt himself drawn by an irresistible force out of his chair. The boy stood up, pale, he knew, and certainly trembling. What would that grim mind of Harrison Loftus conceive as a fitting punishment?

"Friends," said his father, "take that man. He's the one I want."

A pause of amazement ensued, then a rumble of astonishment and determination commingled. Mark Loftus saw his table companions turn suddenly to him and look up. That movement on their part snapped the charm that held him. He swept up a water pitcher and hurled it down the table. Fair and true it struck the great double-burner with which the room was illumined, shattered it to a thousand fragments and instantly flooded the apartment with black darkness and the scent of kerosene.

One yell rose from a score of big throats. Hands gripped at Mark. They gripped with such strength in the dark that, when he tore himself loose, the fingers burned into his flesh. He dropped his left hand on the table and vaulted cleanly to the other side, but, on the way, he crashed into two men who had risen from their places opposite. They went down, yelling curses, and Mark, tumbling head over heels, came to his feet again in the center of the room and alone.

He glanced about him. Against the windows on either side of the room and in the doorway there was a faintly illumined turmoil of heads and shoulders and arms. At least, in spite of all their confusion, they had been wise enough to block the ways of exit. They had fenced and penned him in, and they only needed light in order to fall upon and crush him.

Then a bright ray struck the ceiling, wavered through the crowd, and whipped in to a sudden focus on the face of Mark Loftus. The electric torch of his father had been used to single out his son. From either side the crowd lunged at him with whines of rage, shrill, animal-like sounds that turned him cold. He knew instinctively that those gripping fingers would reach for his throat. Motionless he waited until they were close on every side, a swiftly narrowing circle, and then he leaped back as far as his gymnastic training enabled him to do.

It was the last move they could have anticipated. They were braced to meet his rush from either side or in front, but those behind had simply rushed in blindly with their arms out-stretched. The weight of Mark knocked them away in confusion. Before him the other waves met with a crash, rebounded, and turned with a fearful babel of oaths to destroy him — and always, by the aid of that cursed circle of light, directed by the hand of his own father.

A smashing fist grazed his head. Another landed fairly on his mouth and drove him his own length, staggering back. It was the best thing that could have happened to Mark, that stinging blow. It numbed his lips and sent a little crimson trickle down his chin, and in his brain it roused a peculiar madness. He had boxed before, as he told his father, but always with heavy gloves. Now he leaped into the throng before him and rained blows with his naked fists. And each fist had knuckles like steel, and each arm was a driving piston. The others, untrained with their fists, whaled away with circular blows, or blundered in, merely trying to get to grips, but Mark Loftus smote short and straight, with every ounce of his strong body behind each punch. Where his fists landed, men went down, stunned and amazed, and felt his heels planted on their bodies, as he stepped in for more action.

Now he was happy, riotously, joyously happy. Strange oaths rose to his lips and were poured forth, but in his soul there was a great symphonic music playing from a thousand instruments. Presently he ducked and sprang to one side, sensing by instinct a rush from behind. Now he dove straight ahead, breaking through their legs and surrounding himself with confusion. Their very numbers choked their efforts. They came at him with their shoulders jammed, and he smote the middle man of a trio and threw them all out of momentum. He was never the same. Cat-like surety was in his feet as he darted here and there, never slipping. Sometimes he was erect, smiting long straight-arm blows. Again he was bowed, hitting with lifting punches that smashed through guarding arms as if through breaking straws.

In the light of that single electric torch they followed him as valiantly as they could. They dared not shoot, they dared not draw a knife in such a turmoil, where all were friends except one. Still, half a dozen got out their revolvers and charged to give him the butt. In daylight he could not have stood his ground ten seconds, but in that crowd and in that treacherous light he was like a will-o'-the-wisp. And, oh, the joy of it, the joy of it. Gun butts hissed by his head. Hands crashed against him. Fingers tore at him. But he was whirling and diving and dancing and ducking through them until they cursed brokenly, so great was their labor, so little their reward. His blows were a steady rain, and every blow found a vital landing place. The faces before him were reddened in places. When he smote, they went down in the darkness of the floor, but others rose. Once a pair of arms reached out of the nothingness at his feet and grappled his legs. A jerk of his knees caught the fellow beneath the chin, and he pitched back, out for good.

"Kill him! Break him in two!" they yelled. But it was like catching a phantom. He slipped through their fingers as a football player will drive miraculously through a thick field.

If only that light went out for an instant, he might have a real chance. Now his wind was breaking fast. The terrible efforts, sustained so long, were breaking his heart literally. If he knocked down one man, two more stepped in to fill the breach. They were like bulldogs, careless of pain, and, once they gripped him solidly, like bulldogs, they would finish their work. They would smash every bone in his body, they would trample him to a pulp, for they were now tormented out of all sense of fair play.

In the meantime he worked with some system, edging not toward the windows or the door, but toward the table again. Through their struggling mass he finally dove like a swimmer, passing out of the circle of the electric light. It wavered vainly to find him. As he came up behind them, he saw them still pummeling and yelling. The electric torch still wandered here and there. Mark reached again to the table, scooped up a heavy platter, and hurled it with all his force at the doorway. It struck with a crash, and the electric torch went out. Dimly outlined against the street lights he saw his father topple backward. Then with a yell — "He's trying the door!" — every man in the room rushed to the rescue.

It was providential for Mark. It gave him darkness for at least that priceless moment, and it also gave him a clear path. He ran straight for the window nearest the corral and leaped into it, just as the torch was swung again, and the broad shaft of light focused fairly and strongly upon him. Were his arms and legs made of lead? With one frantic effort he was through, as a dozen revolvers roared behind him, their united chorus singing above his head as he landed on the ground beneath.

He landed running, and he headed straight for the corral where Sally had been kept. Without a horse he would be run down in ten minutes. He could not pause to let down the bars, and he leaped over and ran to Sally who tossed her beautiful head up and greeted him with a neigh. Then she was alert, for around either side of the hotel poured the pursuers, and lanterns were tossing here and there in the columns. A flock of shadows swept across the corral, as Mark leaped onto Sally's bare back. Had she been taught to jump? He put her at the fence. She ran straight to it, then tossed up her head, and reared. He swung her away with a groan, using his hand on her neck as a bridle. Turning her in a short circle, he put her at the jump again.

"Take him alive!" a familiar voice was shouting. "Get horses! Follow him fast, boys!"

"Sally, old girl!" called Mark, and, at the clap of his heels and the call of his voice, she rose like a bird and sailed over the bars.

A yell of consternation and a rattle of guns behind him told that this maneuver had taken them all by surprise, but Sally, the next instant, twisted him into the welcome darkness behind a huge haystack, and now he urged her to top speed. She could jump, and he would use her skill in that direction at once. Half a dozen small fields lay directly in his path. He put her recklessly

67

at the dreaded barbed wire, and gallantly, for a green jumper, she cleared them. Every jump was gaining life-giving time for Mark. The others would have to saddle before they could pursue, and, having saddled, they would have to cut around those fences and make for the gates beyond.

In thirty seconds the clamor was dying down behind him, and the hoofs of brave Sally were ringing on a hard-packed little cow path through the fields. He pulled her back to a dog-trot. He must save her going uphill. If they started him in a straight line, once he had this grade behind him, he would break their hearts if they wanted running. So he halted Sally at the top of the hill, and, riding into a little copse, he looked back through the branches. Out from the hotel the pursuers burst away in two lines, one down the main road, to his left, and one to his right, down the hollow. They had lost him completely the moment he had ridden into the screen of darkness, and they had neither time nor light to look for his trail. After all, they had done the normal thing. They had expected him to stick to the lowlands, the hollows, where a fugitive could put his horse to the best speed. Yelling and shouting, they tore through the night.

Mark Loftus turned Sally, rode calmly back to the deserted hotel shed, picked out his saddle and bridle, mounted, and went again on his way.

X

"FRIENDS OR FOES"

Only then did he begin to feel the pain of his wounds. There were bruises for every square inch of his body. The cut, where the blow had landed on his lips, stung sharply. His clothes were literally torn to tatters. Yet, inside, his very soul was warmed and made happy by the memory of the battle. Even more strange to relate, his heart went out in a feeling of good fellowship to the men who had battered and beaten him. After all, this was life, real life, hot off the stove. Mark felt that he had never truly lived before. The nodding head of gray Sally, as she trotted up the hillside, was a comfort and a joy. He had ridden finer horses, swifter racers, but never had he ridden such a companionable mount. When he spoke to her, and he was talking to her steadily, she had a delightful way of putting one ear back to listen. She was continually turning her head in a friendly manner, from one side to the other, as if she were observing the country and enjoying it, as she went along. There was not a shadow of the sullen, or the fierce, or the proud in her. Yet there was something in her honest faith that was stronger than steel.

"She's like the girl," said Mark Loftus to himself. "She's like the girl."

He saw neither sound nor sight of the pursuit, though he kept on for a full hour and a half, or even more. They must have plunged blindly ahead, waiting until daylight before they would comb the country with care. In the meantime he was growing momentarily more weary, and Sally, with a solid day's work behind her, let her head fall lower and lower. So that, when he came over a hilltop, in sudden and unexpected view of a cabin with a lighted window, Mark Loftus decided to stay on the main road. He went straight to the door, knocked, and, when he obeyed the summons to enter, he found himself in the presence of two men whose clothes were sadly disarrayed, and whose faces bore unmistakable signs of battle. For the eye of the one was as swollen as if a bee had stung him.

At sight of Mark they shouted together: "It's him!"

He tried to leap back through the door, but two huge-mouthed Colts covered him before he could stir an inch.

"Up with your hands," was the order. "Up with 'em, or I'll blow your gizzard out."

Mark obeyed slowly, fighting them with his eyes, but realizing that those grim eyes behind the guns meant business, and that those big brown hands on the gun butts would not waver from the mark.

"You have me," he admitted quietly. "Luck has turned at last."

They came on either side of him without a word. One of them took both guns and covered him steadily while the other bent carefully over him.

"Not even a pocket knife," said the second man, straightening and stepping away. "Can you lay to that, Bill?"

Bill gasped an acknowledgment that he was plumb beat.

"But can't you see their faces, Gus, when we march him into town?"

Gus was apparently interested in other things as he gestured to a chair, and Mark sank wearily into it.

"No funny moves," they cautioned him with one voice.

"No," said Mark, "I'm through. I'll give you my word that I won't try to break away."

"You'll give us your word, eh, and expect us to take it, kid?"

"My word of honor," explained Mark haughtily, lifting his head and frowning at them. He caught them exchanging glances of surprise.

"All right," said Gus suddenly. "We'll take your word. But, say, partner, where'd you get that punch? Where d'you stow it? You lack ten pounds of being as big as me. Bill, where does he get it? I'd've swore I was hit a couple of times with a club."

"For that matter," said Mark good-naturedly, "I think you gave as good as you got. I think it was you, Gus, that landed me here." He touched his bruised lips.

"I done my share, maybe," said Gus, his forehead at once smoothed.

"But the crowd was against you fellows," went on Mark smoothly. "The others got in your way."

"Well," said Bill, from his post of vantage near the door, "it was a great fight. Between you and me, stranger, it done me sort of good. Me and Gus rode down from the shack, wanting to look over the McKringle outfit that we'd heard so much about. All picked men, they say, and all picked for being hard ones. But we sure didn't figure on seeing 'em all licked by one man. We sure didn't." He broke into a roar of laughter. "Next time they start talking big it won't be 'round these parts, eh, Gus?"

"It won't," said Gus, rubbing his hands with an equal elation. "I seen big Sandy, the foreman, go down, *whang*. Up he gets, and slam comes another wallop in the mouth, and down he goes again. It done me so much good that I didn't have the strength to punch our friend, here . . . I was that weak from laughing to myself."

At the memory he began to laugh again heartily, crushing his big arms around his ribs to control the pain of his mirth.

"Well," broke in Mark, "now that you have me, I guess one of you can guard me well enough. Outside I have a gray mare,

71

standing. She's worked hard today, and she's pretty well spent. Will one of you feed her and take her saddle off . . . or let me do it?"

"Worried about her?" asked Bill.

"She has run her heart out for me," said Mark with feeling. "I'd be an ingrate if I let her stand there."

Again his two captors exchanged glances.

"I'll fix her," said Bill quietly, and left the house.

"How did you fellows get here so fast?" asked Mark ruefully.

"We went up the road with Harrison Loftus's part of the gang, but, when they didn't get no trace of you, we cut across and hit back for the shack. Old man Loftus was sure cussing mad."

"Ah," murmured Mark, "was he?"

"I'll tell a man he was. He'll make you step lively, son, when he lays hands on you. That platter you threw at him broke up. One chunk of it cut him across the forehead, and a couple of splinters of it slashed up his hands. Every time he pulled on his reins, he swore that he'd have you skinned. He's got a temper, old Loftus has."

"He's eager to get me, I suppose," said Mark, setting his teeth hard.

Then the door was opened by Bill, returning. "She's a beauty," he said, "that mare of yours. I got something to say to Gus. Step over here a minute, Gus."

Gus obeyed, and the two put their heads together for a moment, murmuring softly. Finally Bill faced their prisoner again.

"Partner," he said smoothly, "seems to me like we got the upper hand."

"There's no doubt of that," admitted Mark.

"But," went on Bill, "we don't see no reason why we should do the dirty work of the McKringle outfit. Maybe Harrison

72

Loftus has a pile of things ag'in' you, but we ain't. Now, stranger, the whole point is this . . . would you leave the gray behind if you was to keep on?"

Mark started violently. The hope of freedom was dangled an instant before his eyes, only to be withdrawn. He shook his head dolorously. "She isn't mine," he said. "Even if she were mine, I'm afraid that I wouldn't give her up. Boys, you saw the way she took me out of the corral tonight, jumping the fences. First time she ever jumped a fence in her life, I guess. Well, would you give up a horse like that, after she's saved your life?"

They were silent, all three staring at the floor.

Plainly the heart of Bill was set on the gray mare. "How'd you get back and land a saddle and bridle?" he asked suddenly.

"Why, that was simple," said Mark. "I went up the hill to the top and saw that the boys were riding on each side of me. They never dreamed that I'd start my horse up a grade like that when I was making tracks to get away. So, when I saw them a good distance away, I simply turned Sally around and trotted back to the shed, took my saddle and bridle, and then started through the hills again." He found the eloquent eyes of the two fixed again upon one another, but they offered no comments. He tried his last and most desperate appeal. It would either save him or ruin him. "Partners," he said, "I suppose you know why I've hit for these hills?"

"Because they take you away from Harrison Loftus. That's easy to guess," said Gus.

"Because," answered Mark, "they take me to Hank Jerney."

It was as if he had set off a bomb in the room. They stiffened in their chairs and glared at him. He thought for a moment that they were going to leap at his throat, but they settled back in a gloomy silence. All friendly admiration was gone from their faces, and he decided at once that he had, indeed, ruined

73

his last hope with them. He was so convinced of it that he made no further effort to talk, and, since they did not proffer any conversation on their part but merely stared at him, as if he were some dangerous and curious animal, he presently wound himself in a blanket and lay down on the floor. The labor of that day made him fall instantly asleep.

Weariness hardens a man. Great fatigue and great courage sometimes bring a man to the same point. Ordinarily he would never have had the courage to mention the name of the outlaw of whom Bill Rafferty had told him such strange and terrible things. And certainly, having proved to his own satisfaction that these were not adherents of Hank Jerney, he would not normally have had the assurance to lie down on the floor and fall asleep. But complete exhaustion gave him the effect of absolute and indifferent courage. In ten minutes he was snoring.

XI

"A DOUBLE SURPRISE"

He was stiff and chill. He had been asleep hours when, at length, he was wakened. A big man was stirring him contemptuously with his toe. Half a dozen others appeared in the background. Among them were Bill and Gus, looking gravely concerned. They had betrayed him, then, to the posse?

"Who are you?" asked Mark, sitting erect.

"Stand up, son," said the other. "I'm Hank Jerney. What you want of me?"

That name brought Mark to his feet like a touch of electric power. He found himself confronting not a rough-bearded, wild-eyed man, not a terrible picture, such as he had conjured in his imagination ever since he began that strange ride for the Chandler Mountains. Instead, Hank Jerney was dressed with a scrupulous neatness. The bandanna at his throat was a sober gray. No finery appeared in any part of his outfit. The band of his sombrero was unadorned leather. His spurs were ungilded steel. On the whole he gave the appearance of an immensely respectable rancher who had brought into the wild West the thrift of a New England conscience.

This was terrible Hank Jerney who had defied the powers of the law and even the formidable machinations of Sheriff Sam Matthews, greatest of manhunters, for nearly twenty years. In age he appeared to be either a young man prematurely aged, or an elderly man well preserved. According as one looked at him, he seemed at one time thirty-five and at another fifty. His face was deeply lined, particularly between the eyes and about the nose and mouth. At the forehead his hair was turning gray.

But his features, if they suggested sternness, also suggested a certain nobility, and the eyes, placed beneath lofty and well-proportioned brows, were large, clear, and straightforward.

Upon this face, so completely dissimilar to his expectations, Mark gazed with concentrated interest. Behind the leader he saw four fellows who were obviously henchmen, and these, to be sure, bore out all that he had heard or dreamed of the bad man at his worst. Unshaven, with a rat-like quickness of eye, prominently armed with revolvers and prominently ready to use them, they lounged carelessly about the cabin, taking stock of what was in it, while Bill and Gus, completely subdued by these formidable visitors, shrank into the background and said not a word. They were adherents of the chief, no doubt, but the alliance was a distant and doubtful one. They served him in fear rather than for their own self-interest.

"I've brought you a letter," said Mark. "But first, I'd like to make sure that you're Hank Jerney."

"If I weren't Hank Jerney," said the other, his face darkening a little, "I wouldn't be standing here like this. Any other man in the mountains would have you tied for the sake of the reward."

This was self-evident.

"Very well," said Mark, "I suppose you're my man. Here's the letter."

He drew it forth, sweat-stained, crumpled, and yellow at the edges. The writing upon it was half obliterated. Hank Jerney looked the bearer over while he ripped open the envelope.

"You're the tenderfoot who busted loose from Jasperville?" he asked. "And you're the same tenderfoot that raised a ruction in town last night?"

He waited for an answer, but, shaking out the paper on which the letter was written, he ran his eyes through the contents, showing not the slightest emotion while he read.

Then he folded it, shoved it into the breast pocket of his shirt, and turned to his men.

"We're starting," he said. And to Mark: "Saddle and come along." He added to one of his men: "Jerry, go out with him."

Jerry detached himself without a word from his companions and accompanied Mark to the shed where they found Sally and saddled her. When they returned to the front of the shack, the others were already on their horses. Jerney was talking to Gus and Bill.

"This may turn out to be the best news that I've ever landed," he declared. "And, if it is, you boys come in on the split. If it turns out a false alarm, I'll remember you, anyway. So long. You'll get more out of me than you'd get out of a reward."

So saying, he waved his hand, and the whole cavalcade started out at a sharp canter.

It was at this hour, on this very night, that Bill Rafferty, thief and ex-convict, was wakened from a sleep as sound as the sleep of Mark Loftus. But it was nothing as palpable as a booted toe, prying at his tender ribs that awakened Bill. It was a faint sound, but it sounded in the sleeping ear of Bill like the closing of a door. He was instantly wide awake.

For a moment he lay there, fighting back his suspicion. He was not in Jasperville. The day before, taking advantage of the general let-down in the vigilance with which he had been watched since the flight of Mark Loftus, Bill had slipped out of Jasperville on an east-bound freight, had ridden eight hours at a rattling clip, and now he was cached away in an obscure little village among the foothills where he was prepared to wait until the storm blew over. Afterward, he would find a way to get to the honest Hank Jerney and get his share of the loot.

So he lay in the bed, fighting back his doubt. There could

be no danger. Even Charlie Clune himself, adroit as a fox hound and dogged as a ferret on a trail, could not have followed him with such speed and over such a distance as this. So convinced was the thief that he even closed his eyes, but, as he did so, he heard a second sound.

It was no greater in volume than the single tick of a watch, and to the ordinary ear it would have meant nothing more than one of those vague noises that continually haunt all frame dwellings. But the ear of Bill Rafferty was by no means ordinary. It had been trained in a wonderful school, where keenness of hearing is often the difference between life and death. Rafferty's remarkable ear told him at once that the sound was made by the pressure of a foot upon the floor.

His own action thereafter was exquisite in precision. In a flash he recalled where every piece of furniture was in the room. He who had entered must now be on the far side of the little table that stood in the corner of the room. To sit up in the bed, without making it squeak and without allowing the bedding to rustle loudly, was one extraordinary feat that Rafferty quickly accomplished. To reach under his pillow and draw forth his revolver was another act almost as deftly and silently performed. Then, hugging the gun close to him and crouching low, so as to present as small a mark as possible, Rafferty reached for the electric light at the head of his bed and snapped it on. He saw, crouched on the far side of the center table, just as he had suspected, the broad face, the heavy jowls, the pig eyes of Charlie Clune.

Strange how swiftly his brain could function. He measured the distance to the window, recalled the distance of the drop to the ground and then the distance to the shed, where he could steal a horse, and he was on his way. All that went through his mind in a single flash, as he fixed his gun on Charlie Clune. Then his mind stopped with a jar. In the hand

78

of Charlie Clune was not a revolver, but a huge, blunt-nosed, shapeless automatic. He saw the forefinger of Charlie whiten around the first joint as it curled on the trigger. Under the touch of that finger, there were seven shots, as the thief well knew, ready to be launched forth in one deadly gust in terribly swift succession. Rafferty stared at it with the feeling that fate had at last overcome him. A revolver, of course, he would not have feared. Clune was an execrable shot. But this horrible weapon — a dying hand could send out with it a spray of death-dealing bullets. Still, he might be able to turn Charlie from his goal with words. Charlie was amazingly stupid. Only when he was confronted with a locked safe did he become a genius.

"Well, kid," said Rafferty, "you sure did give me a start. What's the idea of the gat?"

Charlie Clune grinned slowly. It seemed that that stiff-jowled smile would never reach its full expansion. "I hit Jasperville. I heard everything. I trailed you here. I got you. You're dead."

A wave of cold dread shot up Rafferty's spine and spread in icy tingles to the tips of his fingers. "Why, you fool," he said, abandoning his idea of cajoling the other, "d'you mean to say you'd stand up to me with a gat?"

"You'll get me," said Charlie, "but I'm going to kill you while I die, Bill!"

"You idiot," exclaimed Rafferty. "What about the wife and the kid? If you want to throw yourself away, go ahead and do it. But what about the wife and the kid?"

"Dead," said Charlie Clune, his pig face turning gray. "Dead, Bill, last month. I seen her grave, and then I come on to get you. And I've got you. Except for you . . . her and me would have settled down together. But you were always hounding me. It was always one more game to try, and then we'd all settle down and live straight and clean. Well, you'd never let up, and so I busted her heart, and she's gone. Bill, you got to die."

Bill Rafferty, moistening his dry lips and vainly attempting to speak, knew that his time had indeed come. "When you're so set again' me," he began smoothly, "I dunno. It's true that I sent to old Hank Jerney. But Hank. . . ."

The automatic wavered the slightest bit from its true line as Charlie listened intently to the story. In that instant Rafferty fired. The weight of the heavy slug drove Charlie Clune from his chair and behind the table, as if a strong fist had knocked him down. And Rafferty, kneeling in his bed and whining with savage determination, pumped shot after shot into the shadowy figure that lay spilled on the darkness of the floor. Then he saw a glint of steel. The mass of flesh still lived.

Rafferty threw himself back toward the wall to escape from view, screaming, but as he moved, the big automatic spoke. It was not one shot, but a thunderous chatter that was not stilled until seven slugs had ripped through the bedding.

The gun was hardly silent when the proprietor rushed through the door, a revolver in either hand, but he found that there was no work left for him to do. Charlie Clune was dead, even as he had fired the last shot. Bill Rafferty, face down on the bed, had been literally torn to pieces by that hurricane of lead.

XII

"TIME AND A SMILE"

Ignorant of the fate of him who had sent him on the errand to the Chandler Mountains, Mark Loftus, in the golden light of the late afternoon, rode at the side of the outlaw to the place that Bill Rafferty had so carefully described in his letter. Down three bends of the little river the chief led his party with the letter open in his hand. At length he drew rein.

"There," he said, "is the rock," and he pointed to a big white-sided boulder, scarred, it seemed, by some grinding blast of lightning. "Roll that rock away, boys."

They were off their horses instantly and eagerly. He had not told one of them a single word of his expectations, but they knew they would not be led such a distance as this on a wild-goose chase. Four stout shoulders were applied to the rock, and it staggered and then turned on its side. Beneath they found a hollow, chipped in the bedrock on which the stone rested, and in the hollow was a stout little wooden box, blackened with rain water.

"Give that to me," said the outlaw.

It was presented to him obediently, and he jerked open the hinged cover and exposed a single piece of brown wrapping paper with a few words scrawled upon it. He read it aloud: "Thank you!"

Hank Jerney hurled the box and the paper to the ground.

"We've drawn a blank," he said with the most perfect manners.

Four pairs of grim eyes turned at that word upon Mark Loftus, but Hank Jerney put in at once: "It ain't his fault. He did his work, and he did it well. Somebody was too quick for Rafferty . . . that's all, and we've had our ride for nothing. Now we go back."

There was a growl, but then silence. Plainly they wanted to vent their disappointment on someone, but the puzzled face of Mark Loftus showed that he was as surprised as they. Hank Jerney beckoned him to one side.

"Now, Loftus," he said, "you figuring on playing this game . . . this same game that I'm playing?"

"You know me?" asked Mark, astonished.

"The minute I laid eyes on you," said the other. "It ain't the first time I've run into a Loftus, and I know their look about the eyes. Son, take my advice. I dunno how you run foul of your dad, but get back to him quick . . . quick, you hear? Ask him to forgive you. I know this country, and I know him, and I know that, though you may have beaten him in this one game, he'll beat you in the second. He's too strong for you or anybody else."

"Why?" asked Mark, curious.

"Because," said Hank Jerney, "he's honest, and the whole world knows he's honest. Now, good bye and good luck."

Mark Loftus, as he rode down the mountainside, determined that Jerney was right. The hot anger against his father that had been burning in him since he left Jasperville had been suddenly expended when he learned the night before of the wound he had inflicted on him. Besides, as he looked back on the whole affair, it seemed to him to be a good deal of a comic-opera affair. On the riotous impulse of a moment he had accepted a commission from a criminal. He had labored at the risk of his head to fulfill the commission, and, when the thing was done, it turned out to be a huge jest. All that heart-breaking labor had been performed for nothing.

Yet, after all, there was something accomplished. He had

ridden out of Jasperville, a careless, reckless, soft-handed idler. He had reached the end of the trail and turned back, a man. That, it seemed, was what had happened. He had passed through years of foolish dreaming, and now he turned back, eager, and hungry to take his place among the workers and do a man's share, wherever he might be. There would probably be ample need of such work. Even if he were able to extricate himself safely from these mountains, filled with men hunting for him, he would escape to safety in the lowlands, naked of support. For he could not hope that anything other than time would bridge the gap between him and his father.

He laid his plans, then, to skirt past the main roads and the villages, where he had stopped on his easy journey toward the Chandler Mountains. He dared not show his face in a town because mere bluff, such as had favored him before, would not now serve. He had been exposed, and now he must play a different hand. So he drifted with Sally, slowly and laboriously, down the sides of the mountains, never descending into the valley lands except to reach down, now and again at night, to buy crackers or canned food at some crossroads store. There was little fear that he would be recognized, so long as he did not appear on Sally. A thick beard was growing on his face, and the work of the trail had made him astonishingly lean.

Four slow days were filled in this manner before he turned out of the foothills and rode straight for the town where Mary lived. He must return Sally, at whatever risk. No doubt the girl had learned more about him by this time, had learned everything, in fact, except his real name. How his father, during all of these days, had been able to conceal the identity of the wanderer, when all of Jasperville knew it, was more than Mark could well understand. Doubtless it was simply because he and Larry Day had ridden ahead of all report.

It was a night very dark, with low-drifting clouds, when he

reached the outskirts of the village. He had waited until an hour after sunset before he ventured to approach the town, but now he rode boldly down the main street, relishing immensely the sound of human voices on either side of him, feeling his stomach grow hollow at the scent of cooking food. It seemed to him that half a lifetime had elapsed since he had left the town. But, though shaft after shaft of lamplight struck across him on his way down the street, there was no challenging hail to stop him, and so he came to the farther end of the town and dismounted from Sally before the house of her mistress. There was no light in the front of the house, but there was a murmur in the rear room, the kitchen, perhaps.

At that thought the picture of his first meeting with Mary rolled back upon him, clear in every detail. He would knock at the door, hand the reins of Sally to the person who answered his summons, and then he would disappear into the night.

At his knock he heard the sound of running feet and a girl's voice singing gaily. The door was flung open. He blinked at the flood of light from the lamp that Mary carried. And she, at the sight of him, to his profound astonishment, broke into a flood of laughter. It offended Mark to the soul, for he felt himself to be a somewhat tragic figure, a man alone and defying the world.

"Come in," she said. When he attempted to draw back, she actually caught him by the sleeve and drew him inside the house. "He's come at last," she exclaimed, pitching her voice for those in a distant room. "He's come at last, and Sally's with him . . . dear old Sally."

Then she closed the door behind him and put her shoulders against it to bar his way of flight, her laughter still smiting him. It was puzzling, maddening to see and hear her. In the meantime heavier footfalls sounded. First he saw a very big man with a fluff of brown beard rolling over his breast and bright blue eyes that shone at him. The man was laughing as heartily as Mary. Were they all gone mad? And then, slipping past the bulky figure of the man of the beard, he saw Harrison Loftus, the only sober face of the three.

There was no chance for Mark to make up his mind as to what course of dignified action he should take. Harrison Loftus came straight to him, his arms outstretched, and seized his hands and gripped them in a tremendous pressure.

"Mark, my boy," he said, "now that you've shown me that you are a man, are you going to prove it still more and forgive your hot-headed father? And, when you do that, will you kindly explain why you haven't ridden into a town in the past five days and let me know where you were? I've had every wire hot, asking news of you, ever since the day that Bushy Taylor, the trapper, came in with Larry Day's money."

"Who?"

"Old Taylor found it. Why he pried the rock away in the first place, he wouldn't say. The point is that he did, and the honest old fellow brought in the fifty thousand dollars to Larry Day."

Mark Loftus gasped. News was pouring in upon him almost faster than he could gather it. "But how did you guess . . . ?" he began.

"That you'd come back here? Well, Mark, I followed every inch of the trail you left, and you'll have to confess that you left big signs all around behind you."

"I suppose I did."

"When I came to this house, I found Dan Curtis, here, pretty cut up because Mary, his niece, had given her horse to you. Well, Mark, I talked a while to Mary, and, from certain things she said, I gathered that you most certainly would come back here. And here you are. Mary, was I right?"

But Mary was suddenly abashed and quiet. She had no eyes

for either Harrison Loftus or his son, but looked steadfastly down at the floor. "And I was right, too," she said, "because I told you that he'd get to the end of his trail."

"I've been a fool," said Mark Loftus simply. "But, Mary, as a matter of fact. . . ."

"Take your time, boy," said Uncle Dan Curtis. "They's two things that it don't pay to hurry. One is a balky hoss, and one is a girl. Give 'em time, and they'll come to you."

"Uncle Dan!" cried Mary, tears of rage and shame in her eyes. Immediately she whirled and fled up the stairs.

"Time," said Uncle Dan with imperturbable calm. "Time is all you need, lad . . . time and a smile."

THE STRANGE RIDE OF PERRY WOODSTOCK

In 1932 Frederick Faust's agent was locked in a battle with Street & Smith's *Western Story Magazine*. The Great Depression had had an impact on this magazine's circulation, and the editor wanted to cut Faust's rate from a nickel a word to something less. Faust, during a trip to Egypt that year, wrote three short novels. Instead of selling them to *Western Story Magazine*, Faust's agent offered them instead to the competition, Popular Publications' *Dime Western*. Rogers Terrill, then editor of *Dime Western*, bought all three of them. Terrill changed the title of "The Strange Ride of Perry Woodstock" to "Death Rides Behind" for its appearance in *Dime Western* in the March, 1933 issue. It is interesting, perhaps, to contrast how Terrill was able, by editorial intercession, to diminish this author's poetic imagery and sterling prose into something almost mediocre. Here is how Max Brand opened the story:

An owl, skimming close to the ground, hooted at the very door of the bunkhouse. That door was wide, because the day had been hot and the night was hot, also, and windless. Therefore, Perry Woodstock jumped from his bunk, grabbed his hat in one hand and his boots in the other, and still seemed to hear the voice of the bird in the room, a melancholy and sonorous echo.

The owl hooted again, not in a dream but in fact, farther down the hollow, and Woodstock realized that he had not been wakened by the voice of the cook calling to the 'punchers to "come and get it," neither was it a cold autumn morning at an open camp, neither was there frost in his hair nor icy dew upon his forehead, and his body was not creaking at all the joints. . . .

And here is how Terrill altered that opening scene:

The door of the bunkhouse was wide, because the day had been hot and the night was hot, also, and windless. Perry Woodstock jumped from his bunk, grabbed his hat in one hand and his boots in the other. Something had awakened him. Some sound had come to that door. He stood tense for a moment.

His nerves were on edge, his heart pounding with the effect of some strange alarm. . . .

For its appearance here, Faust's title and full text for this short novel have been restored with all his poetry and magical imagery.

I

An owl, skimming close to the ground, hooted at the very door of the bunkhouse. That door was wide, because the day had been hot and the night was hot, also, and windless. Therefore, Perry Woodstock jumped from his bunk, grabbed his hat in one hand and his boots in the other, and still seemed to hear the voice of the bird in the room, a melancholy and sonorous echo.

The owl hooted again, not in a dream but in fact, farther down the hollow, and Woodstock realized that he had not been wakened by the voice of the cook calling to the 'punchers to "come and get it," neither was it a cold autumn morning at an open camp, neither was there frost in his hair nor icy dew upon his forehead, and his body was not creaking at all the joints. No, he could remember now that he had come down to work on this ranch in the desert unappalled by the fear of heat, for he felt that he could have worked in a furnace the rest of his days and never found the temperature too great.

His nerves were still on edge, however, and his heart pounding with the effect of that strange alarm. He went to the door of the bunkhouse — he was the only person in it — and stood there, making a cigarette and watching the silver flowing of the hills toward the horizon, for it was full moon. He lighted his smoke, blew out the first lungful with appreciation, and then distinctly saw that a man was wrangling the horse herd down in the mesquite tangle in the hollow.

Other than himself and the old man, nobody in the world had a right to work up those horses. Since the old man was snoring with a deep, thundering vibration in the ranch house nearby, it stood to reason that the fellow down there below was either a thief or something perilously close to it. Perry

Woodstock did not hesitate. By the time he called the rancher for whom he worked, the mischief might be done and the fellow fleetly away, beyond pursuit. Besides, Woodstock was not the man to ask for help.

He simply stepped into his boots, then into his trousers, buckled a gun belt around his hips, and went hatless down the slope. As he went, he saw the horses spread out in a flashing semicircle, galloping hard from the mesquite. The soft sandy soil muffled the beat of their hoofs. They gleamed under the moonlight. But the gray mare was not tossing her bright mane in the lead, as usual. No, for the very good reason that she was the one that the stranger had on the end of his rope now. Perry Woodstock nodded in agreement. She was certainly the best of the lot.

A man who could pick horses so well might be able to pick guns even better. Woodstock rubbed the palm of his hand hard against his hip and flexed his fingers once or twice, as a man might do to supple his hand before dealing a pack of cards. In the meantime he saw that a second horse stood in the biggest patch of the mesquite, its dropped head hardly rising above the tops of the brush. It was tired, very tired. The desert dust had been washed from its body by the rivers of its sweat. It was burnished and shone under the moon, but it was dead on its feet.

Yonder fellow who now cinched the saddle on the gray mare and then worked the bridle over her head had been riding hard and long. There was no doubt of that. And that made Woodstock feel all the more nervous about the prospect of the fight. For a man who simply exchanges mounts can hardly be called a thief. All he wins is a little boot perhaps and, if he changes horses often enough, even that works out in the long run. Furthermore, a man who rides through the night in that manner is not apt to be easily stopped.

The progress of Woodstock became slower and slower as he drew nearer the other. He came to a depression that practically covered him from sight. Now he walked with his Colt in his hand. He stalked with long and stealthy strides. He was in pointblank range when he saw the stranger swing into the saddle. Would the gray mare put on her show? She would!

It had cost Woodstock a dozen hard falls to learn her repertoire of tricks, though he well knew how to tie to a horse. Now the brim of that rider's sombrero began to flop violently up and down. The gray had her head and kept it low. She beat the ground as though it were a drum. In mid-air she snaked herself into complicated knots. She never landed on the same foot. Her rider was tall, and his length of leg helped him to get a knee hold, but after half a dozen jumps he was pulling leather, and a moment later the mare whirled, executed a neat reverse, and slammed the stranger full length on the ground.

The reins were hanging under her nose. Therefore the gray did not run off but stood with ears pricked to watch the enemy rise. He was badly shocked. He got up in sections, as it were, first propped on his hands, then struggling to his knees, then to his feet with a final effort. At that point he saw Woodstock and Woodstock's gun.

"Touch the sky, brother," said Perry Woodstock.

The hands of the stranger rose shoulder high, struggled for a moment there, then went up above his head, encouraged by the careless surety of the manner in which Woodstock held his gun. At the hip he kept it, with a half-bent arm. His forefinger was not on the trigger for the good reason that no trigger was there. Instead, the ball of his thumb was hooked over the hammer. Of these points the stranger made himself quickly aware before he hoisted his arms on high. His short mustache bristled a little as his lips pressed together.

"Who are you, brother?" asked Woodstock.

"Name of Joe Scanlon."

"Joe, show me your back for a minute and keep those hands up a little closer to the moon."

Scanlon turned his back. In spite of his slender body he was strong. Now that his arms were raised, his shoulder muscles bulged in hard knots that Woodstock assessed with a competent eye. He slipped a hand under the left armpit of Scanlon and felt the gun that hung there, beneath the loosely fitted coat.

"I thought you were one of those spring-holster boys," observed Woodstock. "Just drop that gun in the sand, will you? And drop it slow, Scanlon."

He put the muzzle of his own gun against the small of Scanlon's back while the revolver was accordingly produced and dropped on the ground. With a few dexterous movements Woodstock fanned his prisoner and found no other weapons.

"All right," he said, "now step back."

Scanlon faced him, but his glance went beyond Woodstock, to watch the silver outlines of the hills in the distance.

"You want money or trouble?" asked Scanlon.

"You got plenty of both?"

"I'll tell you what . . . I'm in a hurry."

"House on fire, eh?"

"I've got a wife and three kids over in the mountains, yonder." He jerked a thumb over his shoulder at the delicate outlines of moon haze and snow that represented Los Diablos Mountains. "The wife writes to me that Bert has diphtheria, and I hit the road. That bronco yonder is a tough bird. It's a roan all the way to the bone. But it played out. I aimed to help myself to a horse right here, when I seen them in the field. If there was any boot to pay, I could fix that up on the back trail."

"Where you from?" asked Woodstock.

"Down on the Fielding ranch. You know? The Fielding brothers."

"How do they feed down there now?"

"Nothing but beans."

"Brother," said Woodstock, "it's not so much what's in a lie as the way it's told that counts. The Fielding outfit is down yonder. You wouldn't ride through here coming from the Fielding place. Not by five points on the compass, if you're headed for Los Diablos range. And Jerry Fielding hates beans so bad that he won't have 'em on the place, boiled or baked or nothing."

Joe Scanlon shrugged his shoulders. "You're one of those particular *hombres*," he said. "But that's all right. If one lie won't suit you, I could try another. But wouldn't it cut things short if I paid my way on this division of yours . . . and paid high?"

Woodstock bumped the iron weight of his knuckles one by one against his broad chin. He cocked his head a little so that the moonlight illumined from a different angle the furrows that labor and pain had worked in his young face.

"I broke that gray mare, brother," he said gently. Even when he spoke so quietly, there was apt to be a soft boom and vibration about his speech. "She's four, and nobody had given her a ride. I rode her. Ever see a kid hammer a doll on the ground? That's the way the mare hammered me. Some of the sawdust and stuffing ran out of me, now and then, but finally she agreed to be friends. Come here, Molly."

The mare came up to him, shaking her head at the tall Scanlon, switching her tail nervously.

"If you'd stolen this mare, I would have followed your trail till my eyes rubbed out, but the trail would have been a blank, pretty soon. I'll tell you what, Scanlon. I'm what they call broad-minded. I can take my whiskey neat, and I can use a beer chaser, too. But I hate a horse thief more than a Mexican hates his mother-in-law. You want to buy her, but your money's no good." He looked askance at the dark muzzle and the white brow of the mare. "Not a damn' bit of good," he added.

"I saw she was the best, but I didn't read her mind," said Scanlon. "I'll make a deal for the next best in the lot."

"I'm a hired hand, and I don't make bargains."

Scanlon's entire body twitched nervously. "D'you aim to hold me?" he asked.

"I aim to do that," declared Woodstock, "until the sheriff hands you on to the jail." He waved toward the tired mustang. "Get your outfit back on that roan," he commanded.

Scanlon obeyed. As he cinched the saddle in place, the tired roan groaned under the pressure and swayed.

"You won't hold me that long, though," observed Scanlon.

"Won't I, brother?"

"Not alive," said Scanlon. "The boys that are riding on my trail now will see to that."

II

Woodstock had lifted Scanlon's revolver from the ground by this time. Like his own gun, it was triggerless, and the sights had been filed away so that they might not catch in leather or cloth in a time of urgent speed. This examination of the Colt made Woodstock squint a little as he stared at Scanlon.

"Who are you, brother?" he asked.

"I've tried one yarn on you. What's the use of trying another?"

"Who's riding your trail? A sheriff and his mob?"

"Put reverse English on that, and you have the idea." Still, anxiously, Scanlon watched the hills that gleamed against the sky. Then he burst through every barrier, exclaiming: "Partner, the law don't want me. Not now. It's wanted me in the past . . . and it's had me, too, had me plenty. Will you give me a break? I've got money on me. I'll pay you five hundred bucks for the worst mustang in that lot, but I've got to get on my way. I'm not a horse thief. The job I'm riding on is so big that things like that don't matter."

"Who are you, Scanlon?" asked Woodstock, frowning.

Into his words came a soft beating of many hoofs. Scanlon whirled toward the sound. It came not over the hills but up the center of the shallow valley, and now they saw five riders coming fast, with the dust of their gallop streaming up into a long cloud that hung motionless in the air like the funnel of smoke that stretches behind a speeding locomotive on a windless day. Over the ground beside them rocked the black shadows of horses and men.

"Look!" shouted Scanlon, throwing up his long arms. "There's what I am . . . a dead man. They've got me."

He drew from his pocket a used shotgun shell which had

been refilled with a paper wadding, as it seemed. This he dropped in the hand of Woodstock. The whites of his eyes showed to the pink. His lips gaped wildly over his words, as he cried: "You've held me for them, damn you. Now, if you're a white man, find Harry Scanlon on the shoulder of Grizzly Peak. Tell him I'm dead. Give him this!" He got to the roan as he spoke the last words, went into the saddle like a mountain lion leaping for a kill, and roused the tired mustang with the terrible rowels of his Spanish spurs.

"Take this!" cried Woodstock, and threw him the revolver.

Whatever life was in the roan responded. He broke away in a gallop that fanned out the tail of Scanlon's coat, and for a minute the bewildered Woodstock thought that there was actually a chance for the fugitive.

Scanlon and the five went out of sight in the draw beyond the mesquite tangle. On the farther side Scanlon appeared, still in the lead, but even in the distance it was possible to see that the roan had ended its race. It moved with a laboring gallop, like a rocking horse, and behind it the five riders swept up the slope on racing horses.

Steel winked in their hands. Scanlon turned with a poised revolver. And Woodstock suddenly bent his head, closed his eyes. The reports of the guns made him look again, in time to see Scanlon falling. His foot caught in a stirrup. He was dragged a little distance, his body flopping, a dust cloud whipping up behind it. Then the roan fell under a fresh volley, and the five closed on their prey. Every man dismounted. They huddled over Scanlon like eager wolves over a dead companion.

"I held him," said Woodstock aloud. "I held him till they could catch up.'

He began to beat his right fist into the palm of his left hand. It was a dream. The moonlight separated the thing from daylight happenings. There was the stillness of a nightmare over it all. And the hoot of an owl had begun it.

The five scattered away from the dead man. It was almost a surprise to Woodstock to see that a body remained. They were on their horses, sweeping off to the left, and again at a full gallop they disappeared among the bright hummocks of sand.

Woodstock, still lost in that dream, hesitated. Perhaps it would be best to rouse the old man, Jud Harvey, his boss. Perhaps it was wiser to go straight toward the place where the body of Scanlon lay, with the roan fallen beside him, small in the distance. He had not quite made up his mind, thoughtfully rubbing his hand over the withers of the gray mare, when he heard again the sound of the hoofbeats. Then, looking up the slope, he saw the five riders coming between him and the house. It was like an Indian charge. Their heads were down. The manes of their horses flew up, glittering in the moonshine. It was all Indian, except the silence, and that silence froze the blood more than the yelling of fiends.

The trance that had held Woodstock snapped. There was no bridle, no saddle on Molly. Never before had he tried to ride her bareback, and the chances were great that she would snap him off her and go frolicking on while he sprawled on his back, and the gunmen swept over him. It was that old used shotgun shell and the paper in it. That was what they wanted. They had failed to find it on Scanlon. If he held it between thumb and forefinger — if he showed it so, and made a gesture of surrender, perhaps they would not shoot him down.

Then before the eyes of Woodstock appeared the contorted face of Scanlon, like a ghost, the whites of the eyes showing to the pink, the lips gaping and gibbering about the words. Woodstock flung himself on the back of the mare and called to her. Her response nearly jerked him off her back. It was sudden as the flight of an arrow from a bowstring, but an arrow does not gather speed through the air, and every bound of the mare was longer. One hand wound into her mane was all that kept Woodstock in place. He sloughed sidewise. The working of her supple body threatened to slide him off. Only by degrees he managed to pull himself into position until his knees had their grip. He had to forget saddles and remember the days of his boyhood.

Still she was gathering speed. The shoulder muscles came back in hard ripples under his knees. He felt the strength of her back pulsing. It was a dizzy thing to look down to the whipping strokes of her hoofs. A bullet kissed the air above Woodstock's head; the sound of the explosion followed on its heels. He risked a glance over his shoulder.

No wonder they had started shooting! Oh, the beauty of speed, and how she pulled away from them. From the tip of her nose to the tip of her tail she stretched in a straight line, quivering with effort. He looked back again. Two of them had dismounted, lay flat on the ground, and steadied their rifles for the distant shot. The other three, still riding hard, fanned out to either side to give the marksmen a fair chance. Woodstock, with a pressure of his hand on the neck of the mare, turned her down an easy slope to the left.

Wasp sounds bored through the air about him. He reached the bottom of the hollow and swung the mare to the right. The shooting had stopped. All the pursuit was for the moment ended. And framed within the walls of the draw he saw far before him Los Diablos range. Grizzly Peak was somewhere among them, one of the lesser brothers in that collection of giants. *On a shoulder of Grizzly Peak, find Harry Scanlon if you're a white man, and give him this!* What was it? One man had died for it this night. How many had died for it in the past? How many would die hereafter — for a bit of paper wadding in a used shotgun shell?

They came over the bank of the draw behind him now, three riding to the front, two far, far to the rear. A foot in a gopher hole, a stumble over one of the rocks would end the race, still. But it was as easy to think of a hawk stumbling in the sky as to think of the gray mare faltering on her home ground. Farther behind, farther behind fell the five. Then, suddenly, they began to drop from the picture, and he knew what that meant. Rather than burn up the strength of their horses, they would cut down their gait to a lope and so try to run their trail into the ground.

There was still plenty of running in the mare, but he called her back by a hand to a gallop. He patted her shining neck, and she turned her head a little, and pricked her ears for him. Suddenly he felt that he was cut loose from all familiar shores and, like a mariner of ancient days, bound for coasts of unknown adventure in unknown seas.

III

To keep to beaten trails would be to invite the pursuers on the way he selected. Instead, he chose a line and held to it over rough and smooth. A good many times he had to dismount and make his own way over the rocks, turning to watch the mare follow him like a struggling cat, her armed hoofs clanging and slipping on the stones. As they advanced into the wilderness, she seemed to draw closer and closer to him. She came to his voice; she came to his gesture.

What would Jud Harvey think when, in the morning, he found his hired man gone, and the gray mare gone also, and that dead body stretched on the hillside opposite the ranch house? Suppose they attributed the killing to Perry Woodstock, now missing? Suppose they loaded him with the name of horse thief, as well?

He could give them, in return, a precious tale about the hoot of an owl and an old used shotgun shell. But he seemed to have turned his back to such actualities. As he climbed into the mountains, he climbed into a new sphere of life.

The desert foothills were marked with spanish bayonet, gaunt figures. He found a valley with a trickle of water running through it, drank it before it ever reached the sands. There were big cottonwoods here. He mounted over rocky slopes spotted with scrub oak. Then he came to the first scatterings of pines. He breathed of them before they met his eyes. He roused some valley quail and heard their three bold notes, without the soft ending of the call of the desert quail. The sound pleased him. On the whir of their wings his spirit was raised also. It seemed easy enough to find Harry Scanlon, deliver the shell — and then? Drop back to the quiet old days and ways again?

The pines grew taller, thickened. They dimmed the moon-light that presently went out altogether as he entered a dense fog. It was one of those clouds that he had looked up to many a time from the heat of the ranch in the desert, seeing them laid along the side of the mountain or over its shoulders like a white feather boa around the neck of a woman.

Rain fell. In the darkness the mare almost grazed the trees, time and again. He had to trust her, often blindly holding out his hands to either side, but so they climbed with the forest until they came to a more scattering growth above, found the moon a dead thing, setting on the edge of a sea of clouds, and the dawn beginning over the upper peaks.

At the top of a great divide Perry Woodstock made his first long halt. He sat on a rock so long that the mare began to graze, sniffing tentatively at the strange mountain grasses before she cropped them. The light grew. Yonder in a cañon a wa-terfall whose song he had heard came arching into view, car-rying the daylight swiftly down into an abyss. Rose entered the eastern sky, moving around the horizon. Off a crag above him, a fish hawk slid into the still bosom of the air, balanced over a hollow where night still lay, and then began to sink into the depth with easy circlings.

At last, all in a moment, the day was there, though the sun had not risen, and from his height Woodstock saw a lake stretched blue as paint between the dark of a pine forest and the golden brown face of a cliff. Up from that lake rose the hawk with something flashing at its feet. It flew so close that Woodstock could see the fish clearly, held by the back and pointed head forward so that it could be steered more easily through the air.

Woodstock stood up. Every mountain had a different face; every one had a different name. He wished with all his heart that he knew them all. When he turned, the clouds were thinning. As through doors he looked down through openings at the desert. It was just beneath him. He seemed to have climbed a sheer wall from the height of which he looked, as it were, into the flat back yard of the world, swept monotonously clean and bare.

He found a way down to the lake with Molly following behind him like a dancer, studying the places where he stepped before she ventured on the perilous slope. Never once did she slip, though she set some rocks tumbling. One of them was a good-size boulder that leaped far out, smote the blue face of the lake, and sent upwards lightning splashes of water. The noise of the impact smacked the ears of Woodstock a long moment later, repeated and repeated by echoes, loud or small.

When they got to the verge of the water, he stripped, plunged as if into liquid ice, then stood on a rock at the margin, laughing at the blue gooseflesh that puckered his body while he whipped away the wet with the edge of his hand. For he had a feeling that he was washing himself clean of the dust of a commonplace existence. A dead man had passed him the key to a new world, and he was determined to try the lock of whatever door he found.

For breakfast he pulled up his belt, smoked a cigarette, watched Molly at work in a rich pasture, and then started again on his journey. He circled the edge of the lake, weaving back and forth among the aspens that fringed the water and by whose presence he judged he was a full seven thousand feet above sea level. Douglas spruce covered the northward-facing slope down which he had just come. Yellow pine grew on the opposite wall of the great hollow; but very few of either of these giant races drew near to the water. They confronted each other like huge armies, and the bright yellow-green of the aspens was pleasant about the blue of the lake.

Woodstock looked twice at the fisherman before he really

saw the man standing at the edge of an indentation of the lake. His boots were as dark as the roots that projected into the water. His trousers were the color of the soil, his flannel shirt a rusted brown like the trunks of trees, and his hat was exactly the color of his gray beard. His body was long and thin, and he had a long, thin, brown face. Out from his hand extended a light pole from the end of which a fishing line dropped to the water, seemed bent sharply to the side, then disappeared far down in the glassy lake. He was watching his rod, not the stranger or the stranger's horse, when Woodstock spoke to him. Then he turned his head and a pair of blue, calm eyes. So an animal, when it is both well-fed and fearless, may slowly move its head and look toward a noise.

"Hello, stranger," said Woodstock. "What's the good word up here?"

"The fish hawks have the fun around these here parts," said the old man. "That one that went shoulderin' by you, a while back yonder on the edge of the mountain, he come down and socked his hooks into the only trout that's worth catchin' in this water. All I've got is small fry. But the smaller they are the sweeter, I guess, and I'm old enough to have patience now. Come back where I got a frying pan, and I'll give you a breakfast."

So he left off fishing, picked up a line with a shining, shivering huddle of fish at the end of it, and walked ahead to show the way. He had a fine carriage and a noble stride — only his step was slow and his knees had not the supple spring of a young mountaineer. Very nearby an old gray mule with legs crooked inward at the knees and a scrawny neck was working without much interest at the grass in a clearing. It was not so much a clearing as a lane that had been beaten and broken into the woods by the fall of an immense yellow pine, a good hundred and fifty feet, perhaps, from its uptorn roots to its head. When at last after a long life some hurricane took it by the top and slowly pried it loose from its deep moorings, it had smashed down many lesser trees of its kind, so that there was a wreckage under and all about its huge body, and in the interstices grew excellent grass, mixed with the sprouts of young trees — not yellow pines, but the lodgepole pines whose seeds fall instantly on every scarred place in the woods.

At a point where the trunk had snapped in two in the fall, leaving a huge face of yellow splinters higher than Woodstock's head, the old fisherman had camped. The mule was hobbled. A light cotton tent was stretched on pegs, and Woodstock saw the black spot of last night's supper. He asked no questions, but set to work gathering firewood. Among green shrubbery he found one pale ghost, so he broke up these dead, brittle twigs and brought them back to the fire that had been kindled already by the fisherman. Two pairs of skillful hands made the work go forward with a magic speed. In a trice they were eating hardtack, fish fried brown, and drinking black coffee.

"They're good and fat," said the fisherman. "You take a fish that ain't got no fat on it, and his meat sort of fills up your belly but don't feed you none. Lean fish is like straw for horses. Puffs you up and keeps you hungry. But you can make a march on food like this, and spare your horse all the way."

He hooked his thumb toward the gray mare. She and the hobbled mule, leaning far forward, stretching out their necks, were cautiously touching noses. When that was done, the mare squealed with a sudden indignation, hitched herself halfway around, and jerked up her heels a time or two as though prepared to batter in the ribs of the mule. The old mule, flattening its ears, lifted its head till its neck was like the throat of a camel, and turned slowly away in disgusted dignity.

"That girl, there, she don't like my Alec," said the old man. "She says he's a worthless nigger. She says that he's poor white

104

trash, is what she says. But that don't matter to you. You like her pretty face, son."

"She saved my life," said Perry Woodstock dreamily. "Come here, Molly."

She came to his hand, and sniffed it. He laid his palm between her eyes.

"I'm Dave Hixon," said the man of the forest. "Who are you? Not that you need to answer. A gent that has to leave without a saddle or a bridle ain't likely to take a name along with him, neither."

"I'm Perry Woodstock." The mare moved away. Woodstock followed her with his eyes, while he asked: "Why did you camp here, Dave, when you could have got closer to the water, and had everything handy?"

The old man pointed to the broken trunk of the tree. "I used to prospect for gold. Now I hunt for the sort of yarns that the mountains can tell you. See where I've chipped into that tree and split it with wedges, here and there? I've only got part of its story. It's eleven hundred years old. Just about exactly. I've counted the rings. I know its starvation years, where the rings are close together. Seven of 'em in a row, when it was a youngster about three hundred years old. That drought must've near killed it. When it was a baby about fifteen years old, the snow bent it over like a bow, and it was that way a coupla or three years. Then it begun to straighten again. God wants trees and men to grow straight.

"I found a place where the ants and the borers begun to wind into it. They meant slow death and sure death unless the doctor come along. But he come. He was Doctor Texas Woodpecker. He laid his ear to the heart of the tree, and he heard enough. So he done an operation with the chisel edge of his beak and took out the trouble, and swallered it for a fee. Life went on for the yellow pine. It wrote its story on him. You read the rings and see. The wounds are filled up with resin, but they're there. It was about five hundred years old when the snow piled up so high on a branch that the branch broke off and took a chunk out of its side. Along about Fourteen Ninety-One an Indian shot an arrow into that tree. I found the flint head, soldered all around with dead resin. Come along about Fifteen Hundred and Fifty or so, somebody tried the edge of an axe on the instep of this tree. Spaniards. They're the only ones that would've had steel in this part of the world. But the Americans come, and forest fires with 'em. Three times that pine got scorched bad, and all within the last eighty years. We're a pretty mean people, son, and we work with steel and fire. When the lightning struck the head of that tree, I don't know, but there's a lot of us that begin to die in the head while the body's still sound."

"That's what you hunt for?" asked Perry Woodstock. "Yarns like that?"

"Yep. They ain't wrote in words, but they're all in the flesh of the stone or the trees or the earth."

Perry Woodstock wondered at him quietly, and the old man endured the gaze like a face of stone, unmoved. "You're telling me that the things we do don't amount to much," said Woodstock. "The trees, even, see a lot more than we do, though they stand still. I guess you're right, but everything that's young is foolish . . . and I'm still young. I want to find a man in these mountains. I don't mean him any harm. I'm just bringing him a message. His name is Harry Scanlon. Know him?"

Dave Hixon stirred in a way that showed his mind was moved as well as his body. "There's a Harry Scanlon living halfway up the side of Grizzly Peak. He's got a blind wife, Theodora, uncommon fast with her knitting. And he's got a daughter, Rosemary. What would you want with him, son?"

"No harm," said Perry Woodstock. He stood up. "Where's Grizzly Peak?"

"They've changed a lot of the names of these here mountains," answered Dave Hixon, "but Grizzly is a name that don't change none too easy. There . . . you can see it through the gap. It ain't more than ten miles, but every one of them miles is worth ten."

"Then I better start. I'm thanking you, Dave."

He held out his hand, and the bony fingers of the old man closed over it, retained it for a moment, while he said: "You're young enough to keep hoping for tomorrow. But it'll be just like today. The trouble is that we always want to hurry things up. We put in the spurs, and we get the blood on our heels. But no matter how hard you ride, all you can get to in the end of your life is a kind of stillness, dead or living, and all the blood you'll have to wash away in the silence, one of these days."

He released Perry Woodstock, and the boy turned instantly away. He called over his shoulder. The gray mare followed him, was seized by a fit of hilarity, and ran joyously before him under the somber trees. But there was no flight of spirits in Woodstock. He trudged straight on for three hours, until a hill raised him above the trees, and he had the rugged height of Grizzly Peak all before him. He stared at it a moment, then took out the shotgun shell, pulled from it the paper slip, and read on this, in ink that time had turned brown:

Walsh and Porcupine on line and Oliver and Gray at the flow find a big stack work one-third down.

IV

Perry Woodstock labored on until late in the afternoon before he heard, far ahead, the clinking of a hammer on iron. He trusted that meant he was close to the habitation of Harry Scanlon. So he paused a moment to straighten his back and shoulders and draw a few deep breaths. The magpie that had been accompanying him for the last half mile, darting in and out among the trees and brush, or gleaming suddenly far overhead, now sat on the tip of a branch and was cradled by the resiliency of the little bough. A shining, tailor-made bit of black satin and murder was that magpie. When Woodstock whistled, it talked back querulously. It kept examining him with an eager eye, as though it expected Woodstock to turn into edible stuff before long.

He went on. The big yellow pines on that southern slope of Grizzly Peak gathered together in dense ranks, as evenly spaced as trees that men have planted. There was no undergrowth. There was no grass, but only the brown, slippery padding of pine needles over the ground. The gray mare grew nervous, and pressed up to the very shoulder of Woodstock. She was at his side when he came to the clearing, and stopped. For in a step he had changed worlds.

Passing through that fence of great yellow pines, he stepped from the wilderness into a tiny farm. For the mountain here put out a shoulder of several acres as level as a floor checked into fields with log fences. The yellow-green of wheat covered one patch; another was newly ploughed; and the sods were still shining, while birds worked among them for roots and worms and insects. Two cows moved slowly at their grazing in a bit of pasture, and near the snug cabin that was backed against the upper slope of the mountain, a girl was spading in a vegetable garden. Beyond her, at the door of the cabin, sat a woman, knitting. The needles flashed with the speed of her work.

The girl was nearest. Perry Woodstock made for her with the mare still just behind him, snuffing down the various fragrances of the pasture and stepping with dainty exactness along the narrow path between the beds of vegetables. Woodstock raised his hand to his forehead before he remembered that he had no hat. And the bare-headed girl returned that salute instantly.

She leaned on her spade, holding it with a gloved hand. She wore a dress of blue gingham, faded to a dirty gray. There was a big patch at her knees, but over her shoulders lay a white collar as clean as snow, and it made the frame for her face. The gentle quiet and beauty of the place seemed to have given birth to her, and her eyes were both soft and fearless, like the eyes of wild creatures before they have heard the hounds baying and the guns of the hunters.

She smiled at Woodstock as he paused, and for pure joy he smiled back at her. But he was sorry that his skin was swarthy and that his wind-entangled hair was black. If he had been blond, he would have been closer kin to her. Now that he was so near, he saw that she was not tall. It was her way of standing and the lift of her head that gave her the appearance of height.

"You're Rosemary Scanlon," he said, "and my name is Perry Woodstock. I've brought your father a message."

From the mountainside behind the cabin the hammer strokes chimed again on iron. She pulled the glove from her right hand and held it out to him, warm and strong to his touch but small. That was how she was — all of her small, but strong and warm with life. She kept on smiling her approval, yet it was only as though she were approving of a fine, strong tree, or a cloud in the sky. There was not a line about her eyes. There was not a line in her face, except what the smiling made. Perry Woodstock began to lose himself in her presence as a convalescent loses himself in the peace and sweetness of the open air.

"I'll take you to Father," said the girl. "He's drilling in the new shaft. What's the name of the mare?"

"Molly," said Perry Woodstock.

"She's beautiful," said the girl. "She's the most lovely thing!"

She stretched out her hand. Woodstock stepped aside and watched the mare lean forward until her knees were trembling. Molly sniffed at that brown hand, and then tried to gather it in with a furtive, thievish upper lip. The girl laughed. Molly tossed her head. And then the three of them went on, with Rosemary Scanlon in the lead. She walked first because the path was so narrow, but she kept turning a little so that he could watch her smile, assuring him she was glad he had come. In her profile he could see more clearly that ethereal beauty of the very young and about her mouth that delicacy of those who drink freely of life and find all of it sweet.

As they came nearer, the woman at the cabin door stopped the rapid work of her needles and dropped her hands on the soft pile of knitting in her lap. Her hair was white, yet it only served to make her face seem younger. Her dark eyes were as bright as those of a girl, but her head was not turned exactly toward them, and Perry Woodstock could have known that she was blind without any further telling.

"Rosemary, what's the trouble?" she asked.

"There's no trouble," answered the girl. "Only a man called Perry Woodstock is here with a message for Father. He's shorter than Father, but his shoulders are heavier. He's about twenty-five, and he has dark hair and dark eyes. He has no hat, and his gray mare follows him without a saddle or a bridle. She's the most beautiful thing. She's nibbling at my hand now."

"No saddle and no bridle . . . that means trouble," said the mother. "What *is* the trouble, Mister Woodstock?"

Her head turned a little from side to side, anxiously hunting for him. He came closer. He bowed a little and spoke distinctly, as though to a child.

"There's no trouble. I wouldn't bring trouble. Only a message to Harry Scanlon."

As he spoke, her eyes found him, and he felt the shock of the meeting. Something was missing from the center of the pupils, and something from the spirit took its place.

"You've come without a hat. There's no saddle and no bridle on your horse," she said quietly. "What drove you here, then? And what can be following?"

Her conviction made him glance hastily over his shoulder; but he only saw the blue, smiling eyes of the girl. "There's nothing following, I hope," said Woodstock. "And I have to see your husband. It's important for me to see him."

The blind woman stood up with the knitting between her clasped hands. "There's trouble," she murmured. "I knew there was trouble!"

"I'll take him to Father," said the girl.

Woodstock was glad to escape from before that questioning face. If she was blind, her touch was all the more sure, and she had found him at once a messenger of evil.

"Little things will worry my mother," the girl was explaining. "She didn't wish to make you unhappy, but shadows we can't see are always crossing her mind. You're not angry, are you?"

"I'm not angry." He looked suddenly at her. "How could I be angry . . . with your mother?" he asked.

Girls are very quick to seize upon compliments. They have a singular perception, a delicacy of apprehension that finds them in the darkest moments, and then they are apt to flush, to turn away suddenly, to brighten all over with agreement and with delighted shame, but Rosemary met that piercing glance of his with an untroubled eye.

"I knew you were kind and gentle the first moment I saw you," she said. "I could tell by the way the mare followed you. And there is something secret and darkened about the eyes of men who are . . . well, unhappy . . . and. . . ."

Words entirely failed her. She was still thinking the unspoken thing as they went up the slope behind the house toward the clanking sound of iron on iron. So they came to the mouth of a shaft with a windlass set over it and a dump sprawling down the side of the mountain. It was a dump that had been worked for many years. The upper part was loose, but the lower sections of débris had been soldered together by the rains and the snows of many seasons. A new shaft was being sunk beside the old one. A man was on his knees in the shallow hole, whanging a drill head with a singlejack, dealing out powerful blows.

He got up to meet them. He looked like Joe Scanlon. He was the same height. He had the same sort of a head and face. He even wore a short mustache. But all of him was made larger and more roughly. The mustache was a shaggy gray brush, and his eyes were buried under the frown of the laborer. He looked a stern and a bitter man who was quite divorced from the peace that covered this mountain farm, but, when Woodstock gazed more closely, he thought he could see, as if through a heavy mist and far away, a resemblance to Rosemary, a fatherhood. There would have been a gulf between them, but this resemblance bridged it.

"This is Perry Woodstock, Father. He's come to give you a message."

The big man strode from the hole and shook hands. His

112

fingers were leathery with calluses. But Woodstock, after greeting him, turned a little toward the girl. She accepted the hint at once.

"I'll go back to the house and cook something. You look hungry, Mister Woodstock."

She was gone at once. Woodstock dragged his eyes away from her and faced the father squarely.

"I've got some bad news to start with, and some other news afterwards that I can't make out," he said.

"Let's get farther back in the woods," answered Scanlon. "My wife has ears that can hear thoughts as they move in your brain. We'll get farther away."

He stepped off quickly through the pines until the green twilight of the woods covered them. One long, golden finger of sunshine slanted through an opening and poured itself on the pine needles until they seemed to smoke and burn. There Scanlon paused and began to stoke his pipe.

"Now let's have it," he said.

"You've got a brother called Joe," began Woodstock.

Harry Scanlon tamped in the charge of cut plug with unnecessary force. "What's Joe been doing now?" he asked. "Are you a friend of his?" He did not lift his head until he came to the last part of his question.

"I never saw him until last night. Something got me out of bed . . . I was working on a ranch yonder in the desert . . . and from the door of the bunkhouse I saw a man rounding up the cavvyard in the moonlight. He picked out this mare here. She threw him. I got down there in time to see him fall. I made him take the saddle and bridle off the mare and put them on his own horse, which was spent. I think I meant to turn him over to the sheriff. I hate horse thieves. But then a gang of five riders came up the hollow. Your brother, Joe, said they were after him. He hopped on his horse and ran for it.

They caught him and killed him . . . and the horse, too. Then they came back and cut in between me and the ranch house. I was standing like a fool. I was sort of sick. I had to jump the mare without a saddle or a bridle, and she took me away from 'em."

"Joe's dead, is he?" said Harry Scanlon. "Well, he never did much good."

His voice was not as his words. There was such emotion in it that Woodstock decently made a pause in which all his attention went to the making of a cigarette. After he had lighted it and carefully put out the match, he went on: "Before Joe Scanlon hopped his horse, he gave me this, and told me to take it to you on the shoulder of Grizzly Peak. That's why I'm here." He handed over the shotgun shell, watched the thick fingers of Harry Scanlon worry the paper out, saw the sheet unfolded, and a blankness come over the face of the big man. "That's why they were chasing your brother. To get that, I guess. It seemed to mean as much as his life to him."

"I've got to get over the mountain and down to the place where they murdered poor Joe," said Scanlon. "This paper . . . did you look at it?"

"Yes."

"Make anything out of it?"

"No. Not a thing."

"Walsh and Porcupine on line," read Scanlon aloud, putting in punctuation of his own. "And Oliver and Gray at the flow . . . find a big stack . . . work one-third down." He shook his head. "It stops me," he said. "I make nothing out of it. It's gibberish."

"It's gibberish a man was ready to die for, and other men were willing to kill him for it," said Woodstock.

"Five men?"

"Yes, five."

"That would be Waley and some of his gang. God knows I told Joe what would come of herding with the brutes, but . . . well, he's ended." The fierceness went out of his blue eyes, and there was only trouble in them. "He was twenty-eight. He was only a kid," said Scanlon softly. In the pause the gray mare turned her head from one man to the other.

"You mean Black Jim Waley?" asked Woodstock.

"That's who I mean." Scanlon crumpled the paper and thrust it into his pocket.

But the name he had heard jumped through the brain of Perry Woodstock like a freezing wind. "Black Jim!" he repeated. "Look here, Scanlon. Whatever you do about this is your own business. I've done what your brother asked me to do, and now I'm going to get out of here. Will you lend me a saddle and bridle?"

Scanlon began to nod his big head, answering: "You're scared, eh?"

"You bet I'm scared," said Woodstock. "I've seen Black Jim. I've seen the Mexican, too, the fellow whose face is all one scar. Who is he?"

"That's Vicente."

"I saw 'em once, and that's enough. If you've got an old saddle and a bridle, I'll hop on the gray mare and get out of here. How they feel about me now, I don't know, but if that's the crowd that wanted my scalp yesterday, I'm taking it for granted that they want it today."

"I don't blame you," agreed Scanlon. "We'll go down to the house. I can fit you out with a saddle and bridle."

They left the woods and saw that the sun was nearing the top of a western mountain. Rosemary Scanlon was at work with her spade again, moving the handle from side to side as she jammed the blade deep enough in the sod. Her mother sat in the doorway with her idle hands still folded on top of her knitting, and her blind eyes fixed upon some future darkness. Scanlon paused, stared at her an instant, and then went on with Woodstock to a shed that was built against the side of the house. A rusty blacksmith shop was fitted up in one end of it. All sorts of harness hung from pegs at the other end of the room, and a saddle and bridle were produced from the trappings.

Woodstock fitted them on the mare, arranged the stirrups at the right length, and led the mare around to the front of the house to say his adieus. The sun was rolling like a great wheel of red gold down the side of that western mountain. With its light it enriched the forest and the green farm and laid a glow upon the face of Mrs. Scanlon.

"What's the trouble, Harry?" she asked, as she heard his step.

"Wait a minute," he said. "And Woodstock, you wait too, will you? I want a little advice before you go. Rosemary, come here!"

The girl came, hurrying. She wore boots; there were clumsy gauntlets on her gloves; and she swung both hand and foot in walking like a true mountaineer; yet nothing could cloud her grace. And still, at a little distance, she looked much taller than the fact.

"Come inside," said Scanlon.

The women passed into the house. Scanlon waited for Woodstock, who squinted into the semi-darkness of the place with an unpleasant sense of entering a trap. However, he could not shy at a shadow. He passed inside the waiting gesture of Scanlon and went into the room.

V

Theodora Scanlon went back into the deeper gloom at the end of this dining room-kitchen and stood by a table with her knitting gathered up under one arm. "We ought to stay outside to talk, particularly if there's trouble," she said. "The sunlight is beautiful now."

She touched her face, on which it had been falling. It seemed to Woodstock that some of the gold remained, glowing upon her. Rosemary had gone to the stove, where she stirred a big iron soup pot that was forward over the fire. The smell of cookery had soaked through the air.

"It's this way," said Scanlon, after waiting a moment to gather his thoughts.

The girl turned from the stove and faced him. She was directly against the light that streamed through the doorway, so that it poured over her rough horsehide boots and cast a deep reflection from the floor over her entire body.

"It's this way. Yesterday . . . last night Woodstock saw your Uncle Joe, Rosemary. He gave Woodstock a bit of paper in a shotgun shell just before five riders came up and murdered him. They chased Woodstock when they didn't find what they wanted on Joe. Woodstock brought the written message to us in spite of the way they hunted him."

Here Scanlon paused. Neither of the women said a word. The girl grew a little taller, that was all.

"We've always talked things over," went on Scanlon, "so we have to talk this over. The message is gibberish, as far as I can make out. It says this: 'Walsh and Porcupine on line and Oliver and Gray at the flow find a big stack work one-third down.' " He refolded the paper, more carefully, because his thoughts were on other things, and added: "The five men who

117

killed Joe were probably Jim Waley and some of his gang. Suppose they had some right to this bit of scribbling . . . or thought that they had. Suppose that Joe stole it away from them. Suppose they killed him because of that. We know that they hunted Woodstock afterwards, and it must have been for that reason. Well, what Waley starts for, he generally finds. He's probably feeling his way through the mountains on the trail that Woodstock left behind him. Now, then, there's two things that we can do. We can try to fight Waley . . . if he's the murderer . . . or else we can admit that he's stronger than we are and give up what he's hunting for. That would save our scalps, and it would save Perry Woodstock here, who doesn't deserve to have any trouble out of it. That's the problem. I want you two to think it over before Woodstock goes."

He laid the folded bit of paper on the edge of the table. A silence began and marched deeper and deeper into the mind of Woodstock. He turned his head nervously and looked from the shadows toward the west, where the sun was out of sight and color was beginning.

Then the girl said: "Uncle Joe died, trying to bring that string of words to you, Father. It may not seem to mean anything, but it *must* mean something. It means a good deal, or Jim Waley would not murder one of his best men on account of it. And if Joe died to give it to us, we're cowards and worthless if we don't try to take advantage of the first and only thing he ever did for us. He always said that one day he'd try to make a return to you, Father, for all you've done for him and all your disappointment in him. He's trying to make that return now. He's trying to wash his hands clean, and we've got to help him do it."

There was not a word of sorrow about the death of her uncle. Her voice remained so perfectly steady that Woodstock began to peer hard at her. He could scarcely believe it, when he saw bright drops issuing from her eyes and running down her face.

"Where does he lie, Harry?" asked the wife and mother.

"He lies in the sheriff's hands, now, most likely," said Scanlon. "What's your word on it, Theo?"

"Rosemary has said all I could say," she answered.

"I might have known that my women would see it that way," muttered Scanlon. "Now, Woodstock, you tell us what it means to you, and how we can help you, the way you've tried to help us? And if you have any advice, I'm a man that's always glad to hear it."

Woodstock said: "I advise you to stop talking this way. You're wondering what you can do to finish out the thing that Joe Scanlon began. But before you've gone ten steps in that direction, Jim Waley, if he's the man behind it, will eat up the lot of you. I know some of the things that Black Jim has done."

"So do I," nodded Harry Scanlon. "I tried to get my brother out of Waley's gang, and I know all about what Waley can do. Rosemary . . . Theo . . . you've heard what Woodstock says? And he's a brave man, at that. He'd give up, if he were in our boots."

The answer of the girl came instantly, indignantly. "He wouldn't if he were in our boots. He's only trying to keep us out of bad trouble. That's all."

"Trouble," said the quiet voice of Theodora Scanlon. "I knew he brought it with him."

"Stick up your hands, all of you," said a man at the doorway. "All of you . . . !"

Swift as a bird pecks a fallen grain, so Rosemary Scanlon leaned and snatched the little fold of paper from the table and thrust it at the big iron soup pot on the stove. From the corner of his eye Woodstock saw this and the flicker of fire shadows that danced on the ceiling above the uncovered flames in the stove. In the meantime he, like Harry Scanlon, was lifting his arms and turning toward the doorway.

Black Jim Waley was there. Two faces like that could not be, so long, so yellow, so filled with timeless evil that the man seemed neither young nor old. The black hat was on his head, and the black scarf wound about his throat, seeming to cut his head off at the chin. He carried a double-barreled shotgun, sawed off short. The big muzzles covered both the men in the cabin.

It was still easier to see the man at Waley's side, for his face glistened as though it were wet. It was a shapeless white blur with a pair of black eyes dropped into the mask. That was Vicente, of course. At the sight of the pair Woodstock grinned like a dead man. He was reaching well for the ceiling. So was Harry Scanlon.

The voice of Theodora Scanlon said quietly: "Now it's come. What is it, Harry?"

"It's Black Jim Waley, ma'am," said the man with the yellow face. "At your service. You, there . . . bring me that paper. Don't think that I'm a whit easier on the women. I'd as soon drill you as your pa. Bring that thing here to me and, when I talk, you jump to it!"

"It's right here over the fire in the stove, Black Jim," said the girl. "If you shoot me, the bullet won't keep me from dropping it into the flame. And there's enough heat to eat it and swallow it whole before you could snatch it out. Do you see the shine of the fire on my hand?"

"Scanlon," said Waley, "tell the rattle-headed fool to bring that to me! You know that I mean what I say."

The calm, deep voice of Scanlon answered: "Rosemary, do what you think best. I never think fast enough when a pinch comes."

At that, out of the straining throat of Woodstock burst a

cry. "For God's sake, give him what he wants!"

His voice shook; his whole body was shaking. The yellow face and the white were double forms of death itself that stared at him.

"The kid talks sense," said the horrible face of Vicente. Only when he spoke, could one see where his mouth was in that mass of scar tissue.

"You!" thundered Black Jim. "Bring it here to me. Western chivalry . . . is that what you're banking on, you fool?"

"You're more afraid of the fire eating the paper," said the girl, "than I'm afraid of you. You won't shoot. You're shaking in your boots now, and I know it."

Black Jim put a long leg into the room. He wore boots of beautiful, shining red leather, with his trousers stuffed into the tops of them. Men said that it was because he wanted the world to know that he walked in blood.

"Tell the damned brat to bring it here, Scanlon, or I'll mop the head off your shoulders. Speak to her!" he commanded.

"Speak to her," echoed the shaking voice of Perry Woodstock.

The calm tones of Harry Scanlon answered: "Rosemary, dear, I guess you know what's best to do."

There was a muttering snarl. It was exactly like the whining voice of a bull terrier. It came from the shapeless face of Vicente, the Mexican.

Black Jim seemed speechless, and it was Mrs. Scanlon who said: "Harry, are you helpless?"

"Aye, Theo," he answered. "It looks that way. They've got the guns on us."

"Then, if we have any hold on them, in turn we must bargain, Harry."

"Bargains be damned!" yelled Black Jim. "If you think. . . ."

Here something stopped him. It must have been something

121

about the girl, for his glance was going straight past Woodstock toward the place where she stood.

"Look out," said Vicente in a half secret aside.

"Hold on . . . you there!" exclaimed Black Jim. "You're singeing the edge of the paper now, you half-wit."

He withdrew the foot that had entered the cabin. The gray mare, as though attracted by these brawling voices, came within the range of Woodstock's view, pricking her ears, stomping with one forehoof raised, like a dog pointing.

"You can give us time," said the girl. She had the calm of her father. To Woodstock there was something terrible in her voice. It was that of one who puts no value on life compared with the brightness of a clean soul. A fantastic simplicity breathed from her, and Perry Woodstock for the first time guessed what martyrs may be made of.

"Time for what?" demanded Black Jim. "You can see that we've got you. D'you think that I'll back down now?"

"I don't know what you'll do. We'll still be in your power if you're not standing there in the doorway with your guns. You could fire the grass and burn us out, if you wanted to. But we have to have time to talk this over. We can't make up our minds all in an instant."

"Rosemary," broke in the voice of the mother, "are you sure that you have a right to what you hold? Are you sure that it doesn't belong to . . . him?" She made a slight pause before the last word, laying a slight emphasis on it.

"It was stole from me," declared Black Jim. "And the man that stole it is . . . well, it's mine. And I'll have it."

"If it's yours, you know what it means?" asked the girl.

"Of course, I know what it means."

"If it's yours, you know what it means, and you can remember the words on it. There aren't many of them. If it ever belonged to you, you know all about it."

"I'm no long hand at remembering," said Black Jim. "Matter of fact. . . ."

Her voice cut straight through his and stopped him. "I don't believe you. I think you lie. If ever you'd had it, it would be printed in your brain now, every word of it."

"There's a way of stopping your tongue," said Black Jim. "There's a way of taking tongues out through the throat."

"We want half an hour . . . alone," said the girl. "Shall we have it?"

"No!" shouted Waley, and his face went insane.

Woodstock groaned. His hip was against the table, and he had to support himself there. He could see the quivering of the trigger finger of Waley, wrapped over the trigger of the heavy gun.

"Get away from the house," said the unmoved voice of the girl. "I'll count to ten, and then you'll be away from that door or else this bit of paper will burn. We ask for half an hour. It isn't much. At the end of that time we'll let you know whether we fight it out or else surrender."

Waley looked at Scanlon hard. He looked a brief time, with more satisfaction, at the frozen face of Woodstock. Then he said: "Well, I don't know that it matters. Half an hour later will serve as well, for us. All I know is that it's a conundrum that none of you can ever work out. You can have your half hour. Use it to try to figure out what the paper says. You haven't the key, and I have. *¡Adios, amigos!*"

He turned and walked from the door. Vicente silently followed him.

VI

Woodstock reached for a chair, slumped into it, and covered his face with his hands. He was still shaking. Through his fingers he was aware of the blood-red sunset that filled the doorway. All of his own blood and strength had gone into it, it seemed. Then there was a trickle of shame that began to fall into the cavern that had been his heart. The cold of it rose in him, and rose. It was more icy than the fear.

"Now, Rosemary," said the voice of the mother, "we have only a half hour. Your wits are better than ours. You will have to tell us what to do, my dear."

"Aye, Rosemary," said the father. "The way you lead us will be the best way. It always is. I thought we were all dead just now, but you've given us a moment for breathing at the least."

A hand touched the shoulder of Perry Woodstock. He looked suddenly up into the face of the girl. There was neither disgust nor pity in it, but only an open friendliness.

"I was a yellow dog. I howled!" groaned Woodstock.

"I've heard a doctor say," answered the girl, "that a lot of people who are afraid before the operation are the bravest when they're under the knife. Besides, Vicente and Black Jim are like things that come out of a grave. They're too horrible to be real. It was like a nightmare, and you weren't prepared for it."

There suddenly was no world whose opinion could shame him, for the only audience that mattered was Rosemary Scanlon.

"Why should the young man have to stay in the trap with us?" asked Mrs. Scanlon.

Woodstock got suddenly to his feet. "I've been sick," he said, "but now I can try to be a man again. I brought the trouble to you, and now I'll try to help you through it."

Big Harry Scanlon pointed a hand at him. "You're not shamed, boy," he said. "And you're not beaten. Anybody can have the shakes. Let's put our heads together."

All four of them drew close. The sunset glowed faintly through the door and showed their faces and their gestures. All the rest of the room was darkness, and the stove gave out a humming sound behind them.

"Joe died to bring us this," said the girl, holding out the torn fragment of paper. "That's the beginning. And Perry Woodstock went through the danger of dying to get it to us. This is a fight, and it's wrong to give up a fight before we're beaten."

"We're beat now," answered the father. "There's five of them. We're in their hands. They could burn us out. They could do anything they want with us."

The blind wife and mother had come out of the darkness with her hands stretched before her to feel the way, but it was as though she were bringing gifts. She said: "After trouble comes, Harry, it has to be met and, wherever we owe a duty, it has to be paid."

"Well, we can all die like pigs in a pen, if that's what you call duty," answered Harry Scanlon, half angrily. "Rosemary . . . she can die with us!"

He turned to her and would have put an arm around her, but she stopped his hand. "I'm not a girl or something that's to be pitied. I'm just one more person in the trap that holds all of us."

A shadow fell over them from the door. It was the gray mare who now stood there, looking into the darkness to find her master. Perry Woodstock stared back at her.

"I've got an idea," he said.

"Go on, boy," urged the deep, gentle voice of Scanlon, the laborer.

"He ought to be free from us. This is not his fight," said Theodora Scanlon.

But the girl said: "He's one of us, because he wants to be."

That gave Woodstock strength to say: "There's the gray mare, waiting. Suppose she could be used?"

"Shall we ask her advice, too?" suggested Scanlon harshly.

"Hush, my dear," said the blind woman, and with a sure touch she found his hand.

Woodstock leaned forward until they could see his face clearly, the pallor and the strain of it. He looked like a man, charging in a lost cause and as a last hope. "Suppose that one of us jumped on the horse and raced for the trees," he said, barely whispering the words.

"He'd be shot down," snapped Scanlon. "Those fellows are marksmen, and Black Jim doesn't know how to miss."

"Suppose," insisted Woodstock, "that they *did* miss. It's the worst light in the world. It's twilight and sunset and moonlight all mixed together. Suppose that they missed and one of us got free . . . wouldn't they feel sure that that one was carrying away the thing that they want? Wouldn't they follow? Would they dare to let one person go? No, they'd all follow."

He stood up straight, having spoken, and gripped his hands hard together behind his back, as though he hoped to crush the trembling out of his body, the uncertainty out of his brain. This idea of his was taking hold on their minds.

Scanlon suddenly said: "Maybe it could be done. Maybe it's the only way. We've got to fight, somehow, and I don't see anything else to do. Because suppose that we give them that bit of paper, they know just the same that we've learned what's written on it, and they couldn't give us freedom till they've collected whatever is to be gained. But if one of us shook loose, they'd all feel that their information was about to be scattered over the world. They'd have to chase." He added:

126

"I'll take the chance. It's my duty to take it."

"You're too heavy," said his daughter. "But I can ride well. And I'm a lot the lightest. I'll take her. I'll ride to get help. . . ."

"Wait a minute," breathed Woodstock. He pumped out the words, one by one. That was what he had known from the first, that if his idea was accepted, he was the only one who could perform the task. "None of you could ride the mare. She bucks like a fiend unless you know her. I'll take her. I'll take the paper along with me, too."

"We can't let him go," said the blind woman. "It's only duty that makes him do it, and what duty does he owe to us?"

"I brought you trouble," answered Woodstock. "Now I'll try to take it away. That's right enough."

"You can't go, boy. I wouldn't let you!" exclaimed Harry Scanlon. "I know my job when I see it. . . ."

"He's going to go," Rosemary said. "You can't stop him. He wants to go through the fire. *I* know how he feels."

Woodstock swallowed hard. He pushed one hand through his tousled hair. He felt for his gun and gripped it hard. The feel of it was reassuring. Then he managed to say: "So long, everybody." He went on, inanely: "I'm glad I met all of you."

"Stop him, Harry! You can't let him go!" cried the wife.

"No, he can't go for us. I won't let him go!" The heavy step of Scanlon came up behind Woodstock, as the latter stood at the door. Scanlon paused. He was saying: "Don't stop me, Rosemary. He'll be gone in an instant if I don't stop him."

"You can't stop a man from being himself," said the girl. "If I were he, I'd want to do the same thing, if there were enough heart in me."

That was what Woodstock heard as he gathered the reins on the withers of the mare and stared about the clearing of the farm. It had seemed a very small place, when he came to it, but it seemed dangerous miles to the secure shadows of the trees. Five men were not enough to scatter about over such a distance, and yet, every time he picked a goal and a harborage, he was certain that the point would be guarded by a rifleman. It seemed as though Black Jim Waley — who could not miss — would certainly be at each of those spots. Where would they be? Well, they would be in the trees on either side, as close as possible to the house. Suppose, then, that he rushed the mare straight down the length of the farm instead of galloping for the nearest cover?

"Let him be, Father."

"Now, Rosemary . . . out of my way."

Woodstock heard that behind him and then made one step outside the door, flinging himself into the saddle. The suddenness of the move made the mare whirl. The drive of his heels into her flanks sent her wildly scampering. But she had her head, and, as she ran, she bucked, pitching here and there as a boat might pitch in a chopping cross current. She was not three strides from the cabin door before voices yelled out of the trees. Rifles exploded. The noises hammered at his very ears. He thought that he could hear men breathing close by, running out at him from the tree shadows, moving faster than the mare, overtaking her.

One red cloud hung in the west like a flag that has flapped itself to sere rags at the edge. The tree tops glistened. There was a soft glow on the pasture — the wheat field was a dull yellow mist. And still the mare bucked, while he cursed her, prayed to her, gasping, biting off his words. Still she jerked him here and there, head down, bounding like a cat at play.

The bullets were all about him. Each sang one note of a song, a brief note. But not one of those fierce voices struck into his body. Then he realized that the wild plunging of the mare was making those sure riflemen miss. Molly, all unaware, was playing his hand for him.

His throat opened; his heart opened; he yelled like an Indian, and the cry suddenly straightened out the mare in a blinding streak of speed. Back there they would be watching from the dark doorway of the house. Hope would be in them, also. Before him, the trees rose higher, the wind of the gallop pulled at his hair, and whispered at his ear. Then the darkness of the woods received him as water receives a diver from a height.

They were slipping, sliding down a steep slope that was sheathed in thick coatings of pine needles. They made only a rushing sound over which he heard voices shouting, and the snorting of horses, and after that the rapid beating of hoofs.

A sort of cold triumph of fear came over him. He pulled up the mare to a walk and moved to the left at right angles to his first course. The noise of the pursuit seemed to rush straight at him.

VII

To flee headlong through the sunset gloom of the woods was dangerous. Also the noise he made would lead them after him, as though he carried a light. Yet the mare in walking made no sound whatever, and, though the river of shouting and hoof-beats seemed to flow straight at him, he would not hurry her. He merely turned in the saddle with his revolver poised. That was how he heard the charge pass behind him, scattering through the woods. He saw only one rider dimly flickering for an instant, among the crowding trunks. That was all.

He let the mare come to a dancing trot, for she was full of excitement. The forest began to move more rapidly about him as he took the same way that he had come up the side of Grizzly Peak. Slipping a hand into his pocket, he touched the crisp bit of paper on which the conundrum was written. How far would they follow him? Or would they turn back to resume their siege of the cottage?

The moon, standing higher, showed him the way clearly enough. The short summer night passed rapidly as he wound through that rough gorge and came at last to the lake set among the aspens. He had intended to ride straight on over the trail that he had taken when coming into the mountains, and, descending to the desert beyond, he could find fighting men in the town of San Lorenz and guide them back to Grizzly Peak to disperse whatever danger hung over the cabin of Harry Scanlon. But now that he was at the lake among the aspens, he remembered old Dave Hixon and went straight to the camp of the mountaineer.

Hixon had not moved. The same rag of canvas was giving him shelter in the same place beside the great column of the fallen pine tree. The hobbled mule stood up and cocked its

130

ears toward the intruders. Then it stretched forth its starved neck, opened its mouth, closed its eyes against the moonlight, and made the hollow roar with its bray. Old Dave Hixon came out from under his little tent and stood erect, at once wide awake and unafraid.

"Sorry to disturb you like this," said Perry Woodstock. "I didn't think that the mule would make such a racket."

"It didn't scare me," answered Hixon. "Old men are like skunks. Nothin' wants to bother us. We walk through the woods, and everybody gives us room, because an old gent like me is likely to ask for a hand-out, and a skunk has things about it that are just as mean. How are things with you, son?"

"Well enough," answered Woodstock. "How does it go with you?"

Hixon pointed toward the fallen tree. "Along about Sixteen Twenty," he said, "there was a whale of a fire that chewed at one side of the tree pretty bad, and must've nigh killed it. But it lived through and put on bigger rings than ever afterwards. And around Sixteen Eighty-Five another tree nearby must have fallen, and it rammed the stubs of a coupla broken arms into my friend, yonder, but the old pine, it just throwed a bed of resin around the chunks of woods that had been whanged into it, and it went on growing just the same. You hit the back trail out of these mountains pretty fast, son, didn't you? Ain't the lay of the land to your liking? Wait till I stew some coffee for you. You look kind of fagged."

He gathered some dead embers, lighted some shreds of barks, and presently had a small fire burning. Woodstock looked rather anxiously among the trees, for such men as hunted him now would notice the smallest sign.

Then he said: "I was stopped by a conundrum."

"What's that?" asked the other.

"Sort of a puzzle in words. A riddle. It goes like this. 'Walsh and Porcupine on line and Oliver and Gray at the flow. . . .' Just nonsense, eh?"

"Walsh and Porcupine on line, eh? And Oliver and Gray?" said the man of the mountains, pausing as he measured out coffee from a bag. "Walsh and Porcupine . . . those would be Hurdle and Thompson."

A door of hope opened in the mind of Perry Woodstock. He stared at that old face, lighted above by the white of the moonshine and from below by the yellow sheen of the fire. "Hurdle and Thompson?" he echoed. "Hurdle and Thompson? What does that mean?"

"They've changed the names of mountains a whole lot lately," pursued the old man. "Hurdle Mountain, that used to be called Mount Walsh, from a gent called Walsh that worked a streak of pay dirt on the side of it in the old days, thirty, forty years ago. And Thompson Peak was called the Porcupine, about the same time. I dunno why. Porcupine ain't a very good name for a mountain, unless it bristles a good deal."

"Hurdle Mountain and Thompson Peak, then. Where are they?"

"Well, wait a minute. Lemme get my bearings. Look yonder. There's old Hurdle. That one with the white top and the two heads and the summit strung in between the two points like a clothes line, hitched up kind of loose. That's Hurdle Mountain. You can't see Thompson from here, but it ain't that far. What's them other names?"

"Oliver and Gray," said Woodstock, beginning to breathe quickly. "Oliver and Gray. . . ."

"That would be Mount Promise and Eagle Mountain, or Eagle Peak some call it, and a fine name for a mountain that is, too. Promise ain't a bad name for a mountain, neither. There's sense in names like that. But old Tom Oliver that got a mountain named after him was a dog-gone trader that got

132

furs for whiskey. God rot him, he was a mean man, I'm here to tell you."

Woodstock got out the bit of paper and, with a stub of a pencil, made the necessary substitutions of names. The script then read: "Hurdle and Thompson on line and Promise and Eagle." Sense came instantly from nonsense. If they were mountains, one was to find the point where Hurdle and Thompson mountains were on a line — a point at which Mount Promise and Eagle Peak were also on a line. After reaching that point there was a flow, and a stack that was to be worked one-third down. Whatever these words might mean, there was now a beginning for him to work on.

He fell into a wide-eyed dream in which he saw five men, riding on his trail, and in the distance the shoulder of Grizzly Peak, and the cottage of Harry Scanlon. He took a cup of coffee from Hixon, regardless of the heat that scalded his throat, for his mind was on fire. He felt that he had placed his foot on the first rung of an important ladder. He could hardly wait to swallow the coffee. Fatigue was no longer in him. He rose to go.

"I've got to hurry on," he said. "You chart those mountains on the back of this scrap of paper, will you?"

It was easily done by Dave Hixon. He marked down Hurdle Mountain and spotted in the others one by one, with short, sharp descriptions that held them in the mental eye of Woodstock. Then they parted. It was already the gray of the early dawn when Perry Woodstock turned the mare westward up the steep side of the hollow where the Douglas spruce met the yellow pines that covered the northern slope, and in the pink of the dawn he had come to a pass that pointed as straight as a leveled gun barrel toward the double top of Hurdle Mountain. There he stopped, at a place where he found the black, round scar of a newly built campfire with a heap of pine boughs, still fresh and green, beside it. Where another man had slept in comfort, he could sleep in turn, and no matter how exposed the position, no matter who might be following him, he determined to have rest. For, after all, the five had ridden long and hard after Joe Scanlon before they took up his own trail. He had against them at least the advantage of half a night's sleep, and perhaps they had paused long before to rest.

He had hardly stretched himself on that fragrant bed before oblivion washed over him in a black wave. It was noon when he wakened with a cloud over his brain, dry thirst in his throat, and above all a ravenous hunger that soon made him forget his other troubles. He had picked up the saddle to put it again on the back of the gray mare when, shuffling through the grass toward her, his foot turned over a rusted axe-head with half its hickory haft remaining lodged in the steel. It seemed to him luck, a stroke of distinct good fortune that placed in his hands a tool without which few men care to travel through a wooded country. When Molly was saddled and bridled, he lashed the axe behind the cantle, half smiling at his folly in doing so.

He rode on now with hunger making him as keen as a wolf's tooth and found the pass, opening out onto a high plateau from which he could spot down every one of the four mountains that Hixon had named and described for him. Porcupine Mountain could have been called The Pig as well, for the summit of it was like a pig's head, thrusting up at the sky, with fat jowls half clothed in a bristling forest. He rode now to get the desired points in line — "Walsh and Porcupine on line. . . ."

That ride took him back on the plateau to a region of mingled darkness and shine that turned out to be the broad, black sweep of a lava flow. He was already well inside the borders of it, sometimes with black cinder dust under hoof, and sometimes the polished gleam of basalt or glass, sometimes things that looked like half-melted boulders, and sometimes huge heaps of clinkers, as it were, when he remembered the last words of the conundrum.

"*At the flow find a big stack, work one-third down.*" At the lava flow, find a big stack, such as one of these clinker-like heaps of melted stone refuse, and work it one-third down in order to find whatever the secret might be. The thought struck home in his mind as clearly as ever a bell-hammer struck home on bell-metal. He forgot the mere hunger for food.

In the meantime he was drawing Hurdle Mountain and Thompson Mountain to a line. When he had established that, Mount Promise and Eagle Peak were still far from lining up. He had to ride on another full mile. The gray mare was beginning to cough from the effect of the whirling wreaths of lava dust before, riding with his head turned back, he was able to check the mare. Now the two lines, cutting across the four mountains, met at a point. He had only to find the big stack. Facing to the front, he saw it rising before him — a gloomy, bristling mass at least fifty feet high, looking as though it had been freshly cast out from the fire room of some enormous steamer.

Beyond any question this was the "big stack," and at first glance the thing seemed an enormous heap of cinders that, in a day or so, one could heave right and left and actually "work one-third down." He had hardly begun to climb, however, when he saw that the entire mass was really welded together. It was a sort of tufa, or stone that had been blown into a porous state when the volcanic eruptions had occurred how many hundreds of thousands of years before? Big knobs and lumps as large as a man could surround with his joined arms projected from the mass. Sometimes he felt the friable stuff crumbling a little under his feet. Once or twice he actually disengaged small fragments that went rattling down to the ground, one of them bounding under the very nose of the mare. She danced away, whinnying anxiously to her master. She even put her forehoofs on the steep slope as though she wanted to climb after him, and he felt that the black desolation around her was enough to make her yearn for any companionship.

Now that he stood on the top, he could scan a great part of the blackness of the flow. Everywhere it was the same, night-dark dust and cinders, or else shining patches of melted rock as brilliant as glass and glaring the sun's reflected light back at him. It was a relief to glance from the lava flow to the dark green of the forests that covered the mountains around the plateau. He wondered what one of them had once been a crater, or what side of a peak had opened to let out the gush of lava, but there was nothing that appeared truncated toward the top except the wide crest of Hurdle Mountain, and that seemed too far away.

The eruption had occurred so long ago that some of the lava had rotted away with time, and now there were various small growths that had taken a rooting on the rock, most of them shrubs that would have been at home on the desert, mere puffs and tawny dust clouds of foliage that could defy long drought. Chiefly, from that low summit, he scanned the pass through which he had ridden toward Hurdle Mountain, half expecting to see five horsemen riding over the lip of it, small as ants with the distance. But he saw nothing, not a living thing.

So he descended, as nearly as he could judge, a third of the way from the top and made the circle of the heap. It was a hard task, for there were a thousand crevices. Some were shallow. In some, the length of his arm and the revolver added to it could not find bottom. In any one of these might be the thing he sought, for which one man already had died, and for which others were ready to imperil their lives. He himself, as he searched, felt that guns must be trained upon him, and that he was no more than the fish hawk which catches the prey and renders it again to the frigate bird that sails in the higher air with a sharper beak and more cruel talons. It was very hot, but he began to sweat with anxious fear as much as with the warmth.

He completed his first circle of the mound and found nothing. He began to guess that he would have to search out one of the shrubs he had seen and use a branch of it as a probing tool among the small-mouthed caverns. He started again around the steep wall of the stack, prying with eye and hand. A crisp, dry rattling with a certain deadly resonance about it that was familiar to him made him start back from one hole. He had probed it, and the muzzle of his revolver had touched something soft, yielding. Now out of the entrance to the hole glided a five foot diamondback. It coiled, almost in striking distance, its terrible flat head couched with the supple curves of the neck ready behind it. Like green jewels were the eyes. Woodstock fired at them, and the twisting, bleeding thing fell in tangle after tangle down the side of the lava to the level below. There it still writhed as Woodstock, when his shuddering ended, thrust the gun cautiously into the hole again.

Where one snake has found a shelter, there may be others of its kind. Scaly horrors wriggled over his back and neck when the gun's muzzle touched again on something soft, yielding. He leaped away, staggered, almost fell in his turn from the slope, but this time nothing issued from the hole. Perhaps the second snake was waiting there. Perhaps it had coiled, and even now the head was ready to strike. But a rattler cannot feel alarm without giving out its natural signal of danger, and there had been no sound from the hole after the issuance of the first snake. There are tales that owls will sometimes live with snakes.

He lighted a match, stretched in his hand a little way, and peered. What he saw was something that looked like cloth. He poked it with the gun again. It was a sort of rough canvas or tarpaulin, so far as he could make out. He reached in, touched the thing with his fingers, and half in horror, as when one grasps an unclean monstrosity, he jerked it forth from the hole.

It was a mere tarpaulin wrapping, worn and battered, but still securely tied. He cut the wrapping open. Within was a second covering of canvas and, within this, three or four sheets of oiled silk, perfectly sound and strong. As he slashed it open, his mouth was working, and his nostrils. His face was like that of a man resolved on a murder. It might have been a throat that he was cutting, when he pulled the silken wrapping wide and looked down at some flat, small bundles wrapped in paper.

He took one out. The size and shape of it were slightly suggestive. He tore open the end of the wrappings, and found under his eyes a thickly compacted sheaf of greenbacks. He flicked a corner of them. They were all fifties. How many?

Twenty — forty — two hundred of them in that one sheaf, and there were other packages of the same size.

No wonder that Joe Scanlon had been willing to die for this thing. No wonder that Black Jim Waley was so hungry on the trail. He would do more murders than one for such a prize. Even the girl yonder in the cabin, even Rosemary, that blue and golden beauty, that brave and gentle soul, might have the life crushed from her, if Waley thought the killing would bring him any closer to the goal. At the same instant that hysterical joy opened the heart of Woodstock, fear closed his throat and froze his tongue against the roof of his mouth.

He turned with cold sweat running on his face and scanned the surroundings. Even the mountains seemed to be spies that watched his actions, that read the denominations of the bills. But there were no men in sight; there were no leveled rifles shining at him.

He snatched the remaining nine bundles from the silken lining of the tarpaulin, and then dropped the lot as though they burned his hands, for underneath them, unwrapped, was a little pool of light, yellow, green, red, and stainlessly bright crystal. He scooped them up in both hands as if he were about to drink. He began to laugh soundlessly. Joy made his eyes wander from side to side. Topaz, emerald, pearl, ruby, diamond, they burned without heat; they shone with lights that danced as fast as the tremor of his hands. Even huddled in a heap, they were so large that they could be picked out, one by one. Any one of them seemed of more worth than all the greenbacks in all the paper packages.

He had not taken all the contents in the hollow of the wrappings. When he looked down again, he saw many more gems and also the grim long body of a revolver. He took out his wallet, poured the jewels into it, stuffed the packages of greenbacks into his pockets, and then lifted the gun. It seemed

139

to say, with a grave and somber voice: *All of this is mine!* It was the dragon on watch over the hoard, but the life was frozen out of it. It was an old-fashioned gun, but it was still capable of business, that was plain. It was an old single-action Colt. Perry Woodstock noted at once that the sights were filed away, and the trigger was gone. Perhaps that gun had belonged to the man who wrote on the paper in ink now time-faded:

Walsh and Porcupine on line and Oliver and Gray at the flow find a big stack work one-third down.

After one knew the key to the riddle, the thing was all too palpable. It seemed a madness that the man had ever written such words. Surely not to imprint the scene on his own memory. Woodstock, in one glance around, burned the picture forever deeply in his own mind. How had the money been gathered together? What dead hands had once counted it with a fondly lingering touch? What dead fingers and what lifeless throats had worn the jewels? Dead, it seemed, they certainly must be. The revolver said that in clear words.

He who had used it, long ago, had known how to fan a revolver, how to turn the small weapon into an automatic from which a stream of death might spring. Perry Woodstock himself had learned that art in his boyhood and practiced it ever since. He had never used it on a human being. He hardly expected that he ever would be called upon to use it, but there was a fascination in working a gun as the great masters of the old time had worked them, as this old Colt had been used surely. He turned it curiously in his hand and on the butt, filed small and close together, he found eleven little notches worked into the steel. Eleven notches! Eleven dead men.

The money stuffed into Woodstock's pockets, those jewels

that made the great, hard lump just over his heart so that he was aware of its beating, had been paid for with eleven lives, at least. And in that count there was no reckoning made of Joe Scanlon. There was no reckoning made of what might happen in the future, for there was no cloud of darkness gathered as yet over the eyes of Black Jim Waley.

He wadded the tarpaulin together, twisted it hard, and thrust it back into the hole from which it had come. Then, with guilty, hurrying steps, he retreated down the side of the stack. He felt now a wild desire to get rapidly away from this place and from these watching mountains, away to some great city where money has more meaning, and the law is nearer at hand for a shelter. But then he remembered the girl as he swung into the saddle. If this treasure were the key that opened the door of the future, two people must pass through it, and not one.

IX

From the high plateau Woodstock could see clearly the outline of Grizzly Peak, looking wonderfully near. Toward it, above timberline and between two lower mountains, opened a pass, and Woodstock made straight for this. In not many hours, he promised himself, he would again be at the cabin of Harry Scanlon, and he would sweep all the family away with him on an avalanche of prosperity. There was enough for all. If he had brought them trouble, he now would bring them an immense reward. There was danger in making that return because, of course, Black Jim Waley might keep lookouts on the ground, but he felt it far more highly probable that Waley would now be feeling his way through the mountains, trying to get on the trail of Woodstock, letting the Scanlons go.

That was why Perry Woodstock laughed and sang so often as he journeyed up the slope through the pines and toward the pass that pointed on toward Grizzly Peak. When he reached timberline, the blue lake of the sky was without a single ripple of wind, only dark edgings of cloud were massed along the northwestern horizon high enough to furnish a perfect foil for the white of the snow summits. From this part of timberline, however, snow had melted away and left the trees and shrubs as the storms had tormented them into wild shapes. Those that managed to stand up a good height had branched only toward the southeast. They looked very like the feather head-dresses of the Indians. But most of the trees never had managed to raise their heads. Time went by them slowly. There were little limber pines of fifty years growth but not more than a foot in height. He saw an Englemann spruce drawn back along the ground by the torturing hands of the wind and turned into a snaky monstrosity full of twists and writhings. Trees hundreds of years old were here on their knees, as it were, or lying prone to endure the force of the storms, and they made Woodstock think of hard-fighting outposts that never can conquer but that will never give up. Among them he managed to recognize some Arctic willows, and there was the alpine fir, the black birch, the quaking aspen.

A ptarmigan in its brown summer suit flew out from a thicket, decided that there was nothing to fear, and lighted on the top of a rock twenty yards away. Woodstock rolled it over with a bullet, toasted and ate the bird at a spot a little farther on, where there was fine pasture for the gray mare. There, as he ate, Woodstock ran his eyes along the timberline as it extended for miles until it was lost in blue haze. It was drawn level as a watermark, as though the lower and duskier air had a weight and color and left its stain upon the mountainsides. Through those lower strata of atmosphere he could look into profound valleys and see distant plains and rolling lands. He sat on a throne not unlike a king but like a tiny pigmy looking out over a vastness.

He finished the ptarmigan. It was a big bird, and a fat one. Without salt, the ravenous fire of his appetite had consumed it half raw with infinite relish, and could have enjoyed another feast of the same size. But now he stretched himself with his back against a boulder, and made and smoked a cigarette. Distances he no longer regarded, but considered instead the ebbing and flowing tide of sound about him, for the bees had come up here on the heights, climbing on strong wings, and afterwards they would blow down the wind, heavy with pollen as they labored toward their hives. For though above timberline where trees could not grow, there were flowers in streaks, in patches, brilliant bands that encircled melting heaps of snow, dapplings of color on the backs of boulders even, and then here and there whole happy meadows of bloom. He knew a

143

great many of their names, such as the paintbrushes and the white-blooming wild buckwheat, the daisy, the purple monks-hood, asters, and goldenrod. He saw gentians, pinks, forget-me-nots, and the blue eyes of columbine. But there were many flowers that he could not name. He never saw them, except up here where the winter was king most of the year and where in the brief summer every plant was forced to bloom suddenly and with all its might before the next wind was iced and the frost came biting at the roots.

The world seemed nothing but a varied beauty to Perry Woodstock when the gray mare came suddenly close to him, snorting, lifting her head. He knew that danger signal well enough to sit up. Over the slope, mounting like ships over the curve of the sea, he saw the heads and shoulders of three men, and then the nodding heads of their horses, and two more riders behind. They were not two hundred yards away when he gained the saddle on Molly and rode for his life.

They were coming like five devils when he glanced back. Their horses seemed fresh in spite of the climbing they must have done, and the gray mare, unused to this altitude, would not last longer than one burning sprint. He thought of the foolish ptarmigan that had sunned itself in the brightness and warmth of this happy world just before a bullet struck out its life, and he himself was a greater fool than that poor bird, for he had known that five men like five wolves were after him.

He dared not ride straight up the pass as he had intended. It was open, easy ground, to be sure, but it was far too clear. If he began to gain in the race, those five rifles would come into play, and this time they would not miss. He chose, instead, to drive the mare toward the northwest through a field of boulders. Looking back, he could see heads and shoulders bobbing behind him, sometimes glimpses of a whole horse and man, and he knew that the good gray mare was at least holding

144

her own. Looking ahead, he saw that the dark clouds were blown over half the sky, blotting out the upper mountains and drowning the lower slopes in trailing shadows of rain or of snow. Golden veins of lightning showed on the forehead of that storm, and thunder began to speak among the mountains. His heart began to fail him. Twice he had escaped them, but the third time would surely be fatal. There is law to chance. One number cannot always be winning.

He was sure of that when, a moment later, the storm reached him, first with some shrewd cuffs of the wind, then with a driving rain that pricked his skin like points of ice. He looked back, and through the gray pencil strokes of that downpour he saw that they were nearer — not all five of them, but two in the lead, one a tall rider, and one a shorter, wide-shouldered man. They would be Black Jim Waley himself and that ghoulish lieutenant of his, Vicente, the 'breed.

Already the mare was beginning to labor. The wind beat straight against her. The thin mountain air was burning out her lungs. He knew that by the flare of her nostrils. Though her heart was gallant, she would have to lose. Then came a thick mist of snow. He was glad of that simply because it shortened the chances of those five marksmen behind him. But they gained still. They drew nearer. Once again he could mark their silhouettes distinctly through the smother of the storm. Five minutes more of that rate of progress would bring them up to him.

On the right he saw a gully opening, its floor slanting up at such an angle that a horse could hardly make headway there. He turned the mare toward it, and asked for the last of her strength. She gave him that with all her brave heart, but a hundred yards of that uphill running stopped her to a stagger. He flung himself to the ground. Running on, he saw through the thickening storm that the men behind him also had dismounted. They were no more than gray shadows that flickered, went out, and appeared again. So he knew that he had gained a little vital distance by his last maneuver — not much, and no safe obscurity, for the eyes of hawks were behind him, straining and red with eagerness.

He thought of snatching out the treasure and dropping it, but he knew that that would never stop them. They wanted the money, but they wanted his life now almost more than the cache he had found. He stumbled into a snowbank. It seemed to him a fatal trap. The snow clung about his legs. He floundered through it and dashed on, blind with fear.

Something thundered before him. He saw a pale thing gleaming and then lightning that jerked from the clouds to the earth, revealing the face of the waterfall that filled the end of the ravine up which he had been toiling. On each side the water, in other ages, had carved out cliffs that were hand-polished, as it were. Not even a mountain sheep could have climbed them. But beside the waterfall, wet and obscured by its spray, there was a jumble of boulders that climbed up. He could not see the top. The driving clouds obscured it, but he rushed at that clumsy ladder with his last hope between his teeth.

He was drenched with freezing water in the first ten seconds. A moment later his left hand slipped from a precarious hold, and he swung on one hand, looking down through coils and swirls of storm clouds at shapes that clambered beneath him, seen in one glimpse and then blanketed away from his eyes again. He swung himself up. A frenzy flowed through him. A dozen times he hung by a fingernail on the edge of his death. He was near the top when the wind struck him like a torrent of water and pushed him to the side over the wet, smooth surface of a rock, until his legs extended under the beat of the waterfall.

One hand by fortune found a crevice that enabled him to haul himself out of that danger. As he rose and stood, out of the white steam of the cloud, he saw a man climbing, lifting head and shoulders high to gain the very rock on which he stood. The lower part of that body was drowned from sight, as though in milk, but Woodstock could see that face clearly, brown as an Indian's, and now contorted with effort and savagery. One arm was bare to the elbow, with a big blue and red design tattooed on it.

Woodstock saw these things while he braced himself against an upper rock with his hands and then kicked the climber full in the face. The weight of the blow knocked the fellow backwards. His hands gripped wildly at nothing. Then the dense cloud swallowed him. His scream sprang up against the ear of Woodstock, but a stroke of thunder overwhelmed all other sound. Woodstock climbed on.

He reached the top of the waterfall, found there a rapidly rising ground, and staggered on up it. Above him the cloud turned brilliant white. It opened in spots to let him see the glorious blue sky above. He was slipping on ice and snow when he came at last out of the arms of the storm and stood in the dazzle and blaze of the upper sky.

X

He went on, always up, stamping his feet to make them bite into the ice and the crusted snow on which he was climbing. Beneath him now the storm had moved from horizon to horizon. Here and there tall islands of clouds rose above the lower masses, but these islands dissolved and were licked away by the billows of mist that ceaselessly beat against them. Out of this whole sea of smoke that rushed endlessly toward the southeast stood the shining tops of the mountains, all encased in gleaming ice. Above and behind all this was the dark blue of the mountain sky, now trembling with the force of the wind.

Perry Woodstock saw all of this without joy. There was in him nothing but the frantic labor of escape, for out of that sea of clouds monsters were about to emerge and fling themselves on him. He glanced ahead, squinting till his eyes were almost shut, in order not to be blinded by the glare of the ice. He saw that the slope above him became broken, here and there, where the rocks arose in sheer cliffs. In the crevices, ice was still lodged, but from the southern smooth faces of the cliffs the sun had eaten away the winter casing. Up a massive tower like a chimney that was about to fall in ruins, Woodstock climbed. The first move was the hardest one. He had to take a run and hurl himself up to grasp with hands the upper edge of the first course of that titanic masonry. After that, the going was easier, yet he was giddy when he gained the top, and his body shook. As he lay flat on his face, looking over the edge of this upper platform, all his muscles twitched, and the breath that had left him would never come back. There was not air enough among all these windy summits to furnish him with a single life-giving breath. And still the others had not come.

There were only four of them now — but what a four!

Thunder exploded beneath him. The rocks on which he lay quivered, the echoes pealing along the valley below, and now they came, Vicente first, Black Jim Waley behind him, and finally two more, rising from the cloudy sea. Yet Woodstock could not rise to flee again. He could not even gain his hands and knees to crawl on. He could only lie there like a trembling mass without bone or nerve in it, while the four followed his sign up the slope.

Once Black Jim Waley paused, shielding his eyes with a hand, and looked straight up at the top of the rock chimney where Woodstock lay. Yet Perry Woodstock could not move enough to withdraw his head from view. If Black Jim saw his quarry, at least he gave no token of the discovery but went on again with small steps, gradually edging up the trail.

They came out onto the rocky shoulder from which the chimney sprang into height. Black Jim leaped twice to reach the top of the first block, and twice he failed. When Vicente offered to heave him up by the legs, Waley shook his head. He pointed at the height of the rock, still shaking his head to deny the possibility that any man could have climbed up this way. That instant Woodstock was able to breathe freely, to the bottom of his lungs, and the strength that had left him poured back through his body.

Still he watched them as they turned their attention to the possible ways in which the fugitive might have traveled. They examined the snow for sign; they examined the rocks that stretched nakedly down, in one place, to the solid sheeting of clouds. They looked at a stretch of ice where footprints of a man would probably make no impression. Then they conferred. Vicente alone went off over the ice, picking his way with infinite care over the slippery steep of it, but Black Jim and the other two climbed down the rocks, and once more the sea of clouds swallowed them.

Vicente was gone from sight around the shoulder of a cliff, and Woodstock sat up with a deep groan of relief. It was the third time, the narrowest call of all, but again luck had favored him. He could think now of that broken body that must be lying, smashed out of recognition, at the bottom of the waterfall. So he would be lying himself, if one of twenty chances had gone against him in that climb. He stood up, found his knees fairly strong beneath him, and scanned the world again.

He could make out nothing at first. Those peaks he had learned to recognize by their entire outline were indistinguishable now that nothing of them appeared except the white summits, clad in ice and burnished by the sun. He remained there, resting, until the storm broke up as suddenly as it had washed across the sky. From the northwest out of which it had come, it broke into irregular masses — in half an hour the entire sea of white had withdrawn, except for certain irregular piles that dwindled in the southeast. The brown uplands appeared again. He saw the flashing arch of the very waterfall beside which he had climbed through the mist. The voice of it, he thought, he heard among the other sounds that trumpeted faintly to his ear through the thin mountain air. He saw timberline, the darkness of forests beneath it, the green of the lowlands beyond. He could recognize several of the mountains now, but he climbed toward the nearest high shoulder of the peak he was on in order to map out the lay of the land more exactly.

It was a steep bit of going in which he had to zigzag back and forth, carefully watching the planting of each foot. If he fell, he might roll a thousand feet, and then drop a thousand more. He was near the top of the slope when he heard a crunching footfall coming over the snow toward him. A mountain sheep, perhaps? Nothing else was apt to be moving at this altitude among the snows. But as he stepped up the last of the

150

incline, he saw before him, looking gigantic against the sky, the wide shoulders and the scar-white face of Vicente.

In the same instant they saw one another. In the same moment their hands leaped for their guns, yet there was time for Woodstock to see the grin of joy begin on the face of Vicente, and to hear the commencement of his animal whine of content. Their guns came out in one flash, but Woodstock's foot slipped and dropped him to one knee. That, he always knew, was why the bullet of Vicente parted his tousled hair instead of splitting open his skull. His own shot struck home on metal. Vicente's gun was flung back against his face, knocking him flat and, as he sat up, stretching his hand vainly toward the Colt, he saw Perry Woodstock, covering him with deliberation.

Vicente began to nod. Blood was running down his face from a cut in the forehead. "That was a good trick, *señor*," he said. "If this were not my last day, I would practice that same trick and use it in the next time I had to fight. But all good things come to an end, even Vicente." He began to laugh, which made his face more horrible than ever. He broke off to say: "*Hai!* Look, *señor!* I part your hair for you. I made a good crease. You won't need a comb, the next time. Only a brush will do."

"Lie on your face," said Woodstock.

"I'll take your lead in the front," answered Vicente. "Make a good steady aim. That is all that I ask. And why should I ask that of a man who is such a master with a revolver? It was a pretty trick, *señor*. By the good God, even Black Jim Waley has no better trick in his whole parcel!"

"I'm not going to shoot you, Vicente," said Woodstock.

"No?"

"No, I'm not going to murder you."

"Murder?" queried Vicente, beginning to gape. "Would you

151

call it that? Shooting Vicente . . . would you call that murder?" At this, he began to laugh once more, more loudly than ever. He held his aching sides as he considered this idea — that the shooting of Vicente might be termed murder.

"Lie on your face a moment, while I fan you for more guns," said Woodstock. "I tell you again . . . I won't shoot you, Vicente, unless you force me to."

"Well," answered Vicente, "not even a sheriff with his oath sworn on a Bible would take Vicente alive if he had a chance to take Vicente dead. However, you are young, and young men can't help being fools." He stretched himself face down, as he spoke, and extended his arms above his head. "I only had the one gun with me, *señor*," he said, his voice muffled by his position. "But there is a little knife in front of my right hip in a scabbard that fits inside the trouser leg. You are welcome to that *amigo*."

Woodstock found it. "You can stand up, Vicente," he said.

The half-breed rose. He began to grin again, his mouth twisting to the side.

"If I tie your hands," said Woodstock, "you won't be able to climb down from here. If I don't tie your hands, you'll take the first chance to shove me off a cliff, and you're likely to have chances like that on the way down."

"Ha?" grunted the 'breed. Then he added suddenly: "Look, *señor*. If you are really such a fool, then Vicente will be a fool, too, for once, and give his promise to be a prisoner and never lift a hand against you."

"I don't want your promises," answered Woodstock. "I wish to God that my bullet had split your wishbone for you. Then you wouldn't be on my hands."

"I understand that, *señor*," agreed Vicente.

"But now that you're here without a gun, I can't very well polish you off in cold blood."

"You are young," repeated Vicente, "and young men are mostly fools. Not Vicente, though. At your age, my hand was well in."

"All I can do," went on Woodstock, "is to promise you that I'm going to watch you as well as I can all the way to the bottom of the mountain. And if I see any move that looks suspicious, I'm going to drive a slug into you, Vicente. Is that fair?"

"*Señor,* if you were a judge in heaven, you could not be more fair and just," said Vicente with another twisted grin.

"We go back this way," said Woodstock, pointing.

"You are doubling back, eh!" exclaimed Vicente.

"For the horses," said Woodstock. "We'll take a longer way around, but I think that's the safest direction. I've an idea that Waley will keep up his hunt for me a long time before he goes back to the ravine where the horses are."

"*Señor,* have I called you a fool?" asked Vicente. "I was wrong. I bow to you."

And he took off his hat and bowed to the snow.

XI

It was the purpose of Perry Woodstock to take a roundabout and therefore an easier way about the side of the mountain in order to get back to the narrow valley in which the horses had been left, and so to climb down the floor of the ravine by an easier stairway than the giant's ladder that ran down beside the waterfall. He merely asked Vicente if the wound in his forehead was painful and should be dressed, but the half-breed pointed out that the bleeding had stopped. So they started on the way.

"Vicente," said Woodstock, "will you talk to me?"

"Shall I tell you stories, *señor?*" asked the half-breed. His eyes narrowed. It was impossible to tell whether he were amused or malicious. The horrible slab of his face was incapable of any subtleties of expression.

"Tell me the story of the money in my pockets, and the jewels in the wallet."

Vicente sighed. He appeared to be thinking for a moment before he answered: "The money and the jewels are worth more than the story that goes with them. If you've got one half, you might as well have the other. How do you pay me for the story, *señor?*"

"How should I?" asked Woodstock.

"Freedom is a beautiful thing."

"Should I set you free if you tell me the story?"

"You should not," said Vicente, making himself a cigarette as he walked along. "Not unless you want robbery and murder to succeed in the world. But although you are brave and wise, *señor,* I think you are not so clever as you are kind."

"Why do you think that?"

"Because you were riding to come again to the cabin of

Harry Scanlon just now. That is true?"

"Yes."

"Instead of taking what you found and using it for yourself, you paid for it with your own danger. They have no claim on it. And I, for one, said that you would be taking the out trail, but Black Jim knew better. He had seen your face. He said that there was too much kindness and honesty in the fool. You would go back to the Harry Scanlon family to divide with them. And he was right! That was how we happened to overtake you on the way from the lava flow."

"Tell me something, Vicente."

"As much as I can."

"How long have you been in this business?"

"Of stealing and killing?"

"Yes."

"Since I was eighteen. I was a beautiful young man, *señor*. When a girl looked at me once, she looked again to make sure that her eyes had not lied to her, and, when she gave me the second glance, I took her heart in my hand and kept it as long as I pleased. I found the prettiest Mexican girl in the mountains, one whose father had two thousand sheep and two houses, and thousands of pesos. Everything could be divided in two for the present . . . half for him and half for Vicente. Afterwards, it would all come to Vicente. So I decided to take her. She accepted me, this only daughter of a rich man. On the wedding day I took my bride as far as the door of the church, and there a cursed wildcat of a she-Indian threw acid in my face. I only had time to throw my left arm in front of my eyes, and after that I was put to bed for a few weeks. They could not help the flesh burning away, but a great doctor turned the scars white instead of red."

Here Vicente laughed without any apparent malice in his voice. He ran the flat of his hand over the flat slab of his face, and in this way wiped away the laughter.

"After that," said Vicente, "the daughter of the rich man screamed when she saw me. But if I could not have her, I thought that at least I should have her father's money, and so I took it. That was how I began, and everything followed in time until I met at last my master, the devil, whom you have seen."

"And then this business of the money? And the note that Joe Scanlon was carrying?"

"Some of us were together in a saloon, *señor,* not long ago, and into the saloon came a man who walked like a cat when a dog is in the room, and he talked from the corner of his mouth. 'Prison!' said Black Jim at once, and therefore bought drinks for this man who said that his name was Mason and that he had been thirty years in prison. Thirty years, *señor!* A life . . . a life!"

"Yes," agreed Woodstock. "A life, I suppose."

"Black Jim asked him what he would do with himself. Mason was a little drunk then. He began to be excited. He threw an arm above his head and shouted: 'With three words I bring into my hands the key to a treasure. Though the key itself is a conundrum.' Joe Scanlon was there and asked him what the three words were. And he shouted back, 'Three Scott forty-eight,' and fell to laughing. Then he had another drink, and, when we looked around, Joe Scanlon was gone.

"Our oldest man came up and said to Black Jim: 'That is Mason, of Partridge and Mason, the bank robbers.' I happened to hear this. And it meant something to me. Does it mean something to you, *señor?*"

"I think I've heard of them," said the boy. "They robbed a bank in St. Louis. They took a quarter of a million in bank notes from the Farmers' and Merchants' Bank, the way I remember it."

"And now that money is making your pockets fat, *señor*," sighed the half-breed, glancing aside at Woodstock. "But after Black Jim heard the name of Mason again, and who he was, his brain began to work, and it worked very fast and sure, as it always does. He knew of Partridge. He knew that Partridge was wounde in the same gun fight during which Mason was captured. It was said that Partridge, after being hurt, took all the loot that belonged to him and Mason and cached it away, and swore that he would never touch a penny of it until his friend was free to spend it with him. He didn't live long to prove that he would be as good as his word. For the wound he had grew worse, and he died of blood-poisoning in the house of his father, who was a rancher. This was the story, and I had heard it, and so had Black Jim, but my mind did not work as fast as the chief's.

"He took us out and made us saddle our horses. There were four of us with him. And he rode hard across country with us for eight miles, until we came to the old Partridge house. Black Jim Waley and I stole into it. It was the middle of night. We found the library. We found a set of books that all looked alike, and the name of Scott was on the back of every volume. The third volume was not on the shelf with the rest. Its place was vacant, and we found the book lying on the table. Black Jim Waley opened it and, between pages forty-seven and eight, on both pages, we found a little impression made, as though a fold of paper had made it.

"Black Jim said to me in a whisper, 'Do you see? The third volume of Scott, and page forty-eight. There was a paper here and in the paper were the directions for finding the treasure that Partridge cached away. The fool of a Mason talked on his way to the place. And Joe Scanlon, the dog, has out-thought and out-run us all. Does he think that he can hunt for himself away from the whole pack of us?'

"With that, he left the house, and I with him, and we struck out after the thief until, far ahead of us, in the moonlight, we saw a horseman jogging. When he saw us, he ran for his life. That was Joe Scanlon, *señor*, and you saw what happened on the rest of that night. That is all the story. It is simple, and the moral is in your pockets and your wallet."

He gave one of his hearty laughs again. One would have said that he enjoyed the oddity of the tale as much as he would have enjoyed the possession of the money.

"I understand," said Woodstock. "Did you manage to trail me all the way to Harry Scanlon's house?"

"No. As soon as you took to the mountains, and we lined out in your general direction, Black Jim guessed that you were riding to Harry Scanlon's place. We all knew where that was."

"When I broke away, you all guessed that I was carrying the paper with me? That was why you followed?"

"The paper, or a copy of it. What would the difference be? We knew that we had to stop you. We tried our best. Then we found your trail and followed it. We knew the sign of the hoofs of the gray mare by that time. Yes, I think they are printed in my mind to endure forever. They are printed in my mind as though in rock. In the lava flow it was hard work. We cut ahead for sign and found the dead snake . . . you had shot it?"

"Yes."

"Then we could see where you had climbed the side of it and, in a little while, we reached the place where you had left the tarpaulin. Black Jim shook out the rags of the oiled silk. And two little sparks of light dropped out of it. One was a green streak and one was red. An emerald and ruby, *señor*, that you had left behind in your hurry, and yet up to that moment you would have been glad to work three years for the price of either stone. After that we started on your back trail and suddenly Black Jim shouts out and began to laugh, and he swore by his own sacred devil that you were riding back with the loot to reach the house of Harry Scanlon. There, *señor*, I have told you the story. You are to judge what it is worth?"

They had come across the ridge and were passing down a steep descent where the snow had been sheltered from the sweep of the wind and lay deep. It was crusted over, but the crust had worn thin, and there crumbled under their steps. Beneath them, this valley head opened on a wide prospect of river and hills and woodland far below. Just to the right was the divide they would follow, when they were a little lower, and come out at the side of the ravine up which the chase had run through the storm not long before.

"The story's interesting," said Woodstock. "I don't wish you harm, exactly . . . but I think you're right . . . I'd be a fool if I turned you loose in the world again."

There was a rushing sound, very much like wind in leaves, but seeming to come out of the very snow over which they walked, and, as Woodstock finished, Vicente broke in upon him with a yell of fear, pointing back. The snow was piled loosely enough, but perhaps it was their passage that had unsettled some of it. At any rate, straight above them and shooting fast down the slope, already throwing up a tail of snow dust high in the air, a snow slide was driving down on a widening front that threatened to engulf them.

XII

There seemed only one haven from the sweep of that danger and this was a group of rocks that thrust their heads up above the surface of the snow on the left, and the two men made for it. Down the slope, Perry Woodstock felt and heard the onrush of the avalanche. He dared not look aside at it while he fled at the heels of Vicente They were already near the rocks when a white arm shot out, picked up Vicente, and threw him into the air like a ball. Then a flying cloud overwhelmed Perry Woodstock. It turned him over, whirled him, beat him, shook him with ten thousand furious and brutal hands.

Up to the surface he shot at the end of that half-second of immersion. He saw that Vicente had grappled with both arms the point of a rock, but he had not yet dragged from the sweep of the snow the lower half of his body. Looking back at Woodstock, as at a swimmer in a flood, the half-breed suddenly lunged out with both legs as far as he could kick.

The utmost reach of Woodstock fastened his grip on one heel, and on that straw he climbed. A comber of snow loomed over them, swelled high, burst, and broke. If there had been any solid part to it, both Woodstock and Vicente would have been swept away, but it was merely the light froth of newly fallen snow. There was a stifling moment, and then the two men found themselves lying face downwards on the red, raw, wet clay of the mountain side.

They got to their feet, Woodstock planting himself firmly against the treacherous inclination of the mountainside, and Vicente staggering a pace or two while they watched the progress of the slide. Widening its front, gaining mass and momentum every instant, it came to a small ridge a quarter of a mile below where, it seemed likely, the sweep of it might be checked.

Join the Western Book Club
and GET 4 FREE* BOOKS NOW!
A $19.96 VALUE!

Yes! I want to subscribe to the Western Book Club.

Please send me my **4 FREE* BOOKS**. I have enclosed $2.00 for shipping/handling. Each month I'll receive the four newest Leisure Western selections to preview for 10 days. If I decide to keep them, I will pay the Special Members Only discounted price of just $3.36 each, a total of $13.44, plus $2.00 shipping/handling ($22.30 US in Canada). This is a **SAVINGS OF AT LEAST $6.00** off the bookstore price. There is no minimum number of books I must buy, and I may cancel the program at any time. In any case, the **4 FREE* BOOKS** are mine to keep.

*In Canada, add $5.00 shipping/handling per order for the first shipment. For all future shipments to Canada, the cost of membership is $22.30 US, which includes shipping and handling.
(All payments must be made in US dollars.)

NAME: _____

ADDRESS: _____

CITY: _____ STATE: _____

COUNTRY: _____ ZIP: _____

TELEPHONE: _____

E-MAIL: _____

SIGNATURE: _____

If under 18, Parent or Guardian must sign. Terms, prices, and conditions subject to change. Subscription subject to acceptance. Dorchester Publishing reserves the right to reject any order or cancel any subscription.

But the head of the slide rushed over that embankment in a single step, sprang out in a mighty arch, dropped from sight, and smote the slope beneath.

The thunder of that impact boomed in the ears of the watchers before they saw the front of the avalanche shoot into view off the lower level. It was transformed now. It ploughed the snow away, cut down to the rock, gathered thousands of tons of loose earth, picked up boulders, hurled them on high, and then used them with terrible hands to beat away whole ledges and add burden to the slide. The landslip — it was a snow slide no longer — reached timberline, still widening its triangle. It swept on through the forest of the valley below. Woodstock could see trees in full plumage and naked masts flung into the air like black ashes that dance above a fire. A continual departing roar poured back upon his ears until the landslide reached the river at the far bend of the valley. That mass of water it dashed into a white cloud that hung long in the air, while the accumulated mass of the avalanche dammed the waterway from side to side.

A long while afterwards the distant roar of those final impacts came hurling back to the ears of the watchers. Then the echoes took up a long, diminishing tale. Still there was a ringing in the mind of Woodstock when Vicente turned to him and said with his horrible grin: "That's like being God, señor. How would it be to go around the world, flaying a valley here, and scalping the hair of a mountain there? Suppose there had been a little town down there in the valley . . . what would it be now except splinters and a little red paste mixed into the heap yonder?" He began to chuckle, slowly rubbing one shoulder, kneading the muscles.

"When I caught hold of your heel, did I almost pull your arms out of their sockets?" asked Woodstock, curious.

"Almost," nodded the half-breed.

161

"What made you save me?" asked Woodstock. "You could have let me go. Nothing could have helped me."

"I would have been sorry to see one man take so much good money to hell with him," said Vicente.

Woodstock grinned. "But if I'd gone with the money, you would have been free. You would not have hanged, Vicente."

"Well," said the other, "when it comes to bargaining, I know how to make a price, but I wouldn't value Vicente at a quarter of a million in hard cash and another half million or more in jewels."

"March ahead of me," said Woodstock shortly. "Keep to the right, and go out along the divide."

So they came out over the narrow ravine at the head of which the waterfall was shaking out its flag of white silk. In the floor of the valley they could see the horses, their heads down as they grazed, but no sign of a man on guard over the small figures.

They found an easy way to the bottom of the ravine. The gray mare came like a dog, frolicking at the sight of Woodstock who put the other five horses on two long leads, fastened the ends of the rope to his borrowed saddle, and mounted. Vicente, meanwhile, sat on a rock and calmly smoked. Woodstock turned last of all to his captive.

"What am I to do now, Vicente?" he asked.

"Put Vicente quickly out of pain. That would be the best thing," said the half-breed. "Or else bring me to the next sheriff. But you will do neither of these things, because you're what Black Jim called you. You remember that I gave you a way out of the snow slide, and that is all you can think about."

"Well," said Woodstock, "I suppose you are right. But tell me one thing."

"A thousand, *señor*. If I can keep you here talking long enough, Black Jim may return. Half his mind must be troubled

162

about these horses all the time that he's away, hunting for you. He may come back at any time."

"Tell me only this . . . if we meet again, are we enemies?"

"Why not?" asked Vicente.

"Well, we have done little services for each other, and things like that make most men friendly."

"What have we done?" answered Vicente. "You have given me my life two times, but my life twice over is not worth the money that I kept from going to waste in the slide."

Woodstock sighed a little as he looked at that inhuman face. "Vicente, you have a clear brain. You read the mind. Now tell me what I intend to do next?"

"That is clear and simple, señor. You will ride hard, now that you have left me and Black Jim floundering on foot. You will go to the house of Harry Scanlon, quickly put him and his wife and daughter in the saddle, and off you will run, the four of you, to get to some big town where money can be turned into land that cannot burn and houses that cannot be stolen. Then you will marry the girl and give the world more honest fools like yourself. She is too good to be amusing, but such men as you, señor, had rather be right than be happy. The newspapers will then publish your picture. You will work hard to become richer and richer . . . and in the end some free man, some happy man like Black Jim or Vicente, will find a way to inherit all of your money."

"Good bye, Vicente," said Woodstock. "I hope your neck is stretched at the end of a rope before long."

"Adíos, señor," said Vicente. "I could not wish for you a sadder life than you wish for yourself."

XIII

When Perry Woodstock came again out of the darkness of the forest and in to the little green farm of Harry Scanlon, he was still a good distance from the house as the girl ran out of it and came toward him, calling out his name. He jumped to the ground to meet her. The gray mare followed slowly behind him, with five fine horses trailing her on the lead — a downheaded lot from weariness were all the six in that group.

Out of the doorway, also, came big Harry Scanlon with his arm about his wife, pointing out to her blind face the direction from which Woodstock was coming. They were laughing with happy excitement, the father and mother, but the girl was weeping. She was trying to laugh, too, but only the tears were real, Woodstock thought. She caught his hand and walked on with him, hurrying a little ahead so that she could partially turn, and so scan him from head to foot.

"We thought that they must have shot you to bits, and that you'd ridden off to die in the woods, and that they'd followed and found you, and gone on with that murdering bit of paper. We've been hunting every minute since, trying to find . . . your body! And here you come back to us safe and sound."

"I whistled at the bullets, and they let me alone," said Perry Woodstock.

The tears kept running out of her eyes, but she dwelt on his face, scanning it like a book. She seemed eager for the good news, but incredulous of it. She was laughing breathlessly, too.

They were close to the house now, and Harry Scanlon's big voice was saying: "Stop crying over him, Rosemary. Don't make a big baby out of yourself. Give me your hand, Perry." He crushed the very bones of Woodstock with his grip. There was a fierce happiness in the face of Scanlon. His eyes, like those of the girl, seemed to be finding something in Woodstock's soul, and taking possession of it.

"I want one of his hands, too," said the blind woman, feeling her way forward.

Woodstock took both of her reaching hands in his. He put his other arm around her and led her back toward the house. Her raised face was close to his shoulder, and she was saying: "When I heard the rifles crashing, and the horse still galloping, I kept asking if you'd fallen yet. And they said that you were still in the saddle. Then I knew that bullets could not strike anything so brave."

"My God," said Perry Woodstock, "how happy I am to be here with you, as if you were all of my own blood. Come into the house. I've something to show you!"

They gathered around the table in the main room of the cabin. By this light Woodstock could see more clearly the big rag rug on the floor and the burnished pots and pans that hung on the wall behind the stove. He thrust his hands into his pockets, fumbling.

"Stop crying, Rosemary!" commanded her father. "You didn't cry when we thought the poor lad was dead. Why should you cry because he's alive?"

"Because I'm too happy," she answered. "Because I feel as though all the happiness in the world had poured into this room, and that we can find some way of keeping it."

Woodstock heaped the packages of money on the table. He opened the mouth of his wallet and poured out the pyramid of jewels. Through the showering exclamations he told all the story as he knew it and as he had learned it from Vicente.

"It's half and half," said Woodstock. "Half to you and half to me."

The big hand of Scanlon dropped on his shoulder. The two women were silent, with puzzled faces.

"If there's a quarter of a million here, stolen from the bank in Saint Louis," said Scanlon, "I guess that money goes back to them, Perry, eh? And as for the rest, none of it belongs to us. It's all yours, if you can't find the owners of the jewels. And after thirty years that would be a hard job, I suppose."

Woodstock stared at him blankly. "I would have kept the money, too," he confessed. "But you're a cut above me, all of you. Well, let the cash go back to the bank. But the other stuff we split half and half. I never would have had a look at any of it, except that Joe Scanlon gave me the message to take to you. It's half and half, man! No other way but that. You're going to get into the saddle now, all of you. You're getting out of this place and coming along with me to some town big enough to make us safe, because Jim Waley and Vicente and the rest . . . bar one . . . are all alive and ready to hunt us. They may be coming near to us now."

"We can't go," said Harry Scanlon. "I wouldn't leave the place. None of that stuff is mine. . . ."

"Rosemary, make him get into a saddle," urged Woodstock.

He hardly heard her words. He only knew that somehow she managed to get her father out of the house, and he was standing alone with the mother.

"I've got half a minute to say something to you, Missus Scanlon," Woodstock said.

"It's Rosemary that you want to talk of," she said. "But you needn't. I've never had eyes to see my dear girl, but I know all that you could want to say."

"I love her," said Perry Woodstock.

"Of course, you do," said the mother. "What a foolish boy you'd be if you didn't."

"When I came back," said Woodstock, "she seemed pretty glad to see me. She seemed so glad that I began to have a crazy hope that she might care a little about me, too."

166

"Dear lad," said Mrs. Scanlon, "do you think there are many men in the world as young and as gentle and as brave as you are?"

"I'm no more than a cowhand. I'm a farm hand and a cowpuncher. That's all I am," said Perry Woodstock.

"Tell her that," said the mother. "And see if it keeps her from giving you her heart as freely as a song."

"We must go," said Woodstock. "We have to start. Come with me."

He guided her carefully.

"You mustn't tremble, my lad," she told him. "It will all be right, the instant that you speak. She's never been taught the lying ways of most girls, never speaking what their hearts desire."

He helped her into the saddle on the smallest and gentlest of the horses. Carefully he fitted her feet into the stirrups. After looking at her with a strange tenderness, he turned to the gray mare, and found the eyes of Rosemary on him. She was laughing a little, but not in a way that made him blush, not in a way that mocked him, merely as though she understood and were happy in her understanding.

"Ride first with me, Harry," said the mother. "You know the way best, and they want to talk together."

"Aye," sighed Harry Scanlon, "I suppose they do. But keep close, Perry."

"Aye, aye," said Perry Woodstock.

He fell in beside the girl. She had not so much as a look for him, but her glance was away among the trees, or up at the blue patches of the sky.

"Rosemary," he broke out at her, "I've got to say something to you."

"Don't," said she, "because words are silly things between us now."

REATA

A Reata Story

Frederick Faust's original title for this story was simply "Riata."
Western Story Magazine, where it was first published in the
August 21, 1933, issue under the byline George Owen Baxter,
retained the title but altered the spelling to Reata to be consis-
tent with their house style. However his name was spelled, Reata
proved to be one of Faust's most popular characters among
readers of this magazine, harking back to the enthusiasm that
had met a previous, very different Faust character, Bull Hunter,
in the same magazine a decade earlier. Like Bull Hunter, who
was accompanied on his adventures by the stallion, Diablo, and
the wolf dog, The Ghost, Reata also gains a mare and a mongrel,
but they are also very different from those found in the Bull
Hunter stories. There would be seven short novels in all about
Reata, of which this is the first and, therefore, heralds the
beginning of his saga.

I

"ROPE MAGIC"

From his head to his ankles Reata looked the perfect cow-puncher. His whitish felt hat was the sort of a genuine Stetson that might have been bought ten years before. The wind and the rain had worked on it. Its uneven brim had been tied down to make ear flaps. It most certainly had saved part of Reata's anatomy from the cold and damp of winter ground. His flannel shirt, too, was a checkered pattern, and the stuff of it had been rubbed and worn out of color rather by much wearing than by many washings. His trousers had the sleek of the saddle inside the knees. Down on his heels were a pair of beautiful spoon-handled spurs, enough to stir the heart of any range rider. As if to show the authentic label, the little round tag of a sack of smoking tobacco hung from the breast pocket of his shirt. His face, too, was coated with that brown varnish that is laid on in successive coats only by many exposures to the scorching sun of the southern deserts and the winds of the northern moun-tains. He was of the rider's ideal build — lean in the hips, with all the weight where it was needed, in the arms and shoulders.

However, there were details in the picture that a very clever eye might notice. The eye of old Pop Dickerman, nevertheless, was the only one in that rodeo crowd which took heed that the feet of those riding boots were not as the feet of the boots of the average cowpuncher who drags on a fitting a couple of sizes too small with a high heel behind it that, to be sure, keeps the foot from becoming too dangerously and deeply committed to the stirrup but also forces a man to walk high on his toes with the stilted gait of an old woman. Instead, the foot part of

Reata's boot was made of the most comfortable and supple leather, the heel was low, and plainly it was designed for the convenience of one who is much upon his feet — and sometimes has need of the utmost in agility. And in that smiling, good-natured face, Pop Dickerman saw the eyes were a little too bright and too changeable. Sometimes they were bluer than gray; sometimes they were yellower than hazel. Otherwise, there was nothing particular about face or features, and in height, weight, and general looks, one might have put Reata down as simply the average man, most readily lost in a crowd of people, whose hair is blond and whose eyes are blue-gray or green-gray.

There was a pause in the rodeo entertainment, and Reata had chosen that occasion to start his own little performance. Before he had made three flourishes, a circle had opened before him, and people were packing closely around to see tricks as clever as were devised on the range by idle men with plenty of wits in the head and in the hands. The tool of Reata was, in fact, the thing that gave him his name, but it was such a reata as never had been seen before. It might be the full length used on the southern range — forty feet — but it was a rope no thicker than a lead pencil. Yes, or even thinner. It seemed to be made of finely braided rawhide. It had the snaky suppleness of rawhide, and it could be made, by Reata, to drop out of the air into a pile in his hand, and thence shifted easily into one coat pocket.

Though it seemed to be rawhide, even the power of that tough leather was not enough, a man would have sworn, to explain the strength of this material Reata used. Some people suggested that into the fabric, or serving as a core, might be a braid of intensely strong wire. Piano wire, for instance, is capable of enduring a great pull, but this wire would have to be more subtle and more supple by far. One thing at least was true — that just as a length of good twine will hold a man, so that very slight rope of Reata's would hold a strong horse. Another thing was patent to all who handled the rope — it was heavier than leather ought to be.

It was a joy to see what Reata could do with that slim length of mystery. As for the rope dance that a good many cowboys have mastered, every feature of it was simple to Reata. He could make his lariat into a walking wheel, into a double and a triple walking wheel, or a wheel that spun with dizzy speed in the air. The crowd gasped and laughed and pressed closer, and little men gripped the shoulders of luckier beholders and pulled themselves up on tiptoe to see Reata throw his lasso into complicated and intertwining curves through which he leaped and danced. For a feature of his performance was that he was rarely still, but seemed as lively, as supple, as lithe as the rope he used.

Now the loop head of the lariat rose suddenly, like an angry snake. Now it coiled its length under that raised head like a snake about to strike. Now the rope stood up its whole length on revolving serpentinings and formed rapidly into various figures, until there seemed to be a stiffening material in it, for the master wielded it so that the rapid ripples which he threw up in it were able to maintain it in almost any position above him. What it could do in the air was wonderful, but that was hardly anything compared with the patterns it made on the ground, when it slithered about in such a snaky way that one or two of the wide-eyed women gasped with something akin to fear.

It all seemed so easy when one glanced into the laughing face of Reata. He made a deft loop that picked the hat of a man off his head, jerked it high in the air, caught it, and then, most marvelously, restored that hat to the man's head, though a good deal awry, to be sure. As the crowd fairly shouted applause after this master stroke, Reata tied into the single end

171

of his rope two bits of lead and asked any one to throw something into the air. A half-drunken cowpuncher responded, in the midst of his excitement, by letting out a loud whoop and hurling his good Colt revolver high into the blue. As it descended, the crowd, scattering back a little from that dangerous fall, a slim streak of shadow darted out of Reata's hand. It was his rope, the double-weighted end of which struck the gun in mid-air, wrapped instantly around it, and allowed Reata actually to jerk the big gun back to him without allowing it to touch the ground. The reata had done the trick, but so swiftly, so subtly, that it really seemed as though a stroke of magic had made the weapon leap into the hand of Reata.

There was a thundering applause for his feat, which might have made some of the people think of those natives in South America who, in the old days, were able to throw a bit of rope weighted at both ends so accurately that they could entangle the legs of running game with it. Reata now caught the gun in a new loop of his lariat and swung the Colt out to the easy reach of the cowpuncher who had thrown it into the air. Then Reata took off his hat from his blond head and waved the sombrero to indicate that the performance was ended. Several of the men told him to pass his hat and they'd make his show worth his while.

"I'm just a 'puncher, having a holiday . . . I'm not a beggar doing tricks," said Reata. He laughed and nodded at them. Then he went off through the crowd, leaving a murmur of delight and wonder behind him.

Only Pop Dickerman looked after him with a glimmering light of real appreciation in his eyes. And old Pop Dickerman put up his hand over his beard, so as doubly to hide his laugh.

In the meantime, getting to the outer edge of the rodeo grounds, young Mr. Reata paused behind a tree and began to produce some small articles from his clothes. He had not devoted all of his attention to his art with the rope. In fact, to see his collection, it appeared that the rope work must have played a very small part, indeed, in occupying his attention. He had two wallets. One contained only ten dollars, but the other held nearly three hundred. He had a roll of bills that once had been coiled up in the vest pocket of a wealthy cattleman who had been staring, like all the others, at the antics of the rope high in the air, unaware that ambidextrous Mr. Reata could continue his rope work with either hand, leaving one set of fingers free to wander and explore — not blindly.

Besides the wallets, he had submitted to temptation and extracted from rather deep in a pocket a fine pearl-handled knife. He had selected for his victims only the most obviously well-to-do of his spectators, and from these he had drawn as contributions no fewer than four diamond tie-pins. One of them would be worth fifteen thousand dollars if it was worth a penny. That was by no means all, for he had picked up a pair of watches, both gold, and one of them from a fine maker. When he snapped it open, the picture of a very lovely girl looked back at him.

Reata frowned. He remembered the fellow from whom he had taken that watch, a big, darkly handsome, proud-headed fellow in his middle twenties, a fellow who was so assured in his position that he was able to venture knee-fitted riding breeches instead of the proper range garb. Out here in Rusty Gulch people would not ordinarily dare to infringe on the old customs. No, that fellow was a person of wealth, of holdings so large that he could afford to do as he pleased, while the rank and file of ordinary men, never knowing when they might need a job on his place, had to treat him with respect. For that very reason Reata had picked on him as a perfect victim. He never used his talented fingers to empty the pockets of hard-working cowpunchers. He only took where it seemed that there might be profit for him and no heartbreak for the loser.

Yet, now he regretted having taken that watch. No matter how high-headed and stiff-necked that cattleman seemed to be, the fact was that he had won for himself — or else why the picture in the watch? — a very lovely girl. The more Reata looked into that pretty face, the more he was stirred. He was, in fact, one of those fellows who lose their hearts as easily as they lose their hats. A pretty face set his blood singing in an instant. And he was as gullible about women as he was keen and sharp about men. Now he drew one long sigh and instantly decided that, for the sake of this charming girl, he would have to return the watch to its owner.

So he ventured straightway into the crowd. When he had been a performer, a mere tilt of his sombrero to the back of his head and a flash of his eyes had been enough to attract attention to him. Now, as he slipped quietly along, finding interstices in the thick groups where none would have appeared to ordinary eyes, rarely jostling so much as an elbow, but melting, as it were, into the mass, he who had been so observed a moment before was now totally unremarked — except by the hawk eyes of old Pop Dickerman who was able to see the very thoughts that stir behind the foreheads of wise men.

Coming quickly to the tall and handsome fellow in riding breeches, Reata slid the watch back into its proper vest pocket. Fate, at that instant, tricked him. It made the big fellow glance down in time to see a slender brown hand with his watch dropping from the fingers. The wrist of Reata was caught, and he was flung heavily to the ground.

II

"RAGE"

Perhaps Reata had been just a little clumsy. Perhaps the charming face of that girl and that delicacy of modeling about her mouth obsessed his mind too much. Perhaps he was a little bit dreamy. As he was caught and hurled to the ground, with the bulk of the big man on top of him, his mind was working cleanly and quickly, like the flashing of a shuttle flung through the intricate shadows of the loom.

There were a lot of things that he could do. If he had educated hands, he had educated feet also. He knew that with a slash of his spurs he could open up the back of the other fellow's leg. Or with his upjerking knee he could paralyze his enemy; or with a cunning stroke of his elbow he could practically obliterate one eye or the other. But all of these methods were brutal, and he hated brutality. When he used any means, it was always just sufficient, no more and no less. So he considered each of these possibilities for perhaps the tenth part of a second and then drew from his pocket that end of his reata to which the two lumps of lead had been tied. With them under the tips of his fingers he slapped the side of the head of the big man just hard enough to collapse all of his strength like a spilled house of cards.

From under that burden of loose flesh Reata arose to find that a veritable forest of hands were reaching for him. They caught him, too, but it was like catching a snake. People were shouting — "Thief! Thief!" Those nearby were reaching with their hands, and some of those at a little distance had drawn guns they poised in the air above their heads, waiting for a

175

chance to shoot. Reata dived through a pair of legs, rose like a swimmer a little ways off, and suddenly twisted into the open. If he ran in the clear, he knew he would be blasted to death with a volley of revolver shots. Instead, he headed straight for the nearest hitch rack, where stood a long line of horses. The men would not fire at him probably as long as he was directly in line with horseflesh. They would rather trust to their speed of foot to catch up with him, and in that matter they would have a lot to do. Most of them were in riding boots, but a few were not, and of those few, one pair held almost even with Reata. It was plain that he could not distance them easily. It was also plain that men would soon be in the saddle to ride him down. Again he had to find an idea in his fertile brain and a trick for his clever hands.

He drew a knife. As he ran, he shouted, and the horses at the rack reared back in violent fear, trembling, striving to flee. As Reata went by the horses, with a powerful, swift slash of his knife he severed several lead ropes by which the mustangs were tethered. They went off immediately, snorting, scampering. Fast as he ran, of course, he could not possibly overtake them, but he had a tool that would bring one of them to a halt. That was the reata, that now shot out, bullet fast, from his hand, and dropped its noose neatly over the head of the nearest mount.

The range horse, knowing well the first lesson of the cow pony — don't pull against a rope — came to a sliding halt. Yet it had not lost fully its momentum when Reata flicked aboard it as a cat might jump on a fence. In half a moment he had that mustang stretched out like a string and sprinting as if for its life. Reata, bending low over the pommel of the saddle, looked back and saw men hastily untying horses, mounting them for the pursuit, heard them shouting, heard guns exploding, heard bullets sing for a few moments in the air about him. He laughed. For he felt his luck on him, and he despised the bullets. An instant later he crashed through a high thicket, and he was well out of revolver range before the riders ever came in view of him again.

A good many of them were better mounted than Reata. A number of them were very excellent riders and not a whit heavier, and yet he managed to keep that mustang going a bit faster than anything that came behind him. He burned up the first three miles, jumped a fence, caught a loose horse of promising appearance in the corner of the great field, and, shifting only the bridle — there was not a second to change the saddle — sped on bareback into the hills.

Behind him the pursuit drew away and away and away. They had burned their horses out in the first stage of the race. Now they would have to settle down to trailing and to patient nursing of their mounts. But they *would* be patient, and Reata knew it, for by this time some of those men had discovered the loss of their wallets, and others had missed scarfpins. Besides, every man in the crowd must have felt that he had a personal obligation to run down the thief.

So Reata rated the speed of his horse to trot or canter and made steady instead of brilliant progress. To save his mount, he did what few Westerners would ever think of doing. When, among the hills, he came to a steep rise, he dropped to the ground and ran beside the gelding, and, when he came to a steep down slope, he did the same thing. That was why the gelding, though it was by no means a fine animal, got through the first cañons at a remarkable rate of speed and was still fairly fresh as Reata came to the bank of a stream, up which he could ride with a fairer footing. Afterward, he would cross it when it grew shallow near the headwaters.

He was so entirely confident now that he gave up jockeying the horse to get greater speed out of it. Instead, he rolled a cigarette and jogged on in comfort, and, to ease his position, threw one leg over the withers of the pony and rode aside. For by this time he and the brown gelding were very good friends. A horse knows a master by those vibrating messages that run down the reins, and by qualities of voice and touch that would never appear to ordinary human audiences. The brown gelding did not feel that it was being forced to labor. It was rather out on a lark.

Then, when all was going so well, trouble dropped suddenly, like a spring shower, on the head of Reata. He was too far away from the pursuit, by this time, to be hindered by it. The thing that injured him was, as usual, his foolishly sentimental heart. As he jogged the mustang up the bank of the stream, he saw a few bits of wreckage that clung to a rock in the center of the stream. On top of the wreckage there was a little mongrel dog, making itself small, with its tail between its legs.

"The devil with it," said Reata.

For he had recognized the terrible, hot thrill of compassion that darted through his heart when he saw the poor little beast. He knew the impulse to go to the rescue ought to be handled firmly and quickly and put behind him. If he wasted time, riding through the width and the danger of that strong current for the sake of the dog, the pursuit would almost certainly catch up with him and bring rifles to bear. The pursuers might have fresh horses by this time, and then things would be very bad for Reata, indeed. That was why he said to himself grimly: "A little mongrel. Not worth five cents. Ugly little fool of a mongrel . . . better in the river than out of it."

He kept his eyes straight ahead of him, like a soldier, marching at a review. Yet all the time his heart was being tugged at, and finally his glance went aside again. The little mongrel dog that was perched on the last remnants of a roof of some kind — perhaps that of a hen house — was not in a blind panic, howling, but instead had braced itself on its spindling legs and was looking down with pricking ears to study the condition of its moored raft and the strength of the current that was battering that raft to pieces. It was like a little philosopher capable of regarding death with a bright and earnest eye, gaining knowledge of the last heart beat.

Reata ground his teeth and pulled in a great breath. At that very moment the dog saw him, stood up, and commenced wagging its slender whip of a tail. It was plainly a cross of many breeds. It had a body as sleek as the body of a rat, and a tail like a rat's tail, but its head was fuzzy, like the head of a very diminutive Airedale. In fact, the dog had not even a color. One could not say whether it were brown or gray or spotted, or roan, perhaps.

When it stood up and wagged its tail, Reata groaned aloud. He swore once, then he turned the mustang and forced it into the water. But even as he entered the stream, he could see, far, far away on the next ridge, a moving dust cloud that was sure to be composed of his enemies.

The mustang, as all mustangs will, swam with courage into the current. It had entered the river a good distance above the dog. Now, fighting bravely, striking out with a will, while Reata swam beside, the good gelding brought its master gradually nearer and nearer to the central rock where the mongrel waited. That tail was wagging so fast now that the eye could hardly see it at all. The eyes of the dog were jade, set in the ragged fur of the face. Rags was the name that came up into Reata's mind. Throwing himself away for a handful of rags — that was what he was saying to himself as his hand reached the bit of life and lifted it.

"No bigger than a jack rabbit, and I'm a fool!" said Reata to himself.

He looked back. That dust cloud that had poured over the

179

ridge had dissolved into a number of galloping riders, who were straining their horses forward. Looking forward to the farther half of the stream, Reata saw at once that he could not possibly reach it without coming under rifle fire. They would be shooting at him before he gained the other bank. When he was sure of this, instead of attempting the impossible, he simply turned the head of his mustang and swam beside it back to the shore that he had just left. The little mongrel, Rags, he put on the back of his neck, where it stayed fast, riding him as a circus monkey will ride a horse.

So the three of them reached the shore and, clambering up the bank, saw a charge of a dozen riders, sweeping down with the leaders hardly twenty yards away. There was no use trying to escape by further flight. The gleaming guns that were ready for him told him that. So Reata simply began to take off his clothes and wring them out.

III

"A LION DOG"

Any Western sheriff has sense enough to know that he may be needed around a rodeo, for wherever horses run for money and bets are placed, there is apt to be trouble, and wherever there is trouble in the West, guns may work. So Sheriff Lowell Mason had been at the Rusty Gulch rodeo, and therefore he had joined the pursuit. He had not been able to ride as fast as the man who had lost the expensive stickpin. He had not be able to ride so fast as Tom Wayland, who had actually grappled with the elusive thief and brought him for an instant to the ground. But before the chase was over, the patient sheriff had saved his mustang so carefully that now he was out in front. He had not been tempted to urge his pony in that ruinous first sprint. The result was that he came first to the thief with big Tom Wayland, handsome Tom Wayland, furious Tom Wayland, half a length behind him.

It was Tom Wayland, however, who got to the ground first. He hit it running and drove a fist with all his might and weight behind it at Reata's head. He was so sure that he was going to knock the head of the thief right off his shoulders that the lips of Tom Wayland stretched a bit and his teeth, set hard, prepared for the shock. But he only lunged his arm through the empty air. Reata's head had dipped suddenly to the side, and the shoulder of Wayland, as he stepped in, bumped softly against the chest of the smaller man.

An unusually odd thing happened then. Not with the keen spurs that armed his boots, but with his heel, Reata kicked Tom Wayland behind the knee in that exquisitely sensitive

181

place where nerves and tendons and straining muscles are laid in a shallow layer over the rounded bones of the joint. Straightway, as an insect is paralyzed by one sting of the wasp, so that leg of Tom Wayland was paralyzed by the blow. A mere twist and thrust then made him fall heavily on his face, so very heavily that he knocked the dust out in a large puff on either side of him.

As Wayland fell and the rest of the charge pushed up, sliding their mustangs to a halt, the sheriff said, without drawing a gun: "Are you sticking them up, brother, or are you going to fight us all one at a time?"

Lowell Mason wore no badge, but young Reata, looking into that battered face, smiled and nodded.

"Hello, Sheriff," he said. "I'm glad to see you."

"The thieving young rat!" shouted the whiskered man who had lost the big scarfpin. "There's plenty of trees over there. I dunno why we ought to take him back to jail. If we string him up right here and now, we'll be savin' the world that trouble later on."

Rags squeezed himself between the legs of his rescuer and began to bark suddenly and sharply at the last speaker.

"You see why I'm glad to have you here?" went on Reata to the sheriff.

"Sure, I see it," answered the sheriff, dismounting last of all his men. "Got to say that you're a mite out of order, Mister Thompson. They don't lynch gents in my county. Not except rustlers and hoss thieves, and they don't count as men. Just back up and give the prisoner a little air, boys, and somebody see if Tom Wayland has busted his face on the ground."

Tom Wayland was picking himself up slowly, and, aside from a thin trickle of blood from the nose and that double lump on the side of his head, he was not injured. He was too dazed and breathless to speak for the moment, however.

"Horse thieves are not men, and this is a horse thief," exclaimed Thompson, his whiskers bristling. "There's the horse that he stole, right under your eyes, Mason! What you got to say to that?"

"I dunno," answered the sheriff. He scratched his head, while Reata went on wringing out his clothes. "What you got to say to that, stranger?"

"This horse?" answered Reata, smiling. "Why, Sheriff, this horse I simply borrowed to try him out. You know how it is. I needed a horse at the time, and I didn't want to buy before I'd tried it out."

"Does he think we're a pack of fools?" shouted Thompson.

"No, but he thinks that maybe we know how to laugh at a joke." The sheriff chuckled. "What name might you be traveling under just now?"

"I never could see," answered Reata, "why a fellow should go sashaying around the world with any set name. Now I leave it to you. Don't you wear a different suit of clothes for the summer than you do in the winter?"

Wringing his articles of clothing one by one, he now stood quite naked and showed a slender body over which the sleek muscles were laid on in intricate entanglements. His stomach lay against his backbone like the middle of a wasp. There was no weight except at the top of the torso, and all the weight was whalebone and India rubber. He began to shake out his twisted garments and dress again, as the sheriff asked: "So you change your name the way you change your clothes, brother?"

"Why not?" asked Reata. "Down south they like to hear one kind of a name. And up in the lumber camps they're partial to something with a Swede sound to it. Why not make everybody as happy as we can, Sheriff?"

"I'm going to make you happy by breaking your head," gasped big, handsome Tom Wayland, wiping the blood from

183

his face. "Sheriff, if the lot of you will turn your back for one minute, I'll give you a different-looking sneak thief."

"How'll you change his looks, Wayland?" the sheriff asked a little sternly. "With your hands? You've tried your hands on him twice before this, and you didn't seem to have any luck. You . . . whatever your name is . . . Reata, I suppose I might call you. . . ."

"Sure. Reata. That's as good as any," he answered.

"Where's my stickpin, you scoundrel?" shouted Thompson.

"It's here. I have everything you people could ask for," said Reata cheerfully as ever.

He took out his spoils and handed them all to the sheriff.

"There's fifty dollars of my own," he said, "but I suppose you'll want that for my board and keep for a few weeks, Sheriff?" He added a separate sheaf of wet greenbacks, and the sheriff took it with a grin.

"There may be some costs or something" said Lowell Mason.

"Some people collect butterflies, and some collect moths. Very pretty, but hard to catch. For my part, I prefer to collect stickpins and watches and such things. Easier to find, and they last longer somehow. You know what I mean?"

At this everyone laughed, even Thompson, putting back his head and shouting. Only big Tom Wayland was silent, his dark eyes eating at the face and the soul of the thief.

"I wanta know one thing," declared the sheriff. "That's this . . . why, when you had a long lead and fresh hoss under you, did you ride out into the river there?"

"Look yonder," said the thief.

He pointed to the last bit of wreckage that was now washing away from the rock.

"I saw a fool of a little dog out there, and just then I was feeling lonely. There was a whole lot of good company back

184

yonder at the rodeo, and after I'd mixed around among all you people and admired you a lot, all at once I found myself riding alone through the mountains. Well, it was kind of a sad thing, and, when I saw the pup out yonder, I thought I'd pick him up." He added: "If I'd known that I was to have all this company right away again, I wouldn't have wasted my time, I suppose."

The sheriff lowered his head a little and stared at the prisoner through the thick brush of his eyebrows.

"It's true," he declared. "It's gotta be true, and it's the damnedest thing that I ever heard in my life. It's got me clean flabbergasted. It's got me ding-busted, by thunderation! You went and chucked your chance for this jack rabbit that's got the head of a dog stuck on its neck?"

"This dog?" said Reata, frowning seriously. "You don't realize what sort of a dog this is, do you, Sheriff?"

"What sort is it?" asked Mason.

"This is a lion dog," said Reata. "This is the best kind of a dog in the world for the catching of mountain lions."

A rumble of chuckling greeted this suggestion.

"Runs the mountain lions right up trees, does he?" asked the sheriff.

"He doesn't have to," answered Reata. "It's this way . . . when he comes in sight, the mountain lion, that could eat a pack of ordinary dogs, just takes two looks and then sits down and laughs so hard that he cries. He laughs so that he can't run any more. It's a sort of funny nightmare for the mountain lion, if you ask me. And all you have to do is to come up and take that lion by the chin and skin him on the spot, because he'll keep on laughing till he's skinned and bare."

"All right," said the sheriff when a big, fresh roar of mirth had rippled away. "I'll have to ask you to climb onto the back of that horse you were trying out with an idea to buy him, and

185

then maybe you'll come back to town with me. But what did you do with your gun, stranger?"

"Gun?" said Reata. "What would I be doing with guns in a world like this, where I can find towns like Rusty Gulch, all full of food and friendship? Why should I need to travel around with guns?"

"You do your job and never use a gun?" asked the sheriff dubiously.

"I never carried a concealed weapon in my life," answered Reata honestly, "unless you want to call this piece of string a weapon."

He took the reata from his pocket and made it spring into the air.

They rode back in close formation to Rusty Gulch, most of the men grouped as close as possible to the prisoner, chuckling at the nonsense he talked all the way. Only Tom Wayland rode in the rear of the party, his face gray and as hard as stone. Every time he saw the broad shoulders and the light carriage of the criminal, a flood of hate rushed up from his heart and congealed all through his blood.

That was how they passed into the little town of Rusty Gulch — where the people came out to see the horse thief pass and to stare and whistle and snarl. There they remained to laugh and gape as Reata rode down the center of the street, surrounded by his guard, keeping his length of rope, jumping and playing and twisting in the air like a living snake. In front of him was Rags, spraddling the withers of the horse, accurately keeping balance, with his ears pricked to the sharpest attention.

IV

"POP DICKERMAN'S OFFER"

When they got to the jail, a considerable crowd had followed and collected in front of the entrance to the building, which was simply a low, squat hut, built of heavy stone. Here Reata dismounted at the command of the sheriff, and he made a little speech to the crowd that encircled him, after taking up Rags in the hollow of his arm.

"Ladies and gents," said Reata, "I am about to retire from you to a rest for I don't know quite how long. Fact is, ladies and gents, that the county *and* the state take a lot of interest in me. They don't feel that I ought to go around from pillar to post, working for a living. They want to have me handy all the time, and they're likely to give me free board and room for quite a spell. Well, friends, it's the sort of attention that a man can't help appreciating. It's a real kindness, even though I've got to say that it has been forced on me. But before I retire, I'd like to lend somebody a mighty fine dog that I have here. Can you all see him?"

He held the little dog up in the flat of his hand, where Rags balanced with some difficulty until he managed to bunch his feet together, his front paws on the tips of the fingers of Reata, and his rear paws clinging to the heel of the hand. Once he was in place, he accepted this perilous position with a perfect content, his small red tongue lolling from his mouth as he panted in the heat of the sun, and his bright little eyes sparkling like black jewels from his furry face as he looked about him, wagging his absurd tail constantly. There was a general laugh at the sight of the mongrel.

"Here's a dog, ladies and gents," said Reata, "that you never saw the like of before. Here's a dog, I can tell you, that's worthwhile. Here's a dog with a lot of variety to him. If a cat sees him from behind, it thinks that it's seeing an overgrown rat, but, when he turns around, he gives that cat the surprise of its life because it sees that he's a lion dog. A regular hunting dog that laughs the mountain lions to death. Take a good look, ladies and gents, and tell me how much I'm bid? Who's going to pay a little money down to have the pleasure of feeding this dog once a day and enjoying him the rest of the time? Here's a dog, ladies and gentlemen, with four legs, a tail, two ears, two eyes, and a mouth full of teeth and a tongue. I'm asking you what you'll pay for him on loan. A low rate of interest is all that I'll charge. What am I bid? What am I bid?"

There was a good deal of laughter during this speech, but there was no answer.

The sheriff said: "He'll be all right, Reata. He won't starve to death likely."

Reata put the mongrel on his shoulder, where the dog sat down. No matter where he was placed, he immediately made himself at home.

"Here's a dog," said Reata, "that you can put down a rabbit hole, and he'll bring you back the rabbit. He'll clean out the rats in no time, and, when he isn't hunting, he'll keep you laughing every minute. Gents, you wouldn't let a dog like that go without a home, would you?"

Even to this appeal there was no answer except noisy mirth for some moments, and the sheriff took Reata by the arm.

"We've gotta go, Reata," he said. "Drop the dog and go in, will you?"

Here there appeared from the back of the crowd that keen-eyed, smiling old man, Pop Dickerman, whose business was that of junk dealer, and in whose junk yard one could find anything from old sacks to a broken-down combination harvester.

Pop put out his hand. "I'll take that dog on trust, young feller," he said.

Reata looked for an instant into those clear eyes. They were too young for the grizzled, shaggy face in which they were set close together. It seemed to Reata that he never had seen a greater possibility of evil in any human face, in spite of the smile that, as a rule, masked the rodent qualities of those features. Intense dislike overcame Reata.

"Who makes a real bid?" he asked. "Here's a gent willing to take the dog on trust, but who's offering a hard cash proposition?"

There was again no answer. And Pop Dickerman held out his hand.

"Come along and shake on it," he said, with a touch of meaning in his voice, "and you'll be glad that you gave the dog to me."

Something made Reata put out his hand, though reluctantly. As his palm met that of the junk man's, he felt the cold, thin touch of a steel blade and another flat bit of metal. Instantly, by an imperceptible gesture as he withdrew his hand from that of Dickerman, Reata made these presents disappear up his sleeve. His sensitive fingers had recognized the rough edge of a very fine saw. So he picked Rags off his shoulder and presented him to Dickerman.

"Take good care of him," he said, "and he'll take good care of you."

"That's the funniest thing I ever heard from you, Pop," said the sheriff. "You got a house full of cats, and how do you think a dog will get along with 'em all?"

"Dogs is like humans, Sheriff," said the junk dealer. "They gotta take their chances and live the way that they can."

Now that this transfer was made, Reata went up the steps into the jail, the door of which had been pulled wide. Already, before he entered the gloomy little building, he had slipped the saw and what his touch had told him was the flat stamp of a key into the lining of his coat, through a small, imperceptible cut inside the lapel. He was taken into the jailer's office and searched thoroughly. A pen, a capped pencil, the knife, a few scraps of paper, and odds and ends of a sewing kit wrapped in a bit of canvas, were all that the sheriff found on his prisoner, aside from the supple length of the reata. The other stuff he laid on the desk. The reata he dangled for a moment, surprised by the weight of it and the absolute flexibility of the coils that were continually slipping through his fingers as though of their own accord.

"Well," he said, "I guess you can't pull out the bars of your cell with this here, so you might as well keep it to amuse yourself, Reata."

"Thanks," said Reata. "It'll kill time for me."

"I've got to fill in the book about you," said the sheriff. "Will you answer some questions?"

"Sure I will," said Reata. "I always answer questions. I was taught to be polite, Sheriff."

The sheriff, with a faint grin, sat down behind the ledger. The jailer, a low-browed brute of a man who looked equal to his profession, gripped the arm of Reata as though to make sure of him without irons on his wrists.

"Nationality?" asked the sheriff, poising his pen.

"U. S. A.," said Reata promptly.

"What state born in?"

"The United States," said Reata.

"That's no right answer," said the sheriff.

"It's this way," answered Reata. "If I picked out one state, all the others would be so dog-gone jealous that you couldn't tell what would happen. All the other states would start in claiming me, and there'd be a ruction. You wouldn't want anything like that to happen, would you?"

"Sure I wouldn't." The sheriff grinned. "Dog-gone me if you don't pretty nigh beat me, Reata."

"I'm sorry," said Reata, "but you see how things are? A real popular fellow like me can't play favorites. It isn't good manners."

"All right, then. Let's see . . . height about five ten. Weight . . . a hundred and fifty? I'd say a hundred and thirty, but I happened to see you stripped, and iron weighs a lot more and harder than wood. Color of hair, blond. No scars or distinguishing marks. Color of eyes. Hey, come a little closer with him, Bob. What color are your eyes, Reata?"

"Medium," suggested Reata.

"All right." The sheriff chuckled. "Kind of gray, I'll put down, but seems to me that they're changing about a good deal."

"They try to please everybody. You know how it is," declared Reata.

"Ever jailed before?" asked the sheriff.

"Let me see," murmured Reata. "Was I ever jailed before? Let me try to remember. Matter of fact, Sheriff, I didn't bring my diary along with me. I can't remember."

"I'd bet that you can't and that you won't," said the sheriff. "But if you haven't been mugged and fingerprinted a few times, my name isn't Lowell Mason. Come on, now, Reata. I'm not getting very far. What would you say your profession is?"

"That's a hard one on me," said Reata. "What should I say? Traveler? That doesn't sound like a professional. Entertainer? Yes, that's nearer to the mark. You might call me an entertainer."

"What kind of an entertainer?" asked the amused sheriff.

"Sunday-school kind," answered Reata instantly and calmly. "Because I'm always showing people the brighter side of things."

At this the sheriff laughed outright. "Let it go at that," he said. "You answer all the questions, but I dunno that I'll ever learn anything from what you say. We'll go and take a look at your quarters, I guess. If we can suit you here, I hope you might be making quite a stay with us, brother."

He led the way into the cell room, which occupied the greatest part of the little building. There was one aisle down the center of the room and three small cells on each side of it. The sheriff went to the central one on the left and unlocked the door.

"Good, hard, tool-proof, is what this steel is," said the sheriff. "I thought I might tell you that to save you time if you wanta make inquiries for yourself. Walk right in and make yourself at home."

Reata walked in, put his hands on his hips, and slowly pivoted.

"Couldn't ask for a better place," he said. "Nice small bed so that it doesn't take up too much room. No strong light to bother the eyes. And lots of scenery." He waved toward the forest of steel bars. "I'm a nature lover, Sheriff, and I'm going to be mighty happy in here."

The sheriff slammed the door. The lock engaged with a loud, clicking noise. The door shuddered for a moment and then was still.

"I'm going to find out what the law may have to say to you, kid," he declared. "I kinda hope that it don't say nothing mean."

V

"THE JAILER"

As Reata very well knew, tool-proof is a term, not a fact. The specially hardened surface of tool-proof steel will, in fact, turn the edges of ordinary instruments, but when Reata had worked out the little saw from the lining of his coat, he was delighted to observe that the edge of it was perfectly set and jewel-bright in hardness. Such a saw as that, he hoped, would be able to make good progress through the bars. But he did not intend to use the saw if there were any possibility of escaping with a light sentence.

It might be that his good-natured behavior, that seemed to have won over both the crowd and the sheriff, would gain for him a very light sentence. After all, everything he had taken had been restored. All would depend on who appeared to press a charge against him, and on the frame of mind of the judge. Tom Wayland, who seemed to be a man of power, might spoil the entire business by the weight of his opinion. But even Tom Wayland might decide to forget and to forgive. At any rate, it was better for Reata to take a term of anything up to sixty days rather than bring too much legal attention to himself with a jail break. Next he examined the flat key. It was well filed and obviously made to fit the big lock in the rear door of the jail. The lock of the front door was of a larger size and a more complicated pattern.

After that, Reata sat down to reflect upon the donor of these important gifts — that rat-eyed, wise-looking, old fellow with the face as shaggy as that of a Scotty. The way the tools had been palmed into the hand of Reata meant a great deal to him, for he had recognized, instantly, the professional touch. There was no doubt in his mind that, as far as jails were concerned, Pop Dickerman deserved a place in one as much as most criminals in this world.

A profound sense of disgust troubled Reata. He was himself a criminal, but he detested his fellow crooks. He would hardly have called himself a thief. He was rather inclined to the idea that he was a mere opportunist who did what he could do as chances were presented to him. When he thought of Pop Dickerman, it was as though he were confined suddenly in a stale garret, smelling thickly of rats.

Well, if Dickerman was taking the dog to his hospitality and offering a prisoner a chance of escape from the jail, it was entirely plain that the old man would expect some return, and a great one. Already Reata writhed a little at the thought of what that return might have to be. He decided that he would take any sentence up to ninety days — yes, or even six months — rather than put himself under obligation to Pop Dickerman. When he thought of the crooked back and the forward-leaning head of the old man, a fresh loathing seized on him. Now the smile, not the rat eyes of the man, appeared to Reata the most disgusting attribute. He was in the middle of these reflections and had just slipped his mind away to the pleasanter thought of the pretty face of the girl as he had seen her picture in Tom Wayland's watch, when the sheriff returned.

His face was very sour. "The Waylands are going to raise hell," said the sheriff. "Why did you have to let Wayland catch you when you were lifting his watch? Why couldn't it have been some other man?"

"He didn't catch me when I was taking it. He caught me when I was putting it back," said the thief.

"Putting it back? What you mean by that?"

"I'd looked it over, and I was putting it back," said Reata.

"How come?"

"You wouldn't understand, Sheriff. I can't explain."

"Try me."

"Well, there was a picture of a girl inside that watch," answered Reata. "You know how it is. She's a beauty, and I thought I was a dirty dog to rob a fellow who had a girl as nice as that. You won't believe me, but that was what went through my fool head."

The sheriff stared. "I dunno," he said. "I've got to a point where I could believe pretty nigh anything about you since I've seen you work in the air with that lariat of yours, and since I've seen you slide through a crowd like a knife and then chuck yourself away for the sake of a little guttersnipe of a dog in a river. I went to the judge and told him about you, and I laid on heavy the idea that you'd not managed to get away with anything . . . that you'd got yourself in prison, when you were practically free and safe, all on account of a fool of a dog. And I had the judge all warmed up and ready to be soft about you. He was beginning to say that a fellow like you just needed a good talk and a second chance.

"But right then, in comes Tom Wayland. And the name of the judge, mind you, is Lester Wayland. He's an uncle of Tom's. And Tom let out a blast about you that would 'a' rattled the sides of a mule. In two minutes he done away with all of my good work, and I seen the judge get black. In two minutes more the judge was ta ing about grand larceny and a term that would be the limit. 'The habitual criminal,' said the judge, 'has got to be removed from society at all costs.' And there you are, partner. If you get out under eight or ten years, you're a lucky man. There ain't much forgiveness in Tom Wayland."

It was not of Tom Wayland, big and handsome, that the thief was thinking. He was remembering the ratty face of Pop

Dickerman, and inwardly sickening. He came to the bars and shook the sheriff by the hand heartily.

"Mister Mason," he said, "you're a mighty white man to me, and whether I have to wait eight years or ten before I get out, I'm going to find a way, some day, of repaying what you've done for me."

The sheriff seemed quite moved. "You never would 'a' started doing wrong things except that you started young," he declared. "And if you get a chance to break away from the business, you'll do it, I think. A man with clean eyes . . . he's always clean-minded, too. I'm sorry for you, kid. I'm going to do what I can for you right to the end."

But the best thing that he could do for Reata during the rest of that day was to give him fried bacon and eggs for supper, together with a big side dish of *frijoles*.

The huge jailer, Bob, came down the aisle, grabbed hold of the bars, puffed on the cigarette that hung from his lips, and breathed the smoke into the cell. Bob looked like a half-breed, but one felt that a good scrubbing with soap and a brush might lighten his skin by several degrees. He seemed to be overlaid by a fine layer of soot and grease intermingled.

Bob said: "Havin' it easy, ain't you, kid? Well, you ain't goin' to have it easy so long. They're goin' to sock you, Reata. You know that?"

"I know that," answered Reata calmly.

"Why, it makes me laugh," said Bob, sneering, "when I think of a gent like you, a kind of a half-wit . . . the only brains you got is in your hands. And it kind of makes me laugh, I say, when I think of you throwin' yourself away for the sake of a dog. And what a dog. It'd make me sick, if it didn't make me laugh so hard."

"I'm glad you can laugh, Bob," said the prisoner. "It must be a pretty sight to see you laugh. It'd do me a lot of good to

196

see that maw of yours gap open and watch your yellow fangs, working up and down."

"You don't like my mug, eh?" demanded Bob. "Well, I'm goin' to make you wish that you was in prison and out of this here comfortable jail before I'm through with you. There's goin' to be sand in your grub from now on, and your coffee is goin' to be worse than a dog would drink. I'll show you where to talk back to me, you sneak thief. And if I get another word out of your trap, you get the butt of this in the middle of your pretty mug."

As he spoke, he pulled out a big Colt, fingered it affectionately, and stared with hungry eyes at his prisoner.

Reata said nothing. He was too patently in the hands of Bob. Moreover, night was closing down. The two wall lamps that lighted the room were blown out by Bob, and the place was left in darkness.

"You want a window open, don't you?" asked Bob before retiring.

"Yes, please," said Reata.

"It'll be closed, then," said Bob. "You can lay here all night and choke like a pig in a pen." And he laughed as he left the room.

Five minutes later Reata was at work with his saw. He knew he would have to make four cuts in order to get out. Even then, with two bars down, he would need to squeeze hard to wriggle through to the aisle. After that, the key to the back door would immediately give him freedom. Afterward would come Pop Dickerman, for, much as Reata detested the thought of the old man, he had not the slightest intention of avoiding his debt. He would have to discharge it. He had no doubt that Pop Dickerman had already thought of profitable and convenient ways.

Once out of this mess, decided Reata, he would keep his

hands clean the rest of his life. It was not fear of the law that moved him so much as the consideration of that leaning figure, that ratty face of old Pop Dickerman. His own future and the whole foul shadow of the world of crime rose over his mind like unclean water when he thought of the junk dealer.

In the meantime the steel of the bars was tough, but so was the patience of Reata. He oiled the saw with bits of the bacon fat he had saved from his supper. If his fingers began to ache, and then his whole arm, he nevertheless continued. And in his patience, instead of scowling with the pain of his effort, he smiled a little.

An Oriental might look the same way when entering a great agony, making his face blank while his soul was on fire. Life had taught Reata the same lesson. Happiness would make him as gay as a playing child in a street, but under pain he grew still as a pool and knew how to endure.

He endured now, cutting gradually through the one bar in two places and leaving the bar attached in its place by only a shred of steel so that it could be twisted away by his hands when he would. He attacked the next bar, finished the top cut, and was halfway through the second one when he heard the sighing sound of a door being pushed open and then a light entered the place.

Reata slipped back to his cot and stretched himself on it. One twist of the blanket gathered it around him. There was only a faint squeaking of the spring of the cot. Now, composing his features, he saw the shadow of the approaching form upon the bars.

A moment later lantern light flooded the cell, and the gross voice of Bob the jailer exclaimed: "Wake up, thief. Stand up and lemme look at you."

VI

"THE BROKEN BAR"

Reata yawned, rubbed his eyes softly with the palms of his aching hands, and then sat up. "What's the matter, Bob?" he asked. "Can't you get to sleep tonight?"

"Yeah, can't I get to sleep?" answered the brute. "I'm tellin' you to stand up. When I tell you to do somethin', you hop to it, kid."

Reata rose instantly to his feet. "How do I look to you, brother, eh?" he said, turning slowly to be viewed on all sides.

"You don't undress, eh? You turn in without undressin', do you?" said the jailer.

"A few new ways in a new place helps the time to roll along?" said Reata. "You know how it is, Bob."

"You lie," declared Bob. "A bird like you, all sleek and clean and full of the smell of soap . . . you'd peel off your clothes before you went to bed. You wasn't in bed. You heard me comin', and you slid in under the blanket."

Reata smiled at him.

"What were you doin', hey?" demanded Bob.

"Thinking about the old folks at home," said Reata, "and the dear face of old Aunt Sally, and the smell of the cornbread in the kitchen, and the sight of the Thoroughbreds in the pasture, and the Negroes toiling in the fields, row after row of 'em."

"Shut your mug. I got a mind to go in there and slap you with a gun right now," Bob declared.

"Have you?" asked the prisoner. "Ah, but you're a good

fellow, Bob. You have a good heart, I know, under your dirty skin."

"I'm comin' in now!" snarled the jailer, jangling a bunch of keys.

"Good old Bob. Come in. Come in. I'll be glad to see you. Come in and make yourself at home."

"Yeah, and you'd like it, wouldn't you? But I've heard about you and your foot tricks and your hand tricks and all your *ju-jitsu*. I'll wait till I get the irons on you tomorrow before I dress you down. After I get your hands safe, then am I goin' to beat the freshness out of you? You wait and see."

"I'm glad to know about it," said Reata. "And I like to see a real hearty nature like yours, Bob. It does me good. Now, if you don't mind, I'll go back to bed again."

Reata's calmness infuriated Bob more than before. Grasping two of the bars, he shook them with an ape-like burst of passion. Behold, one of those bars suddenly wrenched away in his hand. He stood back, gaping down at the thing, stunned, bewildered, unable for an instant to understand the thing that he had discovered.

Reata, that instant, drew the slender, sinuous coils of the lariat from his pocket.

"You snake," whispered the big man in the aisle. "I've found you out. Breakin' jail on me . . . breakin' jail on *me* . . . sawin' through the bars! I'm goin' to sound the alarm. And when I get my hands on you, and my irons snug on your arms, I'm goin' to make a new picture of you, young feller."

He turned, and, as he moved, Reata glided a swift and soundless step closer to the bars. Through the gap made by the cut-away section of one bar he threw his rope. The thing hissed softly in the air, and Bob dodged as though he had heard a snake underfoot. He moved too late, for the coil shot over his head, dropped, and was jerked snug just below the elbows of his arms. The powerful pull stiffened his arms against his sides. It jerked him off his feet and brought him with a thud and a jangle against the bottom of the bars. The lantern, falling, almost toppled over, but then staggered back and forth, gradually coming upright.

Big Bob, parting his lips to screech for help as soon as he had caught his breath, found a slender, steel-hard hand on his windpipe.

"I don't want to choke you," said the prisoner's voice, as calm as ever. "But the fact is, Bob, that I'd rather enjoy it. If you even try to yip, I'll throttle you."

"Don't," whispered Bob. "I'll lie as still as a stone. Don't strangle me, Reata. I don't mean no harm to you. I wouldn't 'a' done any of them things. I was just tryin' you out. I was just talkin'. You sure know how it is with a gent when he wants to see what nerve another bird has. You got a lot of nerve, Reata. You certainly got the best nerve in the world, by thunder."

"Shut up," advised his prisoner. "I don't like your voice even when you whisper. Lie still, and don't bother me."

He shifted a few rapid coils of the reata around the throat of the man, leaving just slack enough for poor Bob to breathe. Then, reaching for his saw, he fell to work on the one uncompleted cut with great rapidity.

"Where'd you get it?" whispered Bob.

"I wished for it, and it came," said Reata. "That's a great thing, Bob. Your mother must have told you when you were just a little chap. She must have told you that, when you grow up to be a big man, all you need to do is to wish with all your might, try with all your might, and you'll get everything that you want out of this good old world. Ever hear that before?"

"You got a funny lingo," breathed the frightened guard. "But what'll the sheriff say when he sees what's happened?

201

He'll think that I been bought and sold. He'll think that I passed you the saw."

"Perhaps he will," said Reata calmly.

"You couldn't 'a' got it from nobody. Nobody but the sheriff himself," exclaimed Bob, but still whispering. "That's it. Honest Lowell Mason . . . why, he's just a crook like the rest."

"Be still," said Reata. "You fellows didn't search the lining of my coat, did you?"

"The lining of your coat? You couldn't . . . yes, you could, and you done it that way," Bob groaned softly. "What a fool I was. And what a fool the sheriff is."

The last cut was completed, and a single twist brought the section of the steel bar away. Reata wriggled through the opening like a snake and stood in the aisle above the jailer.

"I hate to do it, Bob," he said, "but I've got to gag you."

"Gag me? Don't gag me, Reata. Don't gag me and tie me, because I'll sure choke myself to death tryin' to breathe . . . tryin' to get the thing out from between my teeth. Just thinkin' of it makes me start in chokin'."

While he was still protesting, his own handkerchief was removed from his coat pocket and suddenly thrust between his teeth. Bob drew up his feet in an instinctive gesture of protest.

The quiet, rapid voice of Reata stilled him. "I know how to do this to keep you still and to let you breathe, too," said Reata. "But if you struggle, you *will* choke . . . and make a murderer out of me. It's a strange thing, Bob," he went on as he took some lengths of twine from the pocket of the jailer himself and began to tie the man to the bars of the cell. "It's a strange thing that the killing of a brute like you would send a man to the hangman's rope. I'd rather hang a man for killing a little dog like Rags than for killing you, Bob. And one of these days a fellow will agree with me. Some fellow with a knife, or an axe, or a gun in his hand. And he'll pass you off the face of the world and into the long dark. Think it over, old son, and see if you can't use more soap on your skin and more decency every way. It's not a world of pigs, and you're out of place in it."

He stood up, dusted his hands, then rapidly disengaged his reata from the body of the prone man. He saw the wild, popping eyes of Bob strain up at him.

"Lie still," he advised. "Don't struggle. Just concentrate on breathing regularly, easily. Now and then you'll want to swallow, and that will be a little hard, but be patient, and you'll manage it. Even if your throat grows a bit dry, you'll manage to breathe till they find you here in the morning, and when they see you, they'll never think that you were bought up for this job. Never in the world. So good night, Bob."

He walked to the back door and tried the key. It fitted instantly and perfectly, and, pulling the door open, he stepped out under the free stars of the night. The air was clean and good. He drew down a deep breath of it. There seemed to be in that sweetness a remedy for all the ten years of prison life which had been staining his mind and all his hopes of the future. That terrible danger was banished from him, and he knew, when he thought back to the malice and watchfulness of Bob and to the toughness of the tool-proof steel of those narrow bars, that only the forethought and the skill of old Pop Dickerman had saved him from the great disaster. The Waylands were avoided for the moment, but what would lie in wait for the escaped prisoner when he put himself voluntarily in the hands of Pop Dickerman?

He took another breath of that pure, sweet night air and started away. As he did so, he heard a hand knock at the front of the jail. There was, of course, no answer. Then a voice called softly, the sound stealing like a thought into the ears of the listener: "Hey, Bob. Wake up, Bob, and let me in."

Still there was no answer. But what music that calling must be to the ears of Bob as he lay bound and helpless on the floor of the aisle. Or was he in a torment to think that they would enter and discover him shamed and useless? Well, in any case, the discovery would soon be made. The knocking on the front door turned into a heavy beating. And then the voice of the newcomer rose in a loud, frightened yell: "Bob! Bob! Hey, Bob! Where are you?"

Someone else on the street now exclaimed: "What's up, there? What's the matter?"

"There's something wrong, and I can't get a word out of Bob who ought to be in there. Go get the sheriff. I'll try to keep on waking up Bob. Hey, Bob, Bob! Where are you? What's the matter?"

Reata, as he listened to this, had stolen away from behind the jail and well into the shelter of a small grove of second-growth trees. Now he turned into a back alley, a little winding lane, and started for the end of the town.

VII

"DICKERMAN'S INTEREST"

All that Reata knew concerning Pop Dickerman was that, when he had made the pause at the jail there had been, behind him, an old wagon well piled up with junk of one sort or another, the sort of wreckage that accumulates around a decaying house. From his whole appearance, Reata felt sure that he had the junk dealer of the town to handle, and therefore he judged that he might be able to find the yard even by night.

He was right. On the edge of the town, a little set away from the rest of Rusty Gulch by a dry draw, with a narrow bridge across it, he came upon the high board fence and the tumble-down shanty which had a meaning to him as soon as half a dozen little phosphorescent lights ran in pairs across the road before him. Then he saw the shape of a cat, walking along the top of the high fence and looking down at him as though it were a beast of prey about to spring. He had heard that there were plenty of cats at the place of Pop Dickerman. He closed instantly with the idea that he had found the spot.

The gate to the road was shut, but not locked. He pulled the gate open and heard a thin sound of a bell, somewhere in the distance. Before him he saw a wide sweep of ground enclosed by the fence on three sides and the house on the fourth, immediately opposite him. All of this ground was piled over with accumulations of junk. In the starlight he could not make out things very clearly, but he was able to recognize the combination harvester, lying on the ground like an elephant with its huge belly up and its enormous trunk slanting stiffly into the air. He saw the skeleton of a hay press, too, complete, and there were crowds and piled masses of single plows and gang plows all in one heap and another of mowing machines. There were horse rakes in a third, their teeth making them look, in the starlight, like a vast entanglement of spider's webs. But there were more piles of nondescript junk than of anything else. He saw the flats and the rounds of stoves and chimneys in one heap, but on the whole he got very little information out of the heaps except the distinct impression that Pop Dickerman must have worked busily for many years in order to gather such crowds of objects about him.

Among the huge heaps, that seemed like the relics of a ruined city, there were regular little paths laid out like streets, and a broader way, where a large wagon could have passed, straight up to the house of Dickerman itself.

A cat yowled from the roof. Reata looked up and saw the beast, appearing as large as a dog as it stood on the crest of the roof among the stars. Reata recalled tales of witches and midnight evil in other days.

He came to the front door. As he looked about it for a knocker and was about to rap, a voice said, in his very face: "Come right in, partner. There'll be a light as you open the door."

That was old Dickerman, speaking through a loophole in the door, of course.

Reata pushed the door open. He felt a delaying tug, as of a string. There was a sharp, scratching sound, and then a light flickered and flared up, a sort of torch which had been ignited by the striking of a flint.

Dickerman, half dressed in a dirty undershirt and patched trousers and with old, moldering slippers on his feet, stood with his leaning body near the door. His attitude was always that of a man midway in a bow. About his feet were half a dozen cats, some rubbing themselves against his legs, and one of them actually perched fondly on his shoulder. This beast now stood up — a scrawny, red-eyed female — and stretched herself and yawned, showing to the stranger the pink of her mouth and the sharpness of the little white teeth.

"So? So?" said Dickerman. "I'm glad to see you, young man. You've come for your dog, of course?"

"Well, I've come for Rags, if you don't mind," said Reata.

"I'll get him for you. Come in and sit down," said Dickerman.

He pointed to a chair, and Reata went to it. He was in the strangest room that he had ever seen. The place was so big that it must have served as the mow of a barn at one time. The uprights and the thick, squared crossbeams seemed to indicate that it had been a haymow originally. Now it was literally filled to the roof, not with hay, but with odds and ends. With junk! The eye of young Reata wandered over the heaps of stuff on the floor in amazement. One could find a thousand things — a heap of battered furniture, chairs here, tables there in a mighty pyramid that in itself almost reached the roof, a glimmering mound of kitchen tinware, another of great black pots and pans, a stacked confusion of buggy wheels in a corner, smaller mounds of various bits, and, above all, all manner of things hanging in the air.

For the storage purposes he required, Dickerman had had to throng the air, after covering the old wooden floor of his place. There were hanging, from ropes and chains, clusters of harness of all sorts, groups of saddles, snaky ropes, rawhide and hemp. There were carpets, hanging like strange flags and rugs and shawls and bedclothes and Indian blankets, and there a strange, filmy float of color and illusion — party dresses that a woman would have loved to finger and turn over, breathing still a commingling of old perfumes that reached to Reata through the other smells like a ghost of dead delight.

All that he saw on the ground and in the air he could not enumerate. Wherever he turned his eyes, he found something new. He found, for instance, a bundle in which, suspended from various rings, there must have been literally tens of thousands of keys of all kinds, and yonder on the floor appeared a dim, crystal heap of glass lamps, while out of a corner was the smirched flame of a pile of copper articles.

No matter how cheap and tawdry many of the things were, one gradually began to have a feeling that all the wealth that a man could want in the world was here. An entire barbarian nation could have been enriched by the brilliances of glass beads that hung shimmering down through the torchlight, and greedy hands of men and boys would have reached either to the cumbersome arsenal, in which there were revolvers, rifles, shotguns of all sorts and makes, or to the adjacent heap of ten thousand different forms of cutlery, from silver butter knife to Bowie knife.

Reata sat down under the suspended collection of lanterns, great and small. His chair had once been upholstered in good velvet that was worn away at the curves and edges and streaked across with greasy patches. In front of him was a little inlaid round table, and beyond the table a very low couch that squatted close to the ground. He had no chance to see more than these details before there was a rustling out of a corner, and a whole herd of cats appeared — yellow cats, white cats, black cats, striped cats, pinto cats, Maltese cats, tiger cats, Siamese cats — an outpouring of cats, a fountain of them, bursting across the floor, leaping over one another, waving their tails in the air, or flickering them straight out behind. As the cats scattered here and there, a young one rolled on its back to play with the fringe that dripped down off a table. At that moment came Dickerman again with another group of cats — a sort of personal bodyguard of cats — all about him, and, at his heels, was Rags, with head and tail down.

The poor little dog seemed so frightened that he was fairly crowding against the heels of the slippers as they rose before him at each step of the tall man. But when Rags saw Reata, as though he recognized an old, old friend, he streaked across the floor and leaped suddenly into the lap of the thief. Reata put him on his shoulder. Rags laid his weight close against the face of his new master and whined with uttermost joy, while little tremors of delight kept passing continually through the small body.

Dickerman came to the low couch or divan on the opposite side of the table, squatted on it cross-legged, and picked up the long, rubber stem of a water pipe, whose glass bowl on the floor Reata had not noticed before. The first puffs that Dickerman blew out from his mouth refreshed and strengthened the oddest of the fragrances that hung in the air.

"I thought it wouldn't be till tomorrow," said Dickerman. "I thought that you'd wait till you got used to the ways of things in the jail."

"That would have been better," answered Reata, "but there was a thick-necked fool of a jailer who promised to make a lot of trouble for me. On account of him, I had to make a move tonight. This saw is a beauty. And the key is an exact fit."

He laid the two on the table. The old man picked them up in his fingers and stowed them both in his trouser pockets. The torchlight threw shuddering shadows over them, and the eyes of Reata dwelt a little too long on the claw-like fingernails of his host.

"So, here you are," said Dickerman, "and I'm glad to see you. Where would you reckon to be going from here, partner?"

"You might guess," said Reata.

"Guess? Now, how would I be able to guess, I ask you?" said Dickerman.

"Why," said Reata, "I suppose that what I have to do for you will take me pretty far away."

Pop Dickerman sat back on the divan and raised his eyebrows, but not his leaning face, and smiled with his mouth and with his two close-set eyes. His eyes were too bright and young, and his lips were as though they had been freshly streaked with grease paint. The devil was in him, in his shadow, in his soul. "Hello, there," said Dickerman gently. "What did you mean by that, anyway?"

"Why," said Reata, "it isn't something for nothing. I don't think," he added, waving around at the gigantic accumulation of junk, "that you're the sort of a fellow who gives a great deal away."

"No, I don't," Dickerman said. "Giving leads to thriftlessness. That's the terrible thing about it. But there was a minute back there when I couldn't help thinking that I'd hired you to do what you was managing, and that was when you were slammin' Tommy Wayland. Ah, son, that done my heart a pile of good . . . a whole pile of good! I loved you then, brother."

"Well," said Reata, "I'm glad that you liked that part of the show, but now you tell me what price I've got to pay to you."

"What price for you, eh?" murmured Dickerman. "What price for your life?"

"No, what price for getting me out of jail."

"Aye, but that's your life," said Dickerman. "There'd 'a' been a burned-out Reata after eight or ten years of prison. The surface and the shine of him would 'a' been all wore away, I'm thinking. It wouldn't 'a' been you that would 'a' come out of the prison, son. No, it's your life that I've given you."

"Well," said Reata after a moment of thought, "I guess you're right, in a way. Now what's your rate of interest?"

"High," said Dickerman. "I'll have to get three lives for one."

VIII

"KING OF RATS"

When Dickerman had made this pronouncement, as though in agreement or in praise of its master, a cat jumped into his lap and then bounded up onto his shoulder, where it took the exact position of Rags and stared straight across at the dog and Reata. Dickerman began to puff slowly at his pipe, his eyes quite closed, and only the red-lipped smile, lifting the corners of his mouth behind the shaggy screen of the whiskers that covered his face.

Reata, in the meantime, turned the last words slowly in his mind. As he heard them, and repeated them silently to himself, he had felt the sense of a trap closing over him. There was an essential integrity about Reata — not that sort of honesty, unfortunately, that prevented him from putting his hands on the property of others, but the kind of straight seeing that enabled him to face an obligation at its full value. When Dickerman claimed the credit of giving life itself to him, he knew that he could have dodged the issue in one way or another, and he could have mustered up a virtuous indignation and revolted, forthwith, against the proposal that was made to him. Instead, he confronted the thing as a fact. That jail had been enough to secure the maximum penalty for grand larceny.

This part of the case was clear, and, when he recognized it, he merely said: "Three for one is pretty high, Dickerman."

"There's always a price on rarities," said Dickerman. "You take a gent that asks for snow in the desert, and maybe he can get it, but it might cost him a thousand dollars a pound before he's through. Understand? When a gent comes to me and asks for his life, well, he has to pay a price, and a big price. Three for one is what I'm chargin' you."

Reata again allowed a pause to follow. About him he felt hands of impalpable but inescapable force closing in. At last he said: "Put it your own way, then. Tell me what you want me to do."

"I want three men that I've lost," said Dickerman. He took out an envelope. From the envelope he produced three pictures and tossed them across to Reata, who caught them out of the air.

"The one on top is Harry Quinn," said Dickerman.

"Tell me about him," suggested Reata. He was studying a broad, rather good-natured face with a small nose and eyes surrounded with heavy bone work in the brows and the protuberances beneath.

"Quinn's a useful man," said Dickerman. "That's all you need to know. Quinn's a mighty useful man. I want you to get Quinn first. Afterward, Quinn and you might get hold of Bates, who's the next of those pictures."

Bates was an opposite type, one of those men whose features are so extremely thin that it seems to be only a division of a face, half of a face that one looks at. A nervous energy, even from the picture, seemed to radiate out toward Reata.

"Bates," said Dickerman, "is a mighty lot more useful than Quinn, but he's just that much harder to get at. You and Quinn might work together and get him. And then the whole three of you could combine on saving Salvio. He's the third man."

"All right," said Reata.

He looked into the third face, and it seemed to him, at first, that it was the most handsome face of a man that he had ever seen, and the smile that played on the lips increased its attraction. However, there was ground for a further inspection, and that was to be found at the corners of the mouth and the eyes and in something sneering that one perceived without being able to place it exactly.

"Gene Salvio," said the junk dealer, "is far and away the best of the three. He's the fine sword, all right. He's the sort of steel that you might bend, d'you see, but sooner or later it'll straighten itself and run its point between your ribs. Understand that, partner?"

"Aye," said Reata. "He looks sort of like a knife in the ribs. Will you do something for me?"

"What?"

"Stop smoking that perfumed tobacco for a minute. I'm getting dizzy with it."

"Sure, I'll stop," answered Dickerman with his smile that lifted slightly the corners of his mouth.

"These three used to belong to you, eh?" said Reata.

"They used to belong to me."

"What price did you pay for 'em?"

"There's prices and prices," said Dickerman. "I'll tell you what . . . you buy one man by giving him hard cash . . . and another gent, you do him a good turn and he never forgets . . . and another gent, you give him the thing that he ought not to have and he keeps coming back to you to get more of it."

This indirect answer was, after all, enough for Reata. He could use his own imagination in order to fill in the details of the facts. "You break away and outline what's coming to me," said Reata. "You tell me what I have to do, and then I'll have to see whether I can tackle it or not."

"No," answered Dickerman, "you'll gimme your hand that you'll go through no matter whether it's hell in particular and earnest. You'll shake hands with me on the thing, or else I don't talk no more."

"All right," agreed Reata. He got up and moved slowly,

with short steps, toward the old man and felt those bright, snaky eyes, which never winked, fixed steadily upon him. He leaned and held out his hand. At his ear, Rags shrank and shuddered and began to whine pitifully.

"I'm wrong," said Reata to himself, "but I'll tackle the thing, anyway."

He put out his hand, and it closed over the cold, hard, dry claw of Dickerman. At that moment a wicked triumph burned up in the eyes of the junk dealer and made them flame brightly.

"Maybe I've been a fool," said Reata. And he drew back.

"Maybe you have, and maybe you haven't," said Dickerman. "But where there's many a good man that'll fail you, I'll never fail you so long's you're my man. You hear me, Reata?"

"I hear you," said Reata solemnly, for suddenly he knew that he was now hearing truth, and real truth, and nothing but the truth. "And I believe you."

"I'll join to you, son," said Dickerman, "closer'n iron was ever welded and heated and hammered together, so long's you're working for me. There ain't no hell you can slip into that I won't find you and pull you out ag'in by the hand. I'll find you, and I'll save you when you get into trouble. The money that you need, you're goin' to have. The horses you'll want to ride, you'll ride. And everything that a man could ask for and want, I'm goin' to find it for you, Reata. You been having your ups and downs, but you ain't goin' to have nothin' but ups while you're with me. You're goin' to be like a gentleman. You hear?"

"Thanks," said Reata, and something made him smile quickly, brightly, with a mirth that came deeply from the heart.

"Now then," went on the junk dealer, "there's another side to this here business. The other side is what happens to you if you double-cross me or step out of harness. Other gents have tried it, Reata. And those other gents have died. If you try it you're goin' to die as sure as if you drank poison, slow poison, the minute that you done the double-cross."

He went to the heap of cutlery and pulled out of it a little straight-bladed stiletto, a mere tiny icicle down which the light was dripping.

"Take this here," he said. "I went and pulled it out of the side of an old partner of mine that was givin' me the double-cross. I didn't stick that point into his heart, but I was able to name the gent that done it. And so I'm tellin' you, Reata, that if you come in with me, you gotta stay till the job's done. Understand me?"

"I understand you, all right," said Reata. "I could understand you if you didn't show me the knife even. I can see the idea in your bright eyes, Dickerman."

"Aye," said Dickerman with his smile. And he passed his hand over his grizzled, shaggy face. "Aye, I reckon I'm the most ugly man on this earth." He went on: "Folks is simple things, simpler than rabbits, or chickens, or such. They believe the words they hear and the smiles they see. But me, I prefer to have cats around me that always like you for the fish they eat and the milk they drink, and they thank themselves for all the rats they're able to catch. My cats live on rats, mind you, but they thank me for the fun that they got with 'em."

"Rats," said Reata, a horrible interest overwhelming him. "You can't have enough rats on this place to feed that whole tribe of cats."

"Aye, and sure I ain't got enough, but rats is easy fetched. You come and see."

He led the way through the big room, Reata swaying his head this way and that to avoid great bundles of cloth or of metal or of glass that hung down from the beams above his head. They passed out of the main room and into a small chamber beside it where a close, foul, damp odor was in the air. Pop Dickerman lighted a match and held it up, sheltering the flame inside his dirty hands.

"Look at 'em!" he said.

Reata, looking, saw half a dozen great wire cages that were filled with rats. As the beasts saw the light and the men, they began to swarm into life, running around and around like the whirling of foul waters, and running up on the wires with their hand-like feet, and, now and then, one of them would pause in the ugly race and look with bright little devilish eyes at the men.

"There," said old Pop Dickerman. "You see 'em? What you think of 'em for cat food, eh? Fightin' cats is the only kind that I keep, Reata, and fightin' men is the only men that I keep. What you think of that little show now?"

"It's a pretty show," said Reata with cold running through his veins. As for his real thought, he kept it to himself. But what was most strongly passing through his mind was the similarity between the rats and the long, downward, hairy face of Pop Dickerman. He, like a rat, a great king of rats, was keeping cats about him and feeding into their mouths his own race. There was something in the simile that rang profoundly true in Reata's heart. He felt sure that time would enable him to prove what his instinct announced.

IX

"THE ROAN MARE"

When they returned to the main room, Reata simply said: "You tell me where to look, and I'll start for Quinn."

"They're somewhere around Horn Spoon. That's where they want me to send the money, anyway," said Pop Dickerman. "The idea is that Quinn is my last good man, and I sent him out to get hold of Bates for me. You know where Horn Spoon is?"

"I know where it is," said Reata. "The railroad goes through there."

"Quinn got that far, it looks like, and then he got drunk in a Gypsy camp, and when they threatened to use their knives on him, he tells them . . . the fool! . . . that they can turn him into money. So they try the idea out, and they send word to me that they've got a man of mine that says he's worth twenty-five hundred dollars to me, but they'll take nothing under ten thousand. And if the ten thousand ain't in their hands inside of ten days, they'll take and slit his gullet for him. That's the news that I get from a dark-skinned hound that shows up down here one evening a week ago. There's a band of 'em, I guess. Gypsies, they don't travel one by one."

"It'll take me two days to ride across to Horn Spoon," said Reata. "That'll leave one day for the spotting of Quinn and the saving of him. It's a short pinch."

"Sure it is," said Dickerman. "It's a short pinch."

"Quinn means a lot to you," answered Reata. "He's one of your three good men. Isn't his life worth ten thousand to you?"

"There's a value on things, and only fools spend too much,"

said Dickerman. "Five thousand, six thousand, seven thousand even . . . but not ten thousand for Harry Quinn. No, not ten thousand for him. I added him up a good few times this last week, and he never come to ten thousand dollars. Ten thousand? No, not that much. Here, Reata. You step over here and pick out the guns and the knives that you want."

Reata went to the heap of guns and looked them over with a shake of his head. "I won't have one of those," he answered, but, going to the cutlery, he picked out an ordinary horn-handled hunting knife. "This'll do," he said, glancing down the blade.

"You don't never travel with no guns?" asked the old man.

"Never," agreed Reata. "I hate to carry a load."

"Aye," said Dickerman harshly, "and I know a lot of gents that would like to drink, but they're afraid to carry whiskey. What'll you take? Just your hands and that reata? Well, you work it your own way. You ain't got more'n one chance in a thousand of saving Quinn now, anyway. Come along and pick out a hoss, will you?"

He led the way out of the house to a small shed. In the distance across the night Reata could hear the swift beating of hoofs, coming and going. Far, far away there was a rapid barking of guns.

"They've found your ghost," suggested Dickerman, "and they're pumpin' a whole lot of lead into your shadow, brother. Here's the hosses."

He opened the door to a long low shed, and Reata took the lantern out of the hand of his host and stared down a line of a dozen horses.

"You're a horse dealer, too, are you?" asked Reata. "Trade with the thieves and sell to the honest men? Is that it?"

Dickerman laughed. He was capable of laughter, but never of letting the sound finish itself naturally. The laughter always died out with a sudden shock in the very middle of its course, as though danger had suddenly looked him in the face.

Reata, with Rags still on his shoulder, looked over the horses rapidly. Two or three of them were ordinary mustangs. The others were blood horses of more or less quality, and one of them, a big and beautiful gray gelding, was a picture that stood out from the others as though sunshine, not lantern light, were falling on it. Reata stepped back and shook his head.

"You've got a better one than this," he said.

"What makes you think so? Who . . . ?" began the junk dealer. He checked himself abruptly. For an instant a dangerous fire had glimmered in his eyes, but it went out again. In that instant both of the men had faced one another, and the gleam of danger was as bright in the eyes of Reata as in those of Dickerman.

"Well," said Dickerman, "I didn't think. . . ."

He left that sentence unfinished also. Then, going to the end of the stalls, he opened a door set very closely into the wall, and Reata walked into a narrow corridor behind three big, roomy box stalls. There was a silken, polished black stallion in the first stall. There was a golden bay gelding in the second, with the bony head of a Thoroughbred. In the third stood an old-looking roan mare not an inch more than fifteen hands in height, built rather long and low, and with every rib plainly discernible.

The door to her stall, nevertheless, was the one that Reata opened. For the first thing he guessed was that the sunken places above the temples did not truly speak of age. And neither did the hanging head and the hanging lip of the mare. The first thing that he did was to part the lips of the roan, and then he found that the teeth were short, and she was not above five or six years old. At that he put back his head and laughed. For the instant that he knew her age the rest of the picture burned into a bright light for him. She was covered with a stringing of powerful muscles, not big, but ropy and individually developed. Though she was rather ewe-necked, and though her withers stuck up high as a knife, and her hips were like two projecting elbows, she had one really beautiful feature — shoulders perfectly sloped and intricately muscled. Moreover, her hide was roan silk spread over that caricature of a frame. "What's the name of this one?" asked Reata, still laughing.

"Yeah, she's a funny-looking old thing," said the junk dealer. "But there wasn't no more room left in the outside stalls, so I put her in here and gave her room. Sue is her name."

"You're kind to the old, I see," said Reata. "You gave her a good blanket for cold weather, and, while you feed barley to the rest, you give her oats, don't you?"

"How'd you . . . what makes you think that?" asked Dickerman.

"By the smell," said Reata shortly. "This is the nag for me."

"You can't have her."

"Give me a mule, then. I don't want the rest of 'em."

"Well, take her," said Dickerman with a snarl. He came into the stall and ran his hands over her bony ribs. She lifted her head and made it beautiful suddenly, as a horse knows how to do when it pricks its ears and brightens its eyes. She loved Dickerman, and, seeing that, Reata was stunned. We cannot have affection except where we give it. Plainly Dickerman loved the mare also.

"She's gotta be used sometime," muttered Dickerman. "And by a gent that knows hosses." He helped in the saddling silently. Afterward, when the mare had been led outside and Reata was in the saddle, he said: "If you're lost in the desert and don't know the chart of the water holes, let her lead, and she'll take you to a drink. If you're out in bad country, she'll watch you like a dog all night long. If you can't find a trail, she'll smell it out, even if the last hoofs went over it a hundred years ago. She'll never fatten up on you, but she'll keep strong on cactus and the smell of gunpowder." He rubbed the head of the mare between her eyes.

"So long," said Reata.

"So long," said Dickerman. "Good bye, Sue. Good bye, girl. Be seein' you again one day."

X

"THE GYPSY CAMP"

Horn Spoon had been called Great Horn Spoon in the old days, but after the mining booms it shrank to a half-dead village, and the name shrank also, until the point of the old joke was almost lost. Reata rode through that town with no one paying the slightest heed to the down-headed rider who slouched in the saddle on the old, down-headed mare, with the little ragged mongrel dog, trotting just ahead of the reaching hoofs of the horse.

Beyond the town, beyond the railroad, he found the creek that still wore the name of Great Horn Spoon, a little trickle of water that wound among the pebbles and boulders of the dry bed. And here, in a semicircle of meadow hedged in by a great thickness of shrubbery, he found the Gypsy camp. There was a string of wagons that served as shelter also, because canvas covers were stretched over them so they looked somewhat like the old prairie schooners. Half-starved mules and horses grazed the grass — they were starved by years rather than by the lack of fodder. It seemed to Reata that there was not ten dollars' worth of horseflesh in the lot. And mixed with these wretched creatures there was a liberal sprinkling of little velvet-coated, deer-eyed mustangs. One could trust the Gypsies to pick out the best of the horses wherever they were to be found. *Would they recognize the qualities of Sue?* he wondered.

The Gypsies lolled about under the shade. In the center of the meadow smoked a fire over which hung several pots attended by one bulky female who wore a man's sombrero and smoked a cigar. On all the others, men and women and children, there was always some slash of color, one single, bright note at least. Only this heavy creature showed not the least decoration.

Reata noticed these things as he came through the shrubbery by a well-trodden gap and rode the mare at a walk across the green with Rags still trotting a little in advance. Instantly a dozen savage mongrels rushed out. Rags had learned much during that two-day journey, however, and now he turned, leaped up onto the foot of his master, and so gained a place of refuge on the withers of Sue. Into the midst of the yelping dogs, Reata dismounted without taking the least heed of them.

It was a pleasant place, this green meadow. At one side it opened back in a long, green strip down the bank of the creek. Some goats were grazing there. But the pleasure might soon be spoiled, for, as he appeared, all the chattering of the ragged children ended suddenly, as though at a signal, and all the women arose, and all the swarthy-faced men stepped out and shifted quickly into various places so that they ringed Reata. He could not escape now if he wanted to.

The dogs backed away and lost interest in a man who was not even afraid of them. That permitted Reata to walk on toward the cook, who presided over the black pots. He could ask her the name of the head of the tribe. She had the face of an Indian squaw — or an Indian chief. It was a massive pyramid, built up from great jaws across a huge nose and mighty cheekbones to a rapidly receding forehead. The cigar she carried in a corner of her immense mouth. The ashes from it, unheeded, had fallen across her man's coat and down onto her short, wide skirt that revealed big feet in horsehide boots. The moment that Reata had sniffed the fragrance of that cigar, he changed his mind and his question.

"Madame," he said, "I'm looking for a place. I think I've found it here. Will you take me on in the gang?"

She looked him over without the slightest interest. Her eyes were black, but the yellow of the sclera made the iris seem brown. A film of moisture was constantly over those eyes, and some of it was constantly gathering into the deep furrows at the corners of the eyes. "Go talk to the men," she said. "I'm only the cook."

He did not hesitate. Much might depend upon his accuracy in this first guess of his.

"If you're only the cook," he said, "I'll be only the roustabout. I don't want to come any nearer to the head of this tribe than you are, ma'am."

"There's one," said the woman, staring at him in some surprise, "there's one so dog-gone much higher than me as I'm higher'n a grasshopper."

He had seen the glint of a wedding ring, a big, golden ring, on her hand.

"Aye," said Reata, "but he's dead."

At this the immobilized face froze into astonishment. "Who are you?" she asked suddenly, ominously.

Her head jerked back. He became aware that men were approaching him stealthily from the rear. Perhaps he was close to his last glimpse of the blue and the white of the great mountains that soared into the sky all around him. They had him totally in their hands.

"Who are you?" she demanded.

"I'm a lazy man," he said.

"Who told you . . . about *him?*" she asked with a heavy emphasis.

"Nobody," said Reata.

Her face blackened at once.

"Nobody," he repeated.

"Hi! Nobody, eh? And nobody told you that I was Queen Maggie, neither, I suppose?"

"Nobody told me," he replied.

"I think you're a spy!" exclaimed Queen Maggie. "But you're a fool, too. And there ain't no place for fools around here. You tell me what made you think that I was the head of things around this camp."

"The smell of your cigar," said Reata.

"How come? What you talkin' about?" she asked.

"You wouldn't be smoking Havanas," said Reata, "in any Gypsy band in the world outside of your own band. Some man would be on deck to give you a beating for daring to put your teeth in one."

She stared heavily at Reata, her eyes opening little by little. "Who told you, though," she demanded, her anger and her doubt returning in a flood, "that there was somebody bigger than me . . . that he was dead?"

"There's a ring on your hand, and you're not wearing a slash of color. You wouldn't be gay with him under ground."

"Under ground, you fool?" said the woman. "He's in the air and all around me. The fire that burned him took him into the air, and I ask you why he ain't in every wind that touches my face?"

"I care what I eat and drink, and where I sleep," said Reata calmly. "I don't care what you believe."

This moment of high insolence he chose even while he felt with quivering nerves that men were softly closing in on him at either shoulder and at his back. But he kept himself smiling a little as he looked into her empty eyes.

Her lips parted. The angry shout did not issue from between them, however. "You ain't a fool," she said. "And maybe you ain't a spy. And maybe you're a part of a man. It's a long time since I seen one. Now, you tell me what you'd do with this here band of mine?"

"Sleep in the day, gamble at night, drink when I please,"

he responded. "I'm tired of working, and I'm tired of jail."

She grinned. The effect was horrible, for the cigar moved back a great distance in her widening, thinning lips, and her eyes almost closed, and a bright drop of rheum stood up in the corners next to the nose. "Well," she said, "you'd get all of this for nothing?"

"I'll do tricks when you give shows."

"How do you know we give shows? Ever see one?"

"I never saw one of your shows. But you have horse tricks, and I'll do rope tricks such as you've never seen."

"Horse tricks? What you mean?" she asked.

"Why, when you come to a new place, you put on your show . . . you have card tricks and fortune telling, and then you have bareback riding to bring down the house at the end. Isn't that right?"

"And you never seen one of our shows?" she asked him. "You never seen one, and still you know these here things?"

Again he felt, like weights upon the spirit, the presence of the men at his back. He said: "Every lot of loafing Gypsies can tell fortunes and do card tricks. And I see where you've been galloping the horses for the bareback riding."

He pointed to a circular track, so well worn into the turf that, in many places, the grass had quite disappeared.

"That might be a ring for breakin' horses," Queen Maggie suggested.

"Gypsies never break horses that way," said Reata. "They live with 'em. And the horse dies or learns. That's the way it goes."

She stood quite immobile for a long moment. Then she suddenly asked: "What kind of tricks do you do, eh?"

"Rope tricks," said Reata.

"What's your name?"

"Reata."

She scowled again. "Fetch me a chunk of that wood for the fire and then show me one of your tricks, will you?" she demanded.

The rope came out of his pocket. A flying coil of it caught the end of a heavy chunk of wood and jerked it to Queen Maggie's feet. She looked down at the wood, at the rope that had slunk back like a snake into the hand and then into the pocket of Reata, and lastly she stared at Reata himself.

"That's something," she said. "Anything else?"

"Like this," said Reata, and, producing the rope again, he swung its slithering length suddenly around his head so that it flew straight out in a whistling line.

There were three or four loud yells of pain and rage as the rope flicked like a whiplash across the faces of the unseen men. Then snarling voices ran in at him. He did not turn.

"Do you like that trick?" asked Reata, smiling.

She flung up one grimy hand, big as the paw of a man, and shouted out three or four words in a harsh tongue — a language Reata had never heard before — and not a hand touched him. He heard the breathing of those angry men almost on the back of his neck. Then he felt, rather than heard, their withdrawal.

The woman spoke again. A distinct and angry muttering answered her command, but the sounds withdrew. She smiled her horrible smile at Reata. "They'll hate you now," she said. "So will all the other men in the tribe. They'll hate you because you have a white skin, because you've been able to talk to me, and because you've put the whip on some of 'em. All of Romany bleeds when one Gypsy loses a drop of blood."

"Well," said Reata, "Queen Maggie is worth all the men. If I couldn't talk to you, I wouldn't want to be here, easy life or none. As soon as I could talk to you, the rest of 'em would hate me, anyway."

"You can stay if you please," she said. Her eyes looked him

over with a partially amused and a partially cold calculation. "But I'll tell you this . . . if you hope to live with us, you'll have to have a skin tough enough to turn the point of a sharp knife."

"I've seen your men," said Reata calmly, "and I don't think that their knives are made of good steel. I'll stay, Maggie."

"Get out of my way, then," she answered him. "I'm busy here. If you had half an eye, you could see that."

"Where's my place to sleep?" he asked.

"Any place you can find . . . and keep," said Queen Maggie, turning her back on him.

He had taken from Pop Dickerman a thin roll of a blanket and a tarpaulin for bedding. Now, as he unsaddled the mare and let her graze unhobbled — for he knew that she would not stray — he threw the bedroll over his shoulder and walked around the semicircle of the wagons with Rags, jogging before him.

It seemed as though the men of Romany understood exactly what was in his mind — perhaps the bedding itself was a sufficient hint — and everywhere he went he found a man at the head and at the tailboard of every wagon. They folded their arms, and, when he asked them if there was room in each wagon for another sleeper, they gave him utter silence for an answer.

That meant fighting. As he realized how certainly he would have to battle his way, he sighed a little. He had fought all his life, with all sorts of men, from boyhood to manhood, and there was little pleasure for him in the thought of the fighting — his hands and his reata against the knives, perhaps the guns, of the Gypsies. He went back to the fire.

"Maggie," he said, "will they use guns on me . . . or only knives?"

"Go find out. Don't ask me, like a sneaking fool," said

Queen Maggie, stirring some pungent seasoning into the contents of the largest of the pots.

Reata stood back and looked around him at the thin blue of the sky, the deep blue of the mountains, the shining green of the brush. He sighed again and then picked out his man.

There was that strange something in Reata that made him inevitably select the largest of the crowd and the most ferocious in appearance. This fellow had a pair of bristling mustaches that made his face look like that of a cat — a huge six-foot-three cat, with leonine jaws and a lion's power and a lion's triple wrinkle in the center of his forehead. He wore a shirt of red silk, a yellow sash around his hips, and a sort of turban of blue silk twisted upon his head, while great green brilliants hung down from his ears. This was the man that Reata chose and approached.

XI

"THE SHOW"

The big fellow was stunned when Reata stepped up to him and simply said: "Walk into the brush with me, you big, cat-faced brute, and I'll show you reasons why I'm to have a place in this wagon of yours." Then he turned on his heel and went quickly away into the shrubbery that closed in rustling waves behind him.

From the rear he heard a yell of rage. That insult had been so great, so effective, so unexpected, that the Gypsy had needed a moment or two to allow it to soak into his inner understanding. Now he came with a roar that extreme rage made not deep, but shrill. Reata, turning in a ten-foot clearing, stood like a statue while that monster rushed at him with extended hands.

Reata ducked those formidable hands, and, since there had been a knife in one of them, he dropped the loop of his rope over the bulk as it rushed past him. The flashing arc the knife had struck through the air still lived like a solid bit of burnished steel before the eyes of Reata. He jerked on the rope, as the Gypsy turned, and bound those arms helplessly against the ribs of the giant. He sent a swift, wriggling shower of loops through the air and further bound his man, hand and foot.

Utter despair, utter terror, utter rage convulsed the face of the Gypsy, but the rage was greater than the fear. He uttered not a single plea as Reata snatched the knife from the nerveless hand and raised it. But Reata had never intended to do more than break the spirit of the man. Now, shrugging his shoulders, he tossed the knife on the ground, and with two or three swift gestures made his captive free. Through the brush, an instant later, burst a tide of half a dozen of the tribe. The big fellow, catching his knife from the ground, leaped, not at Reata, but at these newcomers, and his howl of rage sent them scattering.

They fled away through the brush, and the man with the knife turned slowly about to face Reata again. He was purple with extreme exhaustion. His face was swollen, as though strangling hands were laid about his throat. These checked and raging forces inside him made his great body waver a little continually from side to side. At last he put up the knife with a brief gesture.

Reata waved a hand.

"Nobody needs to know," he said. "I never talk . . . about friends. Make a place in your wagon for me, and I'll give you the bedroll to put in the spot."

That was what happened. There was no further speech from the Gypsy. He merely stood for a long moment, collecting himself, calming himself, seeming to realize that his disgrace might still be covered from the eyes of men. Then, taking breath, he put back his head and burst into a powerful, full-throated song. With that music he marched back into the clearing. With that song on his lips he climbed into his wagon — the largest of them all — and presently was seen to be flinging blankets, a saddle, a bridle, clothes, boots, in a shower upon the grass.

A slender youth came running, dancing, yelling with rage, picking up one piece of his goods only to have to dodge another bit of his worldly wealth. At last passion got the better of his discretion. He leaped into the wagon, and for a reward he received a driving blow of the fist that catapulted him out and laid him breathless and flat on his back on the green. Above him stood the giant, laughing. The entire tribe took up the jest. At last, pale, gasping, but with his wits about him once more, the youth regained his feet and came slowly up to Reata.

"You buy *him* with a little money . . . you will have to pay *me* with your blood," he said, and went away, limping.

That was how Reata bought a place in the tribe.

He had hardly installed his bedding roll before Queen Maggie shouted out orders from the central fire. Reata went out and, in the golden light of the late afternoon, saw the Gypsies rehearse their show. Altogether, it was quite a performance, and Reata could not help counting the dollars that such entertaining must win out of Western wallets when the tribe moved on to a new town.

There was a little orchestra of three violins and a flute, a drum, and a strange horn that kept up a rapid, gay music throughout. To it, in the opening, an old man with flowing white hair and a glossy black beard danced like a Cossack — leaping, spinning, dropping to his heels, and shooting his legs out before him in rapid alternation. For all his age he seemed to be muscled with watch springs that would not wear out. He finished and walked off the center of the grass, hardly panting from his exercise. And not a single ripple of applause followed him. Only Queen Maggie shouted some harsh words at him.

She sat in a canvas chair beside her cookery, and, with a fresh cigar stuck in the corner of her mouth and a long iron spoon in her hand like a scepter, she ruled over the performance and was chief critic. Now and then, Reata could understand the remarks of the people around him. Only half the time they talked in their own jargon, and the rest of the time — they must have been many years in the West — they talked the exact language of the range, with only a bit of colorful variation now and again. Never once did they protest against a judgment of their queen, whom nothing seemed to please.

After the old dancer, out came two Gypsy girls and two youths, limber as willow wands, with feet as light as the wind.

They went whirling and bounding through another dance that made the little children laugh with delight, no matter how many times they had seen it. The cat-faced man was next, now stripped to the waist, and showing a most Herculean torso. He did feats of weight-lifting and wound up by heaving the rigid bodies of four strong men into the air and slowly whirling them above his head. That any human could manage more than six hundred pounds of weight in this manner seemed to Reata a miracle, but the bulging, straining body of the cat-faced man gave explanation for the miracle. A pair of tumblers now went through antics on the grass, spinning through somersaults. It seemed to Reata that these fellows were amply good enough to perform in a circus, but they got not a whisper of applause from their companions.

The show had been brisk, but it had been short when the final number was brought on. First came a call of — "Anton! Anton!" — from Queen Maggie, and out from the wings of a great stage dashed a fellow on a beautiful chestnut stallion, a flashing wizard of a horse with silk knotted into his mane and tail so that he fluttered and streamed with color. On his back sat as fine a picture of youth as Reata had ever seen.

The tribe had picked up circus tights in the course of its travels, and Anton wore them — blue with a golden fluffing around the hips. His black hair flew behind his head. He laughed as he rode, not a stage laugh for the sake of the audience, but the mirth of one who is lost in the happiness of his work. He rode into the very soul of the music that now broke out into a wilder and more triumphant strain, and from all those indifferent Gypsies came a murmur of profound pleasure. They were seeing the hope of their tribe, the idealization of it.

Anton, leaping from the stirrups, braced his feet before and behind the saddle, and, his body, swaying sharply in to keep its weight against the racing circles that the stallion was drawing, snatched a heavy saber out of a sheath that hung by the saddle and gallantly slashed the air to either side of him. He dropped into the saddle again. He picked handkerchiefs from the ground. He swung himself under the neck of his horse and came up on the other side. And he ended — while the horse went at a much slower gallop, to be sure — by standing on one leg and throwing the saber into the air and catching it again as it fell. But at the third trial of this the saber missed his hand and stuck in the sod.

The voice of Queen Maggie rose stridently in criticism, and she waved the iron spoon to send Anton away.

"Miriam!" she called.

No one appeared for a moment. Then a red-bay mare was led out, bare-backed, without reins, and sent off cantering on the beaten track that circled around the grass. Without varying the easy roll of her gallop, the mare stuck steadfastly to the trail that had been formed, as though an even fence contained it.

"Miriam! Miriam!" screeched Queen Maggie.

She added a torrent of angry words in the Gypsy jargon. But it was not for a long moment — and after heads had begun to turn and bright eyes peer, while a hush fell over the tribe — that the girl came out. And, as she appeared, a universal cry of delight burst forth.

Reata himself started forward a step or two from the tree against which he was leaning.

XII

"MIRIAM"

She had on a circus rider's costume like Anton. She was all in pink and blue, with a fluff of skirts and soft slippers with lacings over the ankles. She did not mince like a girl, but she stepped like a boy, and Reata could imagine the muscle under the smooth of her. She was not quite like the others. She was more finely made. Her hair was as dark, but her skin had been bronzed, not sun-blackened like the rest. She walked with one hand on her hip slowly, with a vast insolence in her posture. When Queen Maggie barked a fierce rebuke at her, she dismissed the criticism with a careless gesture of the whip she carried. As she walked into the circle marked out by the galloping of the bay mare, she was accompanied in every step by the approving murmur of the crowd.

Now, pausing, she watched the mare around the circle and yawned without attempting to cover the flash of her teeth. After that she went forward — one could hardly call it running — and leaped at the mare. The good bay rocked steadily along; the flying slippers patted against her shoulders, slipped up on the smooth barrel, and then clung to the back of the horse. Slanting with the slant of the mare as the bay made the circle, the girl feathered her weight on her toes and let the wind of the gallop blow her. Her sullen indifference was gone. She was smiling like a child.

That was the picture that remained in the mind of Reata afterward. He kept hearing the sweep of the jolly music and seeing the flash of the girl. The other things she did were not important to him. She was as much at home on the back of that pretty bay mare as though she were on a broad dancing floor, and dance she did in good rhythm with the music, and constantly seeming about to sway from her balance as she made the whirling steps, but never coming to a misadventure.

The Gypsies followed this performance with greedy eyes and laughing lips, and the children fairly danced with joy, so that, when the riding ended, they flooded out and swept around and around her like a flutter of leaves in a wind. But chiefly Anton greeted her and took her hand, and they went off together, laughing at each other over their shoulders.

Queen Maggie, in the meantime, had remained silent throughout the latter part of the performance, merely wagging the long iron spoon from side to side in time with the music while she balanced it on one knee, and the cigar in her mouth tilted up at a sharper and a sharper angle.

Reata lay under a tree and tried to think about Harry Quinn and the task of liberating him. There was no Harry Quinn in sight, but, of course, a dozen men could be hiding in those capacious wagons. But he could not think of Quinn. The Gypsy show had ended, and the music had fallen still. The men were gambling on blankets or gossiping under the trees. The women were helping now with the last stages of the cookery, and Reata saw one of them get a resounding clip over the head from the iron spoon of Queen Maggie that was immediately afterward plunged into one of the big iron pots.

Reata merely smiled. He looked up through the entangled green branches above him at the blue of the sky in which the sunset color was beginning, and it seemed to him that there was nothing in the world more delightful than to live as these rascals did, without a thought or a care.

Someone approached; suddenly feet stumbled over him. And there stood Anton, the rider, even more gay in his ordinary clothes than in his riding costume, raving and raging down at him. Why did he stretch himself like a log on the ground and leave no space for men to walk?

Reata sat up slowly, smiling a little. He saw an eager group of the Gypsies, watching. Even in the faces of the children there was a world of malice. Off to the side, contemptuous, but a little amused, stood Miriam. She was not nearly so gay in her dress as Anton. A red scarf, twisted about her hips, was all that she had to distinguish herself. But she did not need color. There was something about her that drew Reata with its difference. He wanted to get closer to see what the strangeness was.

Then he said to Anton: "You want trouble, Anton. Is that it?"

"All the trouble you could give me," said Anton, "would not make a taste on the back of my tongue."

The Gypsies laughed.

"You want to fight," said Reata. "But I don't like to fight."

"Hi!" cried a Gypsy voice, and there was a sneering babble at once.

Miriam turned her back and strolled away from the shameful scene of that admission.

"I don't like to fight," said Reata, "but if you want to send me away from the camp, I'll ride my mare against your stallion over there. If you beat me, I go away."

"*If* I beat you?" Anton laughed. "I'm going to ride the chestnut all the way around you! And after you're beaten, maybe I'll follow you away from the camp."

Rags, sitting up on his master's knees, growled softly. But the Gypsies kept on laughing. They were still rollicking in mirth as they watched Reata saddle Sue and as he rubbed the velvet of her nose and she snuggled her head sleepily against him. As he mounted, Reata saw Anton already in the saddle on the chestnut and drawing through his fingers with a significant gesture a long-lashed blacksnake. No doubt Anton did not expect to use that whip on the stallion, but after the race was ended.

Reata was shown the course. They would ride down the green at the bank of the stream, and so they would come to the white rock that projected above the grass. Afterward, they would turn and swing back to the camp, and the first man across the line, that Queen Maggie was drawing with her heel, would be the winner.

Reata gave Rags to the queen. "Keep him till I get back," said Reata. "He won't bite."

"He ought to bite his master for being a fool," Maggie stated. "Go ride your race and get your whipping . . . and tell me afterward how much money you used to buy Sam."

Sam was the cat-faced strong man, of course.

"You may see in the race," said Reata, "how much money I spent on Sam."

He laughed, in his turn, very cheerfully. Then he brought Sue to the mark. Sam, the strong man, stood to one side, glowering at Reata, the revolver raised from which he would fire the starting shot. Anton drew the lash of the blacksnake through his fingers significantly once more, smiling askance at the stranger.

"Give him the gun," Queen Maggie shouted suddenly. "And if he loses, the whole tribe can put the whip on him till he has something to remember us by."

They gave a short, shrill yell at that. And then the gun barked.

The stallion knew what that gunshot meant as well as any man could do. He went off his mark like a trained sprinter and opened up lengths on Sue in no time. He was away so fast and she so slowly that the triumphant yells of the Gypsies turned into a noisy mockery of the stranger. But by that time

Sue was running at her top. Even in a race there was a sort of mildness in her. Her pull on the bit was just enough to balance her stride a trifle. She was as much in hand at full speed as at a dog-trot. And yet she went like the wind. Those whipcord muscles that were inlaid endlong and athwart her body were showing their power now. The fine stallion began to appear like a hobbyhorse, bobbing up and down on one spot, as that queer-looking Thoroughbred mare swept up on him and caught him at the white rock. The stallion whirled around the marker like a dodging dog. But Sue had her head opposite the saddle girth of Anton in half a dozen jumps.

It was too much for Anton. His amazement was so great that something like fear widened his eyes as he looked back at the ugly, reaching head of Sue. Then, deliberately, he struck her twice across the face with his whip. She did not falter. Her ears did not even go back, in spite of that torment, but before a third stroke could fall, her head was in front of the stallion's.

Anton, quite mad with incredulous rage, raised his black-snake to slash at Reata. That hand never fell. For the swift noose of the rope snared Anton and jerked him forward. He tried to save himself. He dropped his whip and jerked out a knife, but, as the mare drew ahead, the stallion swerved to the side, and one more jerk on the lariat pitched Anton from the saddle.

He showed that he was a fine gymnast and athlete, even then, to break the shock of the fall. Yet, of course, he could not maintain that racing speed for an instant. His knees buckled, and, skidding on his back across the grass with his knife flown away and the lariat snugly about him under the pits of his arms, he was brought swiftly toward the finish.

What a riot of noise there was at the finish line, beside which Queen Maggie stood with her iron scepter, puffing furiously on her long cigar. It seemed to Reata like the screeching of tortured cats as he dragged Anton across the heel mark on the grass and then, freeing the noose of the lariat from the victim, dismounted.

The girl, Miriam, was the first to Anton, babbling shrilly. When she dragged him to his feet, it was plain that it was not about his welfare that she was concerned — it was her demand that he should revenge himself for this disgrace. Poor Anton could barely stagger, however. He had been bumped till his head was ringing and the breath had been crushed out of his lungs. He could merely reel on uneasy legs.

When she saw that, Miriam stopped her appeal. She simply snatched a knife from the belt of one of the nearest Gypsies and went at Reata silently and with the speed of a hunting cat. He stood, laughing, to meet her. Not with the noose, but with a flying loop of the lariat he caught both her hands and jammed them helplessly together.

She tried to draw back then, but a strong pull on the rope dragged her straight up to him until the flat of the useless knife, that was still in her grip, was pressed against his chest. He saw now what it was that made her so very different from the others. It was her eyes, for they were a deep, dark blue, quite free from the night that darkened in the eyes of her fellows.

Reata kissed the lips that were snarling at him. Then he stepped back and let her go. He saw her stamp. He saw her throw up her hands. She ran to one Gypsy man after the other and caught them by the hands and tried to drag them forward into the fight in her behalf. Not one of them could be budged, and, when she saw that, she threw her hands over her head again and fled into the brush with a scream trailing like fire behind her.

XIII

"REATA'S LUCK"

Sam, the giant, had sat at the right hand of Queen Maggie until that supper, which was eaten in a big circle around the fire. On this night the queen had on her right the stranger. And she had actually permitted him to help himself immediately after her majesty's plate had been filled. When she had eaten her fill, poured down a quart or more of scalding coffee, and lighted the half-length butt of a fresh cigar, she drew back a little from the circle and made Reata sit down beside her.

She said at once: "Why did you come out here, Reata? You're too smart and too white to want to spend the rest of your life as a Gypsy."

"I didn't come here to spend my life. I came here to have some fun," said Reata.

"Are you havin' it?" Queen Maggie asked.

"I've had a lot to do since I arrived. It's not quite dark yet, and the afternoon's been pretty well filled."

He stroked Rags, who lay between his feet, keeping his eyes constantly on the face of the huge woman.

"The afternoon's been pretty well filled," agreed Queen Maggie. "But the night may be a lot fuller."

"You mean Anton may help to fill it?"

"Why shouldn't he?" Maggie asked. "Today he was the best rider and the best money-maker in the tribe. The silver used to come out and shine like rain when the folks saw Anton prance around on his hoss. He had the best hoss, the best girl. Now his hoss has gone and got beaten, and he's been dragged like a calf on the ground with everybody to stand by and look

241

on. That's the end of Anton. He's got to kill you, Reata, or he'll never be able to hold up his head again. You can't blame him for that?"

"No," said Reata, readily enough. "I understand what's in his head, burning him up. But that won't keep me from sleeping tonight."

"You're a fool, then," said Maggie.

"No, I'll be guarded," he answered.

"By what?"

"Rags," he said, and pointed to the dog.

At this she leaned a little closer, so that she could make out his face more distinctly in the dim flicker of the firelight. "I guess you mean it," said Maggie. She added: "There's Miriam, too. She's not ended. She'll make all equal with you yet. It's the first time there's been a hand laid on her since she joined."

"How long ago did she join?" asked Reata.

"Too long to remember," Queen Maggie said, grinning.

The blood of Reata went suddenly cold. They had kidnapped her, then? He saw the picture of the child and the dark, reaching hands. But he said nothing.

"She was always a good money-maker," said the queen. "She could only toddle, but she could toddle a dance. Folks like to see a Gypsy gal with blue eyes." She laughed broodingly and went on: "Then she grew up. And she's always made money. She and Anton, they mostly keep the tribe. And now they both want your blood. Why don't you leave, Reata?"

He thought of Harry Quinn. Tomorrow would be the last day of his life unless something were contrived in the meantime.

"I'm staying a few days to see how the life goes," he answered. "Miriam belongs to Anton, does she?"

"She belongs to herself, but she'd have been married to Anton before long, I guess. Since you came and shamed him, I dunno. A gal like Miriam, she's gotta have the best. She's

242

been savin' herself for the best. There's more pride in her, Reata, than in the whole rest of the tribe. Anton wouldn't come out to eat tonight because there was shame in him. She wouldn't come out for the same reason. Anton is sittin' and gloomin' in the dark, but the gal is rollin' around in the dark, bitin' the ground and beatin' her head, and yearnin' for the taste of the blood in your heart. I know her pretty good. Hi! I know her! She's the one and the only one that I've never put a hand on. But you . . . Reata, get out of the camp tonight. I'll see that you ain't followed."

"There may be luck for me here," he insisted. "Why not?"

"Luck for you?" she muttered. "Well, we'll take a look and see."

She pulled from her pocket a pack of cards and shuffled them, then dealt out rapid hands that she picked up, glanced at, restored to the pack, and dealt again and again. A gloom came over her, and her face darkened. At last she jammed the cards back into her pocket.

"The cards say that there's luck for you in the camp . . . and bad luck for the rest of us," she declared. "Luck for you and bad luck for us . . . how could that be?"

"We'll be able to see when the time comes," said Reata.

"I ought to march you out of the camp," said Queen Maggie, "but dog-gone me if I got the heart. There's a part of a man about you, and I ain't seen a man since I started to wear black. But there's meanness in the air. And . . . hi, here it comes! Here comes Miriam with a flower in her hair, and a smile on her face, and a good hot bit of hell in her heart, I can tell you. I could easily warm my hands at the fire inside of her even from clear over here."

Miriam, in fact, walked around the fire, went to the simmering pots where the stew which chiefly fed the camp was never cold, and helped herself to a great, heaping spoonful on

243

a tin plate. She cut off a chunk of bread, poured a tin cup of coffee, and, then, with her hands full, came straight to Reata and sat down at his feet.

Little Rags stood up and snarled at her. She put out her hand and offered a morsel of meat. Rags growled at the offer, trembling with angry suspicion. She coaxed him in a soft voice, and Rags cautiously tasted the gift. Then he sat down, and with his pricked ears made an attentive guard and barrier between his master and the girl.

She had not spoken except to the dog. She sat cross-legged and ate heartily, but not with the noisy, offensive, gluttonous manners of the tribe. She was as natural as a cat; she was as dainty, also. As she ate, she lifted her eyes continually to Reata's face. She did not smile, but there was a brightness better than smiling. He kept thinking that, in spite of the darkness, he could see the blue of her eyes.

"Now," said Queen Maggie, "she's putting out her hand on you. Don't be a fool, Reata. Be scary as a dog with a scratched nose when you're around a cat like her. She hunts wild, and she hunts tame, and there ain't a minute when she ain't dangerous."

Reata said nothing.

The girl said nothing but lifted her head and looked long and steadily at him, as though asking him if he could believe such a thing.

"Well, you fool?" asked Maggie. "Have you got it?"

Reata still said nothing. His blood was working with a dizzy sweetness. Queen Maggie caught him suddenly by the hair of the head, leaned, and stared closely into his face after she had jerked his head back.

"*Bah!*" she said, her wide lips snarling around the cigar. "You've got it already. They'll pull your head back like this to cut your throat before morning. And I hope they do. There's

244

no fool better'n a dead fool!"

With that she immediately stood up and strode away with the wide step of a man, the swaying gait of a horseman.

The Gypsy circle was breaking up. As they went off, they stole glances at Reata and the girl, almost as though in fear,. She had finished eating. She put the plate and the empty cup aside and stroked the head of Rags. But the little dog would not relent. He remained tense with watchfulness.

The moments went on until Reata was aware of the slow drifting of the stars to the west. The universal sweep of the lighted universe seemed to be imparting movement to his own soul that carried the girl with him. She was perfectly silent. She was not staring at him, but simply watching. Now and then her head canted a bit to one side or the other, as though she saw him then from a new angle. So the jeweler watches his most priceless gem — in silence, from many angles, peering into the central fire.

She stood up and held out her hand. There was only a red eye of light from the last embers of the fire, but that glow was enough to suffuse the face of Miriam slightly, and again he saw, or thought he saw, the blue of her eyes. So he rose in turn and took her hand. It was cool, gentle, but he felt the strength of it submitting to the clasp of his fingers.

She did not seem to guide him. It was as though a common volition led them forward, with little Rags at their heels, sometimes running in front and looking up anxiously into the face of his master. They crossed the meadow. They walked down the bank of the stream, far along it where the green narrowed to a path with the shadows of the shrubbery rising up on either side of it. Now and again, off to the side, he saw the faces of the stars in patches of still water. The earth had radiated all the heat of the day and now was giving out coolness. Insects hummed faintly near them. And Reata moved through a dream of happiness with that quiet hand still in his.

He almost stumbled when Rags halted suddenly between his moving feet and darted into a bush with a sharp snarling. A man's voice gasped. A shadow rose beyond the bush, and the girl's hand was gone from the hand of Reata as she leaped instantly to the side. The treason went through him like the cruel pain of a knife. But his nerves were fitted for electric reactions, and his body moved on springs. So, as the girl sprang aside, he sprang also, but not to the side, for he had seen the gleam of the gun in the hand of that rising shadow. And now there were two shadows — another looming beyond the first, armed, also. Low, as into water, Reata dived through the bush. A gun boomed just above his head. Then his shoulders struck hard against knees that buckled, and the weight of the first man crashed down on him. That burden did not matter. It was the second man that counted, as he loomed big and leaning, probing into the dark with his gun to find the right target.

Reata writhed snake-like from under the first Gypsy and caught the barrel of the probing gun in his hand. The revolver spat fire twice, the bullets thudding into the ground, and, as the fellow jerked back, he merely pulled Reata to his feet.

In the background the girl was calling out in the Gypsy jargon words Reata could not understand. He was leaping in, pulling himself strongly by the gun. He tried for the face, but not with his fist. A futile and a foolish weapon is a fist, except when there is sufficient light to give fine direction to the blows. But he jammed the point of his elbow into the face of the big man. He heard a gasp. The revolver came free in his fingers. Incredible hands grasped him and crushed him. At the first touch of them he knew that it was Sam, the cat-faced Hercules of the tribe. And hastily, half blindly — for the grip of those hands seemed to be burning the flesh from his bones — he hammered the gun against the skull of the giant.

Yet the deadly grip of those hands did not relax. The head of Sam swayed to the side as though his neck was broken, but there was still sense in his hands, and they held Reata helpless for the stroke from behind that he felt coming as the first man gained his feet.

"Anton," groaned Sam as the hammer stroke beat down on him.

Reata bent his back in as he felt the knife of Anton coming. Something stopped it. Something had checked Anton, and surely it was not the frightened yipping of Rags.

Anton was cursing, and the name of Miriam was mixed with his curses as Reata beat the gun once more on the head of Sam. The great bulk slid down before him into the dark of the ground, and Reata, turning, saw Anton fling away from the entangling grip of the girl and flee like a deer into the night.

XIV

"THE LAST WALK"

Rags came moaning and mourning to the feet of his master. Reata picked up the little dog whose warning had meant the difference between life and death and put him on his shoulder, and the trembling body of Rags pressed close against his face. Reata could hear two sounds of breathing — from the hurt, stunned giant on the ground and from the girl as she straightened her tousled clothes. But when she spoke, she was immensely calm.

"So . . . the cowards," Miriam spit out. "I thought it would be only Anton, but he was afraid . . . even with a gun, even when he could shoot you by surprise, the way a butcher would shoot a beef. Think of such a fool and a coward, and I was giving you to him so easily. *Bah!* He is gone. He is finished. He's as far from me as the other side of the world."

"Give me your hand," said Reata.

"What will you do? Beat me?" she asked.

"I don't know," Reata said. "Come along with me."

"Well, here's my hand," said the girl, and she walked on down the green path with Reata as quietly as though their stroll had never been interrupted.

He noticed that her other arm, away from him, was not swinging. It was held close to her side.

"Was your right arm hurt by that Anton?" Reata asked.

"No. I'm holding a knife," said the girl.

"You know about men, eh?" Reata asked.

"A little," she answered.

They walked on silently. With every breath that little Rags

drew he uttered a faint snarl, for he was on the shoulder nearest to the girl. On a fallen tree trunk Reata sat down and drew the girl down beside him.

"For that back there," he said, "you have to pay."

"Aye," she answered calmly.

"This is what you'll pay, beautiful," said Reata. "Your camp has been here for quite a time, eh?"

"Yes, too long. Already by one day too long . . . for me."

"But there's been a good reason for the stop, eh? Tell me what the reason is."

"The horses are thin. You could see that," she told him. "And they had to be fattened a little."

"Ah?" said Reata.

"You see, when we go through a town, if the horses look very thin, people yell at us and call us cruel brutes."

"Gypsies are not really cruel, I guess?"

"Yes. But they're cruel Gypsies, not cruel brutes. We can't help being what we are," said the girl.

"You talk better than most of your tribe."

"I use two ears, and they only use one. So Maggie sends me to talk, if any of the men get drunk and into trouble. I've talked a dozen of them out of jail."

"And so the long halt at this camp is because the horses are so thin?"

"Yes, of course."

"That's a lie," Reata said.

There was a pause.

"Yes," she admitted, "that was a lie."

"What's the real reason you keep in this camp, then?"

"We want to go down to the big towns and try to make money. But there's been a real circus . . . a real one-ring circus going through the mountains, stopping at all the little villages. Queen Maggie wants us to wait here a while. Then we'll start when the people have forgotten about the circus a little."

"And what's the real reason you stay on here?"

"That's the real reason," she said.

"It's a lie," Reata insisted.

After a moment she murmured: "Yes, that's a lie."

"Tell me the true reason?" he demanded.

"If you know when I lie, why do you want me to keep on talking?" she asked him without passion.

"Why do you lie so much?" he asked her.

"Because I like it," she answered. "I can be angry, or I can laugh, but the best is that I can cry, and that makes people believe me when I lie."

"The fact is," said Reata, "that you're camped up here because you're waiting for the ransom of a poor devil the tribe kidnapped."

He kept his touch on her hand light and sensitive, but he felt not the slightest betraying tremor.

"We haven't kidnapped anybody," she said.

"That's another lie," he told her.

"No, it's not a lie."

"All right," he answered. "I happen to know the truth. You have Harry Quinn somewhere near your camp under a guard."

"Well, if you know it, it must be true," she answered.

"Then it's a lie that you didn't kidnap him?"

"We didn't. He walked into the camp, drunk, and made trouble. That was all. If we kept him . . . that was his own fault . . . because he talked about money."

"If that money is not paid tomorrow, will Maggie have him murdered?"

"Yes, of course."

"Why do you say, of course?"

"Well, if she didn't keep her promises and her threats, the next time nobody would think of paying."

"How do you feel about it?" he asked her. "D'you think it's a good thing to do?"

"Why not?" she asked. "It's one way of making money."

Reata was utterly amazed.

"You kill grouse, deer, and things like that, and you eat 'em. Why do you talk?" asked the girl.

He saw that words were of no use. "Where is Quinn?" he asked.

"An hour's walk from here."

"Where?"

"Up in the mountains . . . yonder." She pointed. "You see that gorge?" she explained. "There's a cave in the left side of it as you go up. There are two bushes, one on each side of the entrance, so that you can't see the hole in the rock. But it's quite big inside. Harry Quinn is in there."

He looked up at the gorge. The mountains on each side were dim in the starlight.

"That's another of your lies, Miriam," he told her. "They wouldn't keep him so far away."

"Well," she replied, "the truth is that there's a cave under the bank of the creek a ways down. That's where they keep Harry Quinn."

"Come and show me the place."

"I have to go back. The women are talking already," she answered. "Even Gypsy women talk about things, you know."

She shook her head, and the white flower trembled in her hair. He leaned over her and put his arm around her shoulder and tilted her head with the back of his hand. He kissed her.

"Ah, ha," breathed the girl. "That is quite good."

She let her head rest on his shoulder passively, and he saw the glimmer of her eyes as they drifted casually, carelessly over his face. He kissed her again. The fragrance of the flower seemed her own breathing.

"Now I can tell you the truth," she said.

"Yes, tell me the truth," said Reata.

"Well, there is a clearing back in the woods, and Harry Quinn is there."

"How many men are guarding him?"

"Only three," she said.

"Three?" he groaned.

"What are three . . . to you and your dog?" she asked.

"Where is the place?"

"I don't want to talk," she said. "Kiss me again."

He kissed her.

"I don't want to talk any more at all," she said. "Talking is no good."

"Then show me where the place is."

He stood up and drew her to her feet. She hung in his arms, swaying a little.

"They'll kill you if you go there. They'd have to kill you, because if they let Quinn away, Maggie will have them strangled. They know that, both of them . . . both Ben and Frenchie."

"You said there were three."

"There's no use lying to you," said the girl. "There are only two. Ben and Frenchie . . . they have killed men before. They'll kill you, Reata. I don't want to go. I don't want you to be killed."

"Show me where they are," he said.

"If you should be able to get him away . . . hi, how I would love you," said the girl. "Ben and Frenchie are two cats. They never close their eyes. They can throw their knives and hit a line. They can shoot sparrows out of the air. Kiss me again, Reata, and tell me you'll stay here with me."

"No," said Reata. "Show me the place."

"I'll never show it to you."

"You owe something to me," he reminded her.

"Well, here I am," said Miriam.

"I want Harry Quinn," said Reata.

"Ah, how it makes me love you when you say that," breathed the girl. "It crushes my heart. I am happy enough to cry. Let me tell you a funny thing that happened. I opened my heart to hate you. It was a big hate, and my heart opened wide, and all at once love slipped inside, and my heart closed, and the love is in there . . . like whiskey."

"Show me the way to Harry Quinn," he insisted.

"Come with me, then. Keep the dog on your shoulder, because he couldn't squeeze through some of the underbrush. When it is found out that I've showed you the way, Maggie will beat me for the first time."

"Aye, but she won't strangle you," he said.

"Why should she strangle a purse of money, and that's what I am," said the girl. "And when they beat me, I'll laugh. I shall think of you, Reata, and laugh. The burn of the whip will be nothing like the burning in my heart. Come, now. Don't even let your feet whisper. Ben and Frenchie can hear people think miles away. Are you going to kill Ben and Frenchie? Well, they have killed others. It's better for bulls to die young. Afterward, they feed by themselves and get sway-backed, and their bellies are like the bellies of old cows. Put your arm around me and walk slowly. This is our last walk together, and every step of it shall stay in my mind forever."

XV

"THE CAPTIVE"

The moon came up, slanting its light obliquely through the woods, and by that light Miriam said good bye with silent gestures. She moved backward among the trees, and, when she was gone, Reata turned to look once more at the scene in the clearing near which he stood. There had been a spark of fire-light, but the climbing moon drowned that eye of light and showed him Harry Quinn, with legs tied at the ankles, sitting on the ground and playing cards on a saddle blanket with a Gypsy whose silken, black mustache was curled up at the tips. Moving stealthily around the edge of the clearing, generally among the trees, or leaning at a tree now and then to exchange a few words with the other two, was the second guard. He was one of those tall men who have no more weight in their legs than has a crane. When the moon fell on his face, it was distinguished by a gigantic scar that ran down his cheek on the right side, pulling all his features in that direction so that he always seemed to be looking and talking askance.

He was Ben, as the observer soon discovered, and Frenchie was the card player with Quinn. As for Harry Quinn, he was perfectly like his picture, broad-faced with rather a good-natured cast and plenty of brute in his expression. But he was much shorter than his big head and shoulders suggested. The short legs were bowed for greater strength and less length.

Reata, moving by inches, wormed closer and closer to this group. The game was seven-up. In that game the shortness of the hands invites conversation. Quinn was losing steadily. He lost his boots just as Reata got into a favorable position behind a big tree trunk, and at this Ben stepped out from the shadows and burst into a fluent torrent of the Gypsy lingo.

"Hey, wait a minute!" called Harry Quinn. "Gimme a chance to know what you're sayin', brother. I ain't got much time to enjoy things, have I? Lemme have a chance to hear you gents yap at one another, will you?"

Frenchie laughed. "Tell him, Ben, will you?" he demanded.

"Yeah, sure, I'll tell him," snarled Ben. "You wait till it's my turn on guard, Quinn, and then you up and gamble all your clothes away. What good are them boots to Frenchie? But they'd fit me real fine."

"That's too bad," said Quinn. "All I hope you get fitted with is a rope, Ben, you wolf."

"Sure," said Ben, suddenly calm. "Some time I'll get a rope around the neck. I've always knowed it. I've felt it and dreamed it, and I've earned it, so a rope is what I'll get. But not yet for a while, I guess."

"How d'you know?" asked Quinn. "There's a lot of unexpected things will happen to a gent. I've even gone and read that in a book."

"Well," said Ben, "where's the jury and where's the judge? You get a jury and you get a judge before there's a hanging, don't you?"

"I'd be a judge and jury for you if I had a chance," said Quinn.

"Look how he likes you," said Frenchie. "He'd do everything for you, Ben, if he got a chance."

"Tomorrow *he* gets a chance, and maybe I can do something for *him,* then," said Ben. "How will Maggie have him killed?"

"So," suggested Frenchie, pulling his forefinger suddenly across his throat.

"No, kill cattle with a tap on the head," said Ben, and moved softly away on his rounds.

Quinn was not horrified, but deeply impressed. He said: "Now you listen at that, Frenchie. That was kind of bright . . . what Ben said. Kill cattle with a tap on the bean, he said. Well, I'm kind of a bull. I'm kind of heavy in the head and shoulders like a bull. But you wouldn't expect a gent like Ben to have ideas like that up his sleeve."

"Ben, he can use his head a little." Frenchie yawned. "Deal, Quinn."

Quinn dealt.

"Bid," he said.

"Two," said Frenchie.

"Three," Quinn said. "Nope, I'll shoot the moon on clubs. I'm going to go the whole hog."

"What you betting?" asked Frenchie.

"I'll bet my shirt."

"It ain't worth a bet."

"My shirt and my belt," said Quinn.

"All right. Two and a half ag'in' that layout."

"The belt's worth five bucks of anybody's money!" complained Quinn.

"Not my money," said Frenchie.

"Wait for me!" called Ben from the other side of the clearing. "I'll bet three dollars ag'in' that outfit, Quinn."

Frenchie leaped to his feet and turned loose the violence of his tongue. Ben leaped into the circle in an answering rage.

"Go on, boys," Quinn goaded. "Pull out your knives. Wouldn't I like to see you carve each other, though? Go on, Frenchie. Get at him, Ben!"

This urging quieted the Gypsies at once. They glared at one another for a moment, and then Ben said: "Some day, Frenchie."

"Aye, some day," promised Frenchie, adding: "How I always hated your long legs."

"Those long legs will stomp you down in the mud after I've choked you," said Ben.

"Snake eater," Frenchie hissed.

"Shut up, you," said Quinn. "You're spoilin' the game. Come back here while I shoot the moon on you, Frenchie."

Frenchie returned, and, after the draw, Quinn led. His card was immediately snapped up by Frenchie, who laughed loudly.

"There goes my jack for high," groaned Quinn. "I never have no luck in this here game . . . and you'd boost the bets for me, would you, when you was setting there holding an ace ag'in' the shooting of the moon?"

"Why shouldn't I boost the betting?" demanded Frenchie. "What I don't get, Ben'll clean you out of. You can't play cards, Quinn. You got no more head for card playing than any poor fool."

Quinn pulled off his shirt and belt. He sat in red flannel that he promptly rolled to the elbows. Frenchie picked up the shirt and looked it over carefully.

"You been and burned a hole in this here with a cigarette," he declared. "I dunno what's the matter with folks that they can't look where they're dropping the fire off the end of their faces. Here you been and spoiled a good shirt on me, except that it's got a lot of stains all over it."

"Those stains'll come out once it gets a good boiling," said Quinn. "You know how it is when you're out on the road. There ain't any chance to boil up, most of the time."

"The belt's all right," said Frenchie. "But why can't you walk straight? You got the heels all slanted over to the outside. How d'you expect me to walk bowlegged like you do?"

"One of my legs is worth ten of yours, you bum," answered Quinn with a good deal of heat. "Go on and play cards, or shut up and give Ben a chance."

"He can walk the beat till his time's up. I'll have you bare as the flat of my hand by that time," said Frenchie. "Deal, you dummy, deal!"

Quinn dealt.

"Three," said Frenchie.

"All right. On what?"

"Diamonds."

The draw was made.

"I'm gonna skin you like a skunk," said Quinn. "I got a hand full of dynamite here. Play 'em, Frenchie!"

Frenchie played a card that was instantly snapped up by Quinn, who laughed loudly.

"How does that king look for high?" he asked.

"There's still low, game, and jack," said Frenchie. "I couldn't lose to you, Quinn."

Ben stepped out four strides from the tree of Reata, and at that moment Reata made his throw. The whistle of the noose over his head made Ben shrink, but, before he could wince down low enough or throw up his warding arms, the rope was tight around his throat, and he was jerked to the ground with a crash.

A skillful, swift wriggle of the rope enabled Reata to set it free from the neck of the fallen man, who lay prone, turning rapidly from side to side, bubbling sounds pouring out of his throat, and his hands fumbling at his neck.

Frenchie, silently out of his place, springing up and running bent low, gun in hand, gasped out: "What is it, Ben? Hi . . . a snake! A snake!"

For he heard and saw the ripple in the grass as Reata, unseen, drew the rope back into his hand. Frenchie fired twice into the grass, his eyes distending with horror. Then he screamed out with terror as a filmy line of shadow, a mere whisper in the air, darted out at him from behind the tree. He threw up one hand to ward it off, and tried to leap back. He merely succeeded in putting his weight back against that noose which jumped tight around his arms, and the first wrench pulled him flat on his face.

He was not ready to give up without a fight, though, and he was striving to struggle to his feet and regain his fallen gun when Reata ran out at him. Toward the scene came Harry Quinn, leaping like a vast, clumsy frog on his hands and his tied feet, while he shouted: "Mind your back! Mind Ben! Mind Ben!"

Reata had reduced Frenchie to helplessness with two or three running loops of the rope. Now he spun around in time to see that he was too late, for Ben, though half strangled by the first jerk of the rope, had managed to recover a bit of wind and had surged to his feet with a leveled gun in his hand.

Reata saw that, and then Ben was knocked flying, his legs sprawling wide apart like a jack-in-the-box. Harry Quinn had heaved himself at the tall man like a thrown log flung endlong and had knocked Ben into a heap. In that heap the free hands of Quinn found the fallen revolver, and shoved it into Ben's stomach.

"Lay still, you rat!" said Quinn. "Am I believin' my eyes? Have I got you down all at once? Lend me your knife. There . . . and now I got both hands and feet! Hey, partner . . . don't choke Frenchie. Leave me the job of doing that, brother."

Quinn began to laugh in a hysteria of almost womanish joy, and with every breath of laughter he jabbed the muzzle of the gun a little deeper and drew a groan from Ben.

"ON THE ROAD BACK"

They made the two Gypsies show them, in deadly silence, to the place where the two horses of the guards were tied, just away from the clearing in a grassy patch among the trees. Then they tied Ben and Frenchie face to face, but with the trunk of a tree between them.

"If they holler, they'll be heard, maybe. The camp ain't much more'n half a mile away, hardly," Quinn said.

"We'll gag 'em," said Reata.

"Aye, but why would you waste the time?" asked Quinn. "Leave me put a coupla ropes around their necks, and I'll hitch 'em to a hoss and give their necks such a stretchin' that they'll never be able to spit ag'in. The rats! Hold up aces on me when I shoot the moon, will they?"

The honest indignation of Quinn made Reata smile a little. "We'll use gags. We're not murdering anyone, Harry," he said.

Quinn submitted with a groan. "It's a waste of time, when we might use rope so good," he declared.

But he helped in the work, and the pair were quickly gagged and left standing with their arms tied together, spanning the rough bark of the tree. After that, the horses were saddled. Quinn wanted to linger a little in order to lay a quirt on the back of each of the men.

"Why make the noise and take chances?" asked Reata. "It's going to be hard enough to do my last part of this job."

"What part?" asked Quinn.

"I have to go back to the camp."

"Back to the what? Boy, you ain't nutty, are you?" Quinn

asked. "I'd rather fool with rattlesnakes on the ground and hornets in the air than with any more of them Gypsies. Leave them be."

"I've left a horse behind me. But she'll come to a whistle," said Reata. "Ride up to that ridge yonder, Harry, and wait for me half an hour. If I don't come, you hit the trail back to Pop Dickerman and tell him that I was . . . er . . . permanently delayed."

"No," sighed Harry Quinn. "I wish that I could leave you, kid. But damn me if I ever seen a slicker job than you done with them two Gypsies. Besides, the kind of a gent I am, I can't let down a partner in the middle of a mean deal. Come along, and we'll go together."

However, well back from the camp, Reata left Quinn and went in with no more company than little Rags. From the edge of the tall brush, at last, he looked out on the clearing and saw the sleeping camp. From a few of the wagons came muttering sounds of voices, here and there. The horses were grazing the grass. In the very center, near the red, dying eye of the fire, he spotted the outline of Sue, with the slender silhouette of a girl standing beside her. The heart of Reata swelled suddenly in the aching hollow of his throat. But already the past held Miriam.

He whistled, keying the note very low. At the second call the mare tossed her head and turned. He saw the arms of the girl restrain her for an instant. Then Miriam let the mare go, and Sue came straight as a string to the place where her rider waited.

By the mane he led Sue away. She stepped as softly as a hunting cat and made the brush trail almost noiselessly down her flanks. And there was not a sound, not a murmur of pursuit behind them. There was only in Reata's mind the dim picture of the girl, making a gesture of farewell as Sue had moved away. He reached Harry Quinn.

"By thunder," muttered Quinn. "You got it, eh? But what kind of a long-drawed-out god damn' bit of rawhide is this? Hey, man, it ain't Sue, is it? It is! It's Sue! And how'd you ever get her out of Pop? How'd you ever know that she was *worth* gettin'?"

The saddle was placed on the mare, and, side by side, the two rode up the ridge, turned, and headed away for Rusty Gulch.

The night whitened around them. Harry Quinn said: "It was a good job that you done. And you ain't told me much about yourself except your name, Reata. And that was a name that I would have guessed at myself if I'd once seen you work your rope, daubin' it on Gypsies or what not."

"There's not a whole lot to tell about myself," answered Reata. "The main thing is that you're on the loose. And that's one day's work done for Pop Dickerman."

"How many more days are you goin' to work for him?" asked Quinn curiously. "I was kind of thinkin' that the old hound had let me down, and that he'd see me rot sooner than pry himself loose from any hard cash on my account. But here he ponies up and sends you along, and I reckon that you're a lot better than gold. Are you with Pop Dickerman for good, like the rest of us?"

"I don't know," said Reata. "There are two more days of work for me to do. And then . . . well, then, I'll go back and make a call on Queen Maggie, maybe."

"Go back and call on her?" shouted Quinn. "Hey, what you mean by that, Reata? Go back and call on that old devil? Why, she'd throw you to the dogs. She'd laugh herself sick, she'd be so glad to feed you to the dogs."

"You think so?" asked Reata thoughtfully.

"Think so? Sure, and I know so. They ain't nothing but poison in her."

"Maybe not," said Reata, "but I'll have to take the chance one day."

"Hey! But why?"

"Because she's got a claim on something that I want," said Reata. "She's got a claim on something that I've gotta have."

It was not until they were in full sight of Rusty Gulch and saw all the windows of the town flashing in the morning sun that the heart of Reata failed him. He halted the mare suddenly and dismounted. He handed Sue's reins to Harry Quinn.

"What's up?" Quinn asked, as he took the reins.

Reata shook his head. Rags came and sat down at his feet, looking constantly up at the all-wise face of his master, on which a frown was to Rags like the sweeping of storm clouds across the heavens.

"I can't go on with you," said Reata, pointing to the town. "Now that I see the place, now that I think of Pop Dickerman a little more clearly . . . well, there's a smell of rats choking me like an old attic. I can't go on. You tell Dickerman that I'm a liar, that I've broken my word to him, that I won't see him again. Tell him that, and give Sue back to him."

"You're going to break with Pop?" murmured Quinn breathlessly. "Yeah, but nobody breaks with him. It can't be done. If you bust with him, he'll get you, Reata. He'll sure get you. He'll smell out a way to you right through to China. You can't beat him, old son."

"Maybe not," said Reata. "But I'm going to try."

He rubbed the nose of Sue and stroked her neck. Rags had already turned and started back up the road.

"I'm sorry," said Harry Quinn, holding out his hand.

They shook hands cordially.

"You done a grand good job for me," went on Quinn, "and now lookit. Maybe the next time I see you, I'll be looking at you down a gun. But I know how it is. You thinkin' you're thinkin' for yourself, but all it is, is the curse on you from Queen Maggie. She's put the Gypsy curse on you, and you've got to go back."

Reata waved his hand and turned quickly, because he wanted to have the shining windows of Rusty Gulch out of his mind, together with all they suggested to him. He wanted to forget Harry Quinn, and perhaps a good, swinging stride up the trail would ease the longing to have the fleetness of Sue again under him. So he turned a sharp corner of the trail and came in view of the far-distant mountains, and one jagged, white-headed peak that stood up, he knew, above the Gypsy camp.

Toward that goal he aimed himself grimly, and even little Rags slunk down-headed at his heels. Out of the distance behind him the good mare whinnied. It seemed to Reata like a call that summoned him back to his duty, but he put his head down and strode on. His feet went lightly and swiftly. He had a queer certainty that they would find their way blindly, because the devil was guiding them. But after that he began to think of Miriam, and that thought started him singing up the trail.

IN MEDIAS RES

MEN BEYOND THE LAW

These three short novels showcase Max Brand doing what he does best: exploring the wild, often dangerous life beyond the constraints of cities, beyond the reach of civilization . . . beyond the law. Whether he's a desperate man fleeing the tragic results of a gunfight, an innocent young man who stumbles onto the loot from a bank robbery, or the gentle giant named Bull Hunter—one of Brand's most famous characters—each protagonist is out on his own, facing two unknown frontiers: the Wild West . . . and his own future.

___4873-6 $4.50 US/$5.50 CAN

Lockwood

LAURAN PAINE

In the Wyoming town of Derby, Cuff Lockwood is wounded in a gunfight and has to stay long enough to recuperate . . . and meet the pretty widow Lady Barlow, owner of the Barlow ranch. The ranch is in need of a ramrod, but Lockwood refuses the job. After all, Wyoming isn't what he had in mind. But it looks like Fate—or someone else—doesn't want Lockwood to leave town. When he tries he's ambushed and forced to stay again. It seems to Lockwood like his journey's ending, but sometimes life leads you down trails you never expected. Some mighty dangerous trails.

___4906-6 $4.50 US/$5.50 CAN

LAURAN PAINE

THE KILLER GUN

It is no ordinary gun. It is specially designed to help its owner kill a man. George Mars has customized a Colt revolver so it will fire when it is on half cock, saving the time it takes to pull back the hammer before firing. But then the gun is stolen from Mars's shop. Mars has engraved his name on it but, as the weapon passes from hand to hand, owner to owner, killer to killer, his identity becomes as much of a mystery as why possession of the gun skews the odds in any duel. And the legend of the killer gun grows with each newly slain man.

___4875-2 $4.50 US/$5.50 CAN

TREASURES
OF THE
SUN
T.V. OLSEN

The lost city of Huacha has been a legend for centuries. It is believed that the Incas concealed a fantastic treasure there before their empire fell to Francisco Pizarro's conquistadores in the 16th century. So when Wilbur Tennington comes upon a memoir written by one of Pizarro's men, revealing the exact location of Huacha, visions of gold fill his eyes. He wastes no time getting an expedition together, then sets out on his quest. He should have known, though, that nothing so valuable ever comes easily. He will have to survive freezing mountain elevations, volcanic deserts, tribes of headhunters, and murderous bandits if he hopes to ever find the . . . treasures of the sun.

___4904-X $4.50 US/$5.50 CAN

THE SHADOW IN RENEGADE BASIN

LES SAVAGE, JR.

The novels and stories of Les Savage, Jr., have always been famous for their excitement, style, and historical accuracy. But this accuracy frequently ran afoul of editors in the 1950s. Only now is Savage's work finally being restored and presented in all its original glory. Finally, the realism, the humanity, and the honesty of his classic tales are allowed to shine through. This volume collects three of Savage's greatest tales, including the title novella, a brilliant account of a cursed basin where the mineral deposits look like blood, and where treachery has wiped out all the residents . . . except one.

___4896-5 $4.50 US/$5.50 CAN

Dorchester Publishing Co., Inc.
P.O. Box 6640
Wayne, PA 19087-8640

Please add $2.50 for shipping and handling for the first book and $.75 for each book thereafter. NY and PA residents, please add appropriate sales tax. No cash, stamps, or C.O.D.s. All orders shipped within 6 weeks via postal service book rate. Canadian orders require $2.50 extra postage and must be paid in U.S. dollars through a U.S. banking facility.

Name_____
Address_____
City_____ State _____ Zip_____
I have enclosed $ _____ in payment for the checked book(s).
Payment <u>must</u> accompany all orders. ❏ Please send a free catalog.
   CHECK OUT OUR WEBSITE! www.dorchesterpub.com